UNFINISHED BUSINESS

D1188657

BY LESLIE A. FIEDLER

Nonfiction

An End to Innocence
No! in Thunder
Love and Death in the American Novel
Waiting for the End
The Return of the Vanishing American
Being Busted
To the Gentiles
Cross the Border—Close the Gap
The Stranger in Shakespeare

Fiction

The Second Stone
Back to China
The Last Jew in America
Nude Croquet

Unfinished Business

LESLIE A. FIEDLER

STEIN AND DAY / *Publishers* / New York

First published in 1972
Copyright © 1971 Leslie A. Fiedler
Library of Congress Catalog Card No. 72-81820
All rights reserved
Published simultaneously in Canada by Saunders of Toronto Ltd
Printed in the United States of America
Stein and Day/*Publishers*/7 East 48 Street, New York, N.Y. 10017
ISBN 0-8128-1482-7

Acknowledgments

The author wishes to thank the editors and publishers of the following firms and periodicals under whose imprints parts of this book originally appeared:

COMMENTARY for "Henry Roth's Neglected Masterpiece," August, 1960; "John Peale Bishop and the Other Thirties," April, 1967.

EDIZIONE DI STORIA E LETTERATURA for "Caliban or Hamlet: A Study in Literary Anthropology," from *Friendship's Garland,* ed. V. Gabrieli, Rome, 1966.

FOREIGN SERVICE for "John Barth: An Eccentric Genius," January 7, 1961.

FREE PRESS for "Voting and Voting Studies" from *American Voting Behavior,* Glencoe, Illinois, 1959.

JOURNAL OF THE CONFERENCE ON COLLEGE COMPOSITION AND COMMUNICATION for "On Remembering Freshman Comp," February, 1962.

THE LISTENER for "The Shape of Moby Dick," 1967.

MONTANA OPINION for "Montana: P.S.," June, 1956.

NEW AMERICAN REVIEW for "Toward a Centennial: Notes on *Innocents Abroad,*" 1966.

NEW LEADER for "The Pleasures of John Hawkes," December 12, 1960.

PARTISAN REVIEW for "Our Country and Our Culture," May-June, 1952; "An Almost Imaginary Interview: Hemingway in Ketchum," Summer, 1962; "The New Mutants," Fall, 1965.

PLAYBOY for "Academic Irresponsibility," December, 1968.

RAMPARTS for "The Antiwar Novel and the Good Soldier Schweik," January, 1963.

SOUTHERN ILLINOIS UNIVERSITY PRESS for "The Two Memories: Reflections on Writers and Writing in the Thirties," from *Proletarian Writers of the Thirties,* 1968.

Contents

Acknowledgments v

Introduction 3

1. The Rosenbergs: A Dialogue 7
2. Voting and Voting Studies 18
3. The Antiwar Novel and the Good Soldier Schweik 32
4. The Two Memories: Reflections on Writers and
   Writing in the Thirties 43
5. John Peale Bishop and the Other Thirties 64
6. Henry Roth's Neglected Masterpiece 79
7. Our Country and Our Culture 88
8. Caliban or Hamlet: A Study in Literary Anthropology 93
9. Toward a Centennial: Notes on *Innocents Abroad* 104
10. The Shape of *Moby Dick* 120
11. The Pleasures of John Hawkes 127
12. John Barth: An Eccentric Genius 133
13. Montana: P.S. 139
14. Montana: P.P.S. 145
15. An Almost Imaginary Interview: Hemingway in
    Ketchum 151
16. On Remembering Freshman Comp 163
17. Academic Irresponsibility 169
18. The New Mutants 187

Index 209

UNFINISHED BUSINESS

Introduction

IN THIS VOLUME, the reader will discover all I shall probably ever get down of two books I have dreamed through most of my life as a writer. It seems clear to me now that I will never produce either the full length study of the thirties which I have been promising myself for so long, or that inclusive and conclusive book on the university with which I have been teasing myself for a somewhat shorter time. My essays on Henry Roth and John Peale Bishop, as well as a more general one called "The Two Memories," will have to make do for the first; while a little piece on freshman composition, plus the longer essays called "Academic Irresponsibility" and "The New Mutants" will have to substitute for the second.

I cannot write a full scale work on the thirties, I discover, not now anyhow, because I am still too deeply involved with memories and feelings still out of my control; while a full and formal treatment of the university seems inevitably to end in banalities, which I cannot bear to sign with my name and send forth into a world weary almost to the point of death of precisely such banalities. Perhaps, all the same, I may someday grow detached enough to do the first and inspired enough to do the second, who knows.

Just six months or a year ago, I would have included among these scraps from unfinished books an essay or two on Shakespeare, but suddenly I am in the process of writing that presumably unfinishable book. Still I could not forbear including in this volume an essay called "Caliban or Hamlet," in which Shakespeare is treated not so much as a literary subject as a source for metaphors capable of redeeming politics from the clichés which usually dog it.

I have also occasionally proposed to myself a surely unwritable book on the "non-Ethnic" American writers of the twentieth century to whom I have responded passionately, but who have tended to fall out of the categories around which my longer work is usually organized. I have therefore included essays on two such writers, John Hawkes and John Barth, leaving out with regret (because I do not feel that what I have written on them so far is substantial or amusing enough to be preserved) essays on two other "non-Ethnics" whom I equally admire, Wright Morris and Kurt Vonnegut.

Finally, I must mention that I have included in this volume the two brief postscripts to my early essay "Montana, or the End of Jean-Jacques Rousseau" and the article I wrote on Hemingway after a tragic confrontation with him at the moment just before his death. Hemingway and Montana are inextricably intertwined in my own mind, and the conjunction of these two essays may serve to illuminate the mingled piety and horror, love and rejection with which I regard both. These have been hard essays for readers with a taste for simplicity and the single vision to understand, and I sympathize with their confusion, though their failure to make due allowance for my own has led to their difficulties in the first place.

Equally ambivalent and confusing is my attitude toward the Rosenbergs, whose case is treated at length in an essay reprinted in *An End to Innocence,* and which I take up again here in an article that is really a prescript rather than a postscript, having been written some half-year before the former. That prescript, which I wrote from Italy as a kind of message home as well as a preparation for returning, seemed to me at the moment of its composition too personal and passionate and somehow naked to be printed then. But I discover that I have preserved it over seventeen or eighteen years, and I print it now for the first time, at a moment when the Rosenbergs have become the heroes of a play on Broadway and my own earlier comments are being quoted widely in the press by conservative commentators quit sure I have not changed my mind. Radical students, on the other hand, keep asking me hopefully, "You don't *still* believe that stuff about the Rosenbergs, do you?" The answer to which is, "Yes, I do." But I suspect that neither the conservative journalists nor the radical students quite understand what I said about the Rosenbergs to begin with, and I, therefore, have decided to publish my two Rosenberg pieces in order to make clear just how divided was the mind out of which both came. Let me add only one word from the present, a commentary on the little dialogue reprinted here. Though the character I call "C" has the final word in that dialogue, "A" and "B" also represent the author, which is to say, me. In this piece, therefore, as in so many others which I have written before and since, my attitude finally is as simple as A-B-C, which is, of course, not very simple at all.

ONE

The Rosenbergs: A Dialogue

(The scene is the house of A., where A. himself and B., C's two oldest friends, are waiting eagerly to pick up again their twenty year long political wrangle, interrupted by C.'s two years abroad.)

A: Welcome home! (holding out a drink)

B: Home! Home! I hope you're not such a victim of clichés that you take this word too seriously. Just because you go away from a place and come back, that doesn't make it home. What man who respects himself could feel at home in the U.S. in 1953!

C: (He takes the drink, and motioning in salute to his two friends swallows it down.) American whiskey! *I* feel at home—and it's not only the bourbon. You have no idea what a pleasure it is to come back to the same arguments, the old familiar language of disagreement and misunderstanding. I haven't felt so much at home for two years—except in my dreams.

B: Some dreams! Nightmares is more like it. The tidal oil lands turned over to private industry, Stevenson beaten, the campaign against the "eggheads" in full swing, snoopers in every college and university, McCarthy—the Rosenbergs—

C: The Rosenbergs! You make me feel as if I were back in Europe again. This is the Europeans' America—the legendary land of horror they *have* to believe in so they can continue to

7

despise us while they sustain what freedom they have left with our money. Rosenberg! I haven't heard that name mentioned since I got back; but in Europe there are posters on every wall, announcements of mass meetings, and every communist cab driver or clerk asking you, "What about the Rosenbergs?" As if you were killing them personally, as if their sentencing were an answer to all the charges against Russia, two people to balance against the millions in the concentration camps!

B: Well?

C: Well, what?

B: In a sense you *are* personally responsible for their deaths—you and all the rest of those who think communism is the main enemy, who don't have the time to protest against McCarthy!

C: I'm bored with the whole business. It's all too obvious, the same arguments over and over.

A: They have to be repeated over and over. Take me. I approve of the death sentence, and I don't hesitate to admit it. If that means personal responsibility, I accept it. These are traitors who acted in the interests of a foreign country and who are too cowardly or too stupidly sly to admit it. They delivered information that may bring destruction to thousands, to millions of their own countrymen, to those very kids of theirs that are being publicly wept over by the professional commie sob sisters. They're guilty as hell—and they should die! Why not?

B: Don't change the subject. For years now all you ex-communists and ex-liberals have been howling for blood. Now you have it. How do you like it?

A: Fine! I like it just fine. Thank God, I've faced up long ago to the part of me that's guilty in the same sense the Rosenbergs are. Fortunately, I never had the chance to do what they did, though once I would have given a lot to have had it. So I don't have to pay publicly for a crime, only internally for an intention.

B: Fine, fine—they should die like scapegoats for your moral benefit, two real human beings, not literary examples, *real* people, with mothers, friends, children—so you can feel clean and smug.

A: That's not the point at all. The real question is: do you think they're *guilty?*

B: Guilty! What does the word mean?

A: I don't mean anything metaphysical. Just the legal fact. Did they pass certain information through Greenglass that—

C: In a sense, I *know* they're guilty, but—

B: You know, you know—did you read the whole transcript?

B: To tell you the truth, I hardly even read the newspaper accounts, but the pattern is so obvious, once you know the types involved, it's clear that it *must* be true, that Greenglass can't be lying. It's the old pattern, classic by now. All one has to do is remember himself of ten or fifteen years before, and the verdict is—

C: Guilty, I know. *You're* guilty, but you're not on trial. It's easy enough to try yourself in a figure of speech—you won't burn. Listen, aside from this look-at-yourself business, it's just one man's word against two others; the word of a man who contradicted himself, a man who hated his relatives, who's trying to save his own skin—

A: The whole point is that it's not just one word against another. As B. says, there's a pattern, a context, a whole framework of possibilities which we can't pretend we don't know, we three, who have in common our experience in the movement, whatever our later differences—

B: Is that proof in court? Why are so many distinguished people convinced that they're innocent? I won't even mention the Pope, but take Urey—Urey isn't satisfied, and he read the whole transcript. Is it proved, *proved!*—not just probable?

C: Jesus, B., you know why most of the protesters are protesting. It has nothing to do with the Rosenbergs. They only want to save *themselves* in their own eyes, to acquit their own youth: pretend to themselves that *they* really wouldn't have done it —or that their communist friends whom they sponsored and protected in the Popular Front days, wouldn't have done it, couldn't have done it, *didn't* do it. Talk about trying yourself!

A: Those are the same people, or at least the same kind of people who protested for Hiss, for Judith Coplon, for all the latest Communist Tens and Twelves and Elevens, and always for the same irrelevant reasons: to clear themselves, to refuse to admit that what they were once so proud of, what they thought of as their "highest principles," should lead only to lying and betrayal and piddling evil.

B: Stop ganging up on me, you two. "Evil"! this is the new fashionable word. Once it was "the class struggle"—now it's Good and Evil—and I suppose you've got Original Sin up your sleeve. Put all your cards on the table!

A: Talk about red herrings!

B: All right, let's talk about this "evil," then. Suppose for a minute the Rosenbergs did it, that they passed on the information, whatever it was worth. The question is what they did it *for,* Is this an irrelevant point? Were they paid? Hirelings, sadists, bullies or what? They—

C: You can never be sure about motives. What do you think *we* were in the movement for? For the pure, disinterested reasons we would have given once, or—

B: Listen, hells bells, let's not go too deep. Maybe all virtue is vice disguised, I can't discuss such crap anymore—this is for the college dormitory. But speaking in an ordinary, human, un-clinical way, these were people who acted for the *best* motives: for Internationalism, for Peace, for Humanity. Don't you think this should be taken into consideration?

A: There you go. Just what I've been waiting for you to say, part two of the standard justifier's gambit: one, they didn't do it at all—they were framed like Tom Mooney, Sacco and Vanzetti, Guy Fawkes, God knows who; and two, they had a *right* to do it, because—

B: I didn't say they had a right. If they betrayed their country, be-trayed us, *me*—they were wrong. This much I know. I'm only saying that they *may* have done it not because they were worse, but because they were better than their neighbors, those fake patriots and black marketeers, who will probably watch the Rosenbergs' execution on television!

A: If you don't say it, the Rosenbergs do. They at least want it both ways: they're innocent spotless lambs, and they're heroes of the struggle against American imperialism. Like Hiss and Remington and all the rest—and because they want it both ways, they're nothing in the end, *liars!*

B: But still you can't deny they began with a desire for peace, a love of humanity—

A: They were always what they are now, stooges, who gave up their minds to the party bureaucrats, stupid and proud, victims of pride, like we were once, like you still are, B.

C: I can't agree. In this respect, B. is right for once. They acted stupidly, certainly, but for motives which I would hate to deny, for ends that may have been practically unattainable, but which I'm glad, *proud* (I'm not scared of the word) I yearned for when I was young and foolish—for Humanity! Is that just a dirty word for us now?

A: We couldn't tell the difference between Humanity and the Soviet Union. We kept saying Humanity—but what we really dreamed of was an eruption of force, getting even, wiping out in blood the world we felt despised us. There was a lot of hate—

C: It's no use. I just feel guilty. I want to cry when I think of their dying—really cry, because *I'm* not dying, because they're paying alone the bill for the rest of us. To hell with their foolish or hypocritical defenders, and with their hypocritical or foolish opponents. I know what they mean!

A: I don't understand it, C. Europe seems to have softened you up. Why all this sentimentality? You certainly didn't talk like this about Hiss.

C: Hiss! But he wasn't sentenced to death. What did he get, after all? A measly couple of years; and the whole respectable world, everybody blessed enough to have gone to Harvard, secretly convinced he couldn't have done it, because he was one of them!

A: What difference does the sentence make? The principles are the same; the sides line up the same way—

C: No, damn it all, the Rosenbergs are the precise *opposite* of Hiss. Take the same twelve people who would have believed at first sight and despite all evidence that Hiss was innocent (so clean-cut!)—and they would swear at the same first sight and on a stack of Bibles that the Rosenbergs are guilty! That they *look* like communists—the dirty kind, not the polite ones you can meet at the Harvard Club.

B: Why don't you say it right out, C. The Rosenbergs are *Jews;* they look like Jews—ugly, drab people with their comical Jello boxes and Bronx background. Why don't you say the word anti-Semitism, my friend?

C: Because it's not anti-Semitism. They were given a fair trial— presided over by a Jewish judge, the case against them conducted by a Jewish lawyer—

B: There were also Jews who helped round up the Nazis' victims in the Warsaw Ghetto!

A: Please, spare us the quotations from the *Daily Worker!*

C: Yet, somehow, no one can deny that the fact of their being Jews had *something* to do with their deaths. That they should be the only ones to pay in this way with their lives, two Jews, it can't be entirely an accident.

A: I'm ashamed of you, C. You're really a racist at heart. That's why you talk so differently about the Rosenbergs than you did about Hiss. Because they're Jews, fellow Jews—that's the only difference. You're just like the Harvard lawyers in their attitude toward *their* boy. You identify completely with these people, who—

C: Who I'd hate if they were in this room, whom I couldn't say three words to without losing my temper, who haven't thought one thought of their own in years. But so harmless, so middling, so unattractive, so much out of a world I know, so *made* to be victims! Why the hell should they pay for being born in the wrong situation, for having just the right combination of guts and stupidity to be caught out for something the Browders and Fosters ought to be paying for. Who's *really* responsible?

A: But don't you see where this leads you? Why stop with Foster? Why not Molotov or Malenkov, the Central Committee of the Russian Party, who really make the policy all their American stooges act out. Or why not Roosevelt himself (okey, he's dead, but just for example) because during the war years, when the crime was committed, he led the propaganda to convince us that Russia was our simon-pure friend—

B: It's true, after all, that Russia *was* our ally in those days. And that shouldn't be forgotten either. The Rosenbergs gave the information, *if* they gave it, to an ally.

A: Let's take one thing at a time. For every crime, society and its leaders are responsible in some sense. But also the individual! Isn't this the whole point, C.? That for all our good intentions, for all our being misled, we were each responsible for what well-meaning evil we did? You wouldn't plead (or would you?) that no one should be executed for anything, since all guilt is spread thin over all of us?

C: Your question is too general. This is a *special* case. It's not just a matter of the diffused overall responsibility of all of us for each other but of a deliberately sponsored political policy whose purpose was to lead such dull individuals to crime— and of an almost equally criminal stupidity, which—

B: Admit it! They're dying because they're Jews; and you're feeling a twinge because their death is a threat against you, C., and you, too, A., if you'd only face facts. If, at least, they hadn't had a Jewish judge, who had to lean over backward, to prove that all Jews weren't accomplices and Bolsheviks! A gentile judge—and we would be having another discussion. Let's even admit that they should have been found guilty, but such a sentence! It's lynch spirit—lynch law—

C: It's true that the sentence is excessive, a scandal! Why should they die, when someone like Fuchs, much more directly, more terribly guilty, is already free? When a Hiss, a real power in our political life for years, is almost ready to leave jail—

B: Naturally, these were not Jews!

C: That's not the point—

A: It really is the point, C. B. gives away your whole racist game

C: No, no—such perilous matters aside, the sentence is absurd. Why does it shock the whole world?

A: Communist propaganda—subtle enough even to influence you.

C: And the Pope? No, no. There's obvious injustice. First of all, Russia *was* our ally at the time of the crime. And then, nobody can be *sure* that the piddling information Greenglass dug up for the Rosenbergs really helped the communists—Urey says no. And most important, no real harm has been done yet . It's all speculative. A sentence for possible murder—if the victim doesn't commit suicide first.

A: Why do you bring up the issue of murder? Treason is enough. They spied in wartime; they gave information to another country. And let's not kid ourselves. Sooner or later, Russia will find an excuse to attack us—and you can be sure they won't hesitate about using against us the atomic weapon they have in their hands thanks to Ethel and Julius Rosenberg. You don't have any illusions about that? Maybe you think that Russia's having the bomb is an aid to world peace?

C: You know I have no such illusions. It just seems *wrong,* that's all. I can't find the arguments against what you say—it's just irrelevant. The whole thing has a disgusting feel to it, the feel of fear and vindictiveness. It makes me ashamed of my country; and I don't like to be. Naturally, I give answers to the communists—when they bring it up, but—

B: And now the latest move—did you read about it? How they promised immunity to the Rosenbergs, if they would confess. Confess! Exactly like the Russian trials—

A: It isn't exactly like anything. In the first place, they didn't ask for a confession, but for identification of accomplices; and in the second place, it wasn't a promise of immunity, but of conversion of the death sentence, and—

C: Don't let B. bait you with these party line arguments; he knows as well as we do that turning State's evidence is an old democratic procedure—and yet—

A: And yet, what? How can you even consider for a moment comparing this isolated case with the thousands of farcical trials, judicial executions is better, of the communists. Not to mention—

C: You don't have to convince me of the hypocrisy of the communists; even B. knows that!

B: Even! Thank you.

C: I don't give a crap for what the communists say—or how loud their stooges and made-to-order meetings howl and scream in forty countries. Whatever the United States does, good or bad, they'll twist into something good enough to use as propaganda against us—good enough to convince those who are convinced in advance of anything they read in the *Daily Worker* or *Unità* or *Humanité*. I don't even care about the noble statements of the Catholic hierarchy; after all, they're professionals, mercy is their business! But for our own sake as Americans, because it's against our traditions to kill for political dissent—

A: Political dissent! Treason is what you should say.

C: You know what I mean. Politically, practically, a million absolutely unjust executions are infinitely worse than one half-unjust one—but morally each single instance has the same weight. And against this one, against our injustice or excess or mistake, America's act and *mine,* what can I do? What can I feel but guilt! They shouldn't die, that's all!

B: It's hysteria, McCarthyism, the beginning of the end. Naturally, we're nowhere near as bad as Russia now, but one thing leads to another. You start with Red-baiting (even if the communists are wrong, even if they're vicious—they're such small potatoes in the U.S.) and you go on to Jew-baiting and worse!

C: This is not what I feel. It's only that—well, after all, a piece of all three of us will be dying with these Rosenbergs; we should at least have the decency to say out loud that it hurts.

A: Sometimes I just don't understand you, C. I'll bet anything that if the Rosenbergs had been acquitted, or were given some nominal sentence, you'd be howling against the stupidity of the courts, the sentimentality of the American people, our moral immaturity—

B: What do you mean—an old Red-baiter like him (he puts a friendly arm around C.), he'd be yelling for their blood.

C: You're both right—but—I only wish I were! I only wish I were!

Rome, Italy
—1952

Voting and Voting Studies

IT IS A terrible thing to be a lion in a Daniel's den; but a humanist fallen among social scientists can scarcely help seeing himself in that absurd role. I have been interested for a long time in voting: in the meaning of the act itself and of the choices which that act involves. My interest has been especially poignant because so Platonic; I have, that is to say, actually voted only once in my life—and regretted it immediately afterward. There are, I tell myself, good superficial reasons for my failure to go to the polls: changes of residence and a consequent lack of knowledge of local candidates and issues, an early Marxist indoctrination against the whole notion of parliamentarianism. But I am not really sure why I have so strong a reluctance to vote; and I have sought to answer my questions about myself by speculating on my neighbors. Do they really believe that they are acting meaningfully when they put a cross before one of two names on a printed ballot? Do they vote to make a choice or make a choice in order to be able to vote; that is, is voting an act of social conformity, a symbolic gesture of belonging rather than a way of influencing government? Why do societies succeed in getting more and more people to vote as they become more and more totalitarian? Has the act of voting in its modern mechanical form (I see the voting machine as the visible and outward form of an invisible and inward process of dehumanizing choice) anything to do with traditional democracy at all?

I was disconcerted in turning to the three recent studies of voting I have been looking through *(Straight Fight, Voting,* and *The Voter Decides)* not so much by their failure to ask some of the questions that strike me as fundamental, as by their method. Different men must ask different questions, I know; for a study, whatever its pretenses at objectivity, is an attempt to define oneself as well as a social problem. But the dispassionate, scientific air of these approaches left me feeling inadequate, overwhelmed by their modesty and impersonality, and dazzled by the charts and diagrams, the clinical vocabulary (no one "thinks" or "guesses," but "conceptualizes"), the sophistication in the matter of statistics, and the precision of the sampling methods. I am almost ashamed to admit that the very notion of the "panel" interview was unknown to me; and that I had vaguely assumed all my life that a "random sample" was one made at random.

In the face of such professionalism and abstract concern, my own interest seems not merely amateur but almost animal, that is, passionate and instinctive; and so I have been indulging in the sentimental image of myself as a member of a lower species trapped in the lair of the prophets of science. Yet when I have turned to their prophecies, that is, to the results of their investigations, I have been disconcerted once more in quite an opposite direction. *Straight Fight,* for instance, informs us that, in one English urban constituency at least, a greater portion of the old, of women, and of the upper classes vote for the Conservative Party, though, indeed, all three factors may be reducible to the single one of social class. To which the only adequate response is, "Uh-huh," or in more literary terms: we need no prophet come back from the grave (or panel interview) to tell us this! And when the same study goes gravely on to observe that "the behaviour of electors may perhaps be classified in terms of long-term trends and short-term fluctuations," the modest "perhaps" with which this platitude is proffered seems the final insult to one trained to wince at belaboring the obvious. I am similarly offended when it is ponderously established in *Voting* that Catholics tend to vote Democratic, or noted, with the air of having discovered some arcane truth, that "opinions are really formed through the day-to-day exchange of observations and comments which goes on among people." This even the naïvest of poets has observed, as he has also observed, merely by living, what *The Voter Decides* includes in its summary: "the results of both studies may be said to conform to the basic psychological principle that when strong and opposing forces act on an individual the resultant behavior will demonstrate the characteristics of conflict." This assertion, stripped of its technical vocabulary, does not even make the grade of a platitude but remains a simple redundancy: where there is conflict, there is conflict! And such a pleonasm is scarcely redeemed by applying it to the political situation and producing the further conclusion that a voter with contradictory convictions is less likely to vote and more likely to vacillate in his choice than one without them.

I do not wish to appear Philistine on this score; and I want to go on record as believing that sociology will yet survive such self-evident "discoveries," as it will survive parallel ones in other sub-fields, i.e., that rumors are less accurate as they spread out from a center, that people who talk about moving move more often than those who don't, and the like. I feel, however, that such banalities are the price American social science is paying for its current anti-intellectualism, its flight from theory; and I cannot help making some observations on the sociology of such sociology from the point of view of a not wholly unsympathetic outsider. I feel obliged to preface those observations with a note on the sociology of my own sociology of sociology; this is a process which opens up possibilities of endless regression, but here I promise I shall stop!

The humanist's image (or as we prefer to say, "myth") of the contemporary sociologist is that of a heavily subsidized, much-touted and honored scholar, torn at each moment between offers from industry and government—scarcely knowing, indeed, whether to take the rewards offered by the Coca-Cola Company or the Air Force—for his latest documentation of some weary cliché about man, long since a commonplace of literature. The humanist, made especially aware of the spiritual dullness and lack of intellectual curiosity in contemporary society by its indifference to great art, cannot help thinking of the sociologist's statistical wisdom as an ersatz for real insight into the social being of man; and he is likely to be caught muttering bitterly: "Sufficient unto the day is the social science thereof." Perhaps the wittiest expression of this rather unfair, but thoroughly understandable, reaction is found in two lines of Auden, a new commandment for modern life:

Thou shalt not sit with statisticians
Or commit a social science.

The humanist's case must, then, be discounted a little for the professional pique of the excluded which lies behind it; yet it is not without merit. The sort of statistical sociology (or political science) represented by these texts seems to him the result of two phenomena, both peculiar, in their strongest forms at least, to contemporary America: an almost neurotic impulse to self-examination and an almost religious regard for "scientific method." The spiritual hypochondria, the eternal feeling of his own pulse by the contemporary American is a standing joke among Europeans; and this eternal self-examination (rivaled only, if we can believe Dostoevski and Chekov, by nineteenth-century Russians) is not merely a matter of maudlin self-exposure at cocktail parties, but of endless polls, interviews, exposures, and candid statements to the press, ranging from the crassest journalism to the most cautious and methodical research.

These, the average American is not only delighted to participate in, but is pleased to spend his leisure time reading. From Kinsey's improbable best-seller to the latest Gallup or Roper report in the daily newspaper, the American is at once creating and consuming a never-ending "Song of Myself": a monument to obsessive self-concern beside which Whitman's poem seems a masterpiece of selflessness. His voting habits are of especial concern to him since the act of balloting tends to become his only even remotely political activity; and he wants to be told first how he is going to vote, then how he is voting (at two in the morning, he is still up beside his radio; and the great electronic gadgets of which he is so proud are adding him to all the other nameless units awake beside their sets), at last how he has voted. And he is not even averse to being told why, though the simple, gigantic figures are what interest him most. Like the sociologist on his more sophisticated level, the man by the T.V. believes that only quantitative truth is real.

Once given official sanction (and large budgets), such organized curiosity is insatiable; from the polls, to the altar, to the sickbed, to the grave—the experts we have hired to tell us all pursue us doggedly, notebooks in hand. I presume that the only reason we did not drop sociologists and psychologists into Hiroshima with the Bomb was a technical one; and I sometimes have a nightmare of our world after its final war, in which the sole man and woman left alive turn out to be a pair of sociologists, who after questioning each other scientifically, instead of getting down to reproduction, separate to write rival studies of "The Single Survivor." Yet the interest in self which lies behind such phenomena is not, however untrammeled, in itself really reprehensible. As a nation, we come by it honestly enough, out of the tradition of soul-searching so unexpectedly handed down by the Puritans to the emancipated, contemporary American of whatever origin. There is something really satisfactory and amusing in the notion of the social scientists as our Last Puritans.

It is only what the "self" becomes in the electronic calculating machines that gives me pause; for what the IBM cards can record or newspapers report is a statistical datum, abstract and unreal. I cannot finally convince myself that in our desire to know first especially and then exclusively the existence we share with others, experience that is *statistically* meaningful, there is a retreat from inwardness and the person as defined in literature and art. There is a kind of comfort, I am aware, a delightful sense of actuarial helplessness in learning that we are Democrats because of certain probabilities inherent in our generation and ethnic group—or adulterous because of our level of education. The panel method, for all its avowed desire to come to grips with individuals rather than with rows of figures, cannot handle those individuals except as instances of, say, the male sex, the forty-year age group, the Protestant religion. The sort of peace with himself that man used to seek in the conviction that we are all sons of God, he seems now to find in the conviction that we are all specks on a bar graph between the covers of a scholarly book.

I do not believe, of course, that the studies I have been reading are the work of conscious or deliberate enemies of inwardness. They are written by men doing a job as conscientiously as they can in a society organized on the lines of a rigid division of labor. They are, in short, "specialists" rather than men at the moment that they write, and in that sense, the victims of a general panic in our culture, a flight from the person. A first symptom of this is their resolve to attest to their objectivity by drawing their metaphors for the individual from science rather than the humanities. The "sciences of man" (as they are sometimes called in the phrase that already gives away the game) hesitate between the natural sciences and literature and philosophy; but the poles do not stand still. And how can one blame the sociologist for abandoning traditional notions of man, when critics and philosophers, too, are abandoning insight to statistics, poetry to methodology—and even the professor of literature likes to boast that he is producing "research."

The embarrassment of the scientizing political philosopher and literary man alike is that he deals with a field in which there is (in a sense analogous to that of the physical sciences) nothing new to discover; though, indeed, certain older wisdom has to be taught again and again in new languages. I think at this point of Freud's plaint about having to tell men as if it were a revelation what every nursemaid knows. Both poet and social scientist are, therefore, necessarily engaged in redeeming platitudes; but the method of the poet is to specify and complicate the cliché, while the method of the sociologist is to quantify and simplify. A poet's pondering on the problems of filial ingratitude produces *King Lear*. A sociologist might by a series of panel interviews decide that ("perhaps" and "at least in one rather typical small court of pre-Christian England, selected because of etc., etc.") there is more of a tendency among grown daughters of kings showing signs of senility to evidence open hostility, if such kings give over their property completely to such daughters. A really canny investigator might even be able to show, within the normal statistical margin of error, of course, the percentage of such cases in which the father would finally be shoved out into a storm. To put it mildly, such information is irrelevant to any central human concern; though, to be sure, more than one Department of Welfare might be persuaded to put up funds for a continuing study along the same lines.

Yet the notion that knowledge about the relations of men to each other is not useful—not even really *true*—until it can be quantitatively expressed has taken over not only in the social sciences. The accidental (from any philosophical point of view) predominance of physical science in our culture and the confusion of that science in the popular mind with technology have lent prestige to all graphs, mathematical formulations, and equations, however meaningless. The social sciences, precisely because they have come late into the field to which they aspire, and because they are suspected of continuing fraternization with such outmoded elite disciplines as religion, philosophy, and literature, feel obliged to ape especially sedulously the outward appearance of the more prestigeful methods of investigation. In the way a schoolgirl imitates the hair style of the reigning movie actress, so the social scientist imitates the mathematical statement and laboratory attitudes of the physicist. His world, too, can be reduced to numbers! *Wie m' goyisht sich, azoi m' yiddisht sich* (As the gentile is a gentile, so the Jew is a Jew)—the folk saying puts it.

Of course, there are rationalizations. "True," the sociologist retorts, "everyone always knew that things fell when one dropped them; but until such knowledge was quantitatively expressed as $S = \frac{1}{2}gt^2$, that knowledge was not practically of any consequence, and in the same way. . . ." But it is, alas, never the same way; at least, I have never seen any "sociological law" of the order of the law of gravity emerge from the most statistical analysis of a platitude. Indeed, one could scarcely look for such an event until the vagaries of the individual man become as indifferent to us as the wanderings of individual atoms. At this happily scientific stage, I trust we shall never arrive; and, indeed, it is because I feel an impulse in such a direction in statistical sociology and political science that I am a little wary of those disciplines.

One does not have to move to such large objections, however, because of the lack of smaller ones. The "quantitative method" as exemplified in these three studies leads to an insidious sort of half-conscious falsification, disturbing, I am sure, even to advocates of the method. For instance, in *The Voter Decides,* there is a striking instance of the tendency to hypostatize imaginary psychological categories, which can then be statistically manipulated in their interrelationships. In this case, the "manageable number of variables" turns out to add up to the fairy-tale number of three: issue orientation, party orientation, and candidate orientation; and though the writers begin by speaking of these as names, convenient labels, they end by the logic of their method in treating them as *things.*

More disturbing to me and more inevitable, I fear, is the way in which all three books are driven, for the sake of merely getting on with the problem, to treat all Republican or Democratic votes as equivalent to each other. I suppose that if one is to make any generalizations at all on this level about voting behavior, one must assume that all voters are making a choice between two relatively constant and distinguishable alternatives. Yet such are the complications of our party system to begin with, and of human motivation in the second place, that two people who are "black radicals," opposed passionately and ignorantly to the educated and rich, may vote one Democratic ("for the party of the people") and the other Republican ("for the party of the investigators who showed up those Harvard boys in the State Department"). Each of these may be paired off with a quite genuine conservative, one of whom takes the Whiggery of Eisenhower to represent his ideal, the other of whom finds the same ideal better personified in the genteel New Deal nostalgia of Stevenson. In such cases, is it not more bewildering than informative to treat arbitrary labels as indications of a real choice? The same impulse to make quantitative lists rather than qualitative discriminations leads to a lumping together of all nonvoters, though certain refusals to vote may be real political acts, just as certain resolves to go to the polls may be abject surrenders to conformism, the rejection of politics. Such distinctions are perhaps impossible to make inside such an approach as we are examining; and I suspect that many of the investigators would find them as pointless and finicky as a qualitative distinction between orgasm and orgasm would seem to a Kinsey.

My final and chief objection to the statistical method in the social sciences in general is that it represents the triumph of an antitheoretical drift, which seems to me one of the most regressive aspects of American scholarship. It strikes me, to put it as bluntly as possible, as yet another facet of a widespread, academic anti-intellectualism—part of the (real American!) quest to find a democratic substitute for something so aristocratic as ideas, some bureaucratic ersatz for the insight of the individual thinker. Sociological investigation becomes not merely quantitative in method but bureaucratic in its organization, not the child of pure science it would like to claim itself but a hybrid offshoot of mass production and industrial engineering, with techniques as impersonal and ultimately mindless as the production methods of a movie or a news magazine. One imagines the director of research with three phones on his desk, dreaming of the day of complete automation.

"Specialization" first and now "bureaucratization," these have been in the American university, in the schools of a country notorious for its resistance to general ideas, the respectable methods of substituting technology for theory. Such a retreat from speculation to "fact" begins with a healthy desire to escape the "ivory tower," to bring political science, say, down to the level of practical politics —to be immediately useful to ordinary men in their everyday concerns. This is not on the face of it an ignoble ideal; but it turns out to be merely the noblest disguise of the heresy of practicality which has turned our colleges into trade schools. To be sure, the investigation of opinion formation is *useful,* and it is no accident that it blurs into big business on the one side and journalism on the other; but such a usefulness is not the usefulness of science or of pure mathematics. It is the hallmark of the technological: and technology is the slave of the system it serves; it cannot challenge or teach, only blindly implement.

I suppose that below such theoretical levels, the development of mass faculties in mass universities has created an economic pressure for the invention of cooperative disciplines to replace individual talent. Only in an academy of the elite, can one expect Platos and Aristotles; we must find, and are finding, ways in which the mediocre can at once maintain their self-respect and be useful to their society. This is a necessity in a day in which the university is becoming more and more overwhelmingly a refuge for men of indifferent talent in search of status and security. In the beginning, the fact-compilers and the statistics-gatherers were humble and spoke as temple servants. They were mere collectors bringing in a fresh harvest of data against the day when some great, synthesizing mind would make of their harvest a new theory. But let anyone now dare to try to synthesize with the proper rashness and brilliance, and hear the vituperation heaped on him as a popularizer and robber of other men's ideas. The fact-snufflers, the truffle-hounds of science, have come to think of themselves as their own masters; the temple servants have set themselves up in the inner sanctum as priests.

And who is there to challenge them in a society that more and more thinks of "facts" as more honorable than theories, of impersonality as more acceptable than personality, of graphs as more worthy than poems?

Of the three books I am discussing, *Straight Fight* is by all odds the worst offender in this regard: no idea contaminates the purity of its research. *Voting* is, in many respects, an honorable exception. Certainly, in its last two chapters, especially in the latter on "Democratic Practice and Democratic Theory," it moves out freely and interestingly into the realm of speculation; but, truly, I must confess that I find it hard to see how the detailed documentation that precedes those chapters is necessary to the posing of a question of which most of us are surely aware: How is it possible to maintain a belief in classic democracy now that we are conscious (and weren't the formulators of that doctrine conscious of the same thing, after all?) that the individual voter does not come up to the ideal qualifications they dreamed for him? The book does, however, resist the temptation to stay safely ensconced behind its figures and easy clichés, asking finally some of the questions at least which properly follow such an investigation.

It seems to me, however (speaking with all the irresponsibility of one whose primary commitments are elsewhere), that some theoretical speculations must be engaged in before *an investigation*. No one can begin, of course, without prior ideas and expectations; if he is not conscious of those ideas and expectations, he is likely to begin with ill-perceived general assumptions that will betray the finest sampling methods and questioning techniques. There are two areas especially where the lack of insight and theory seems to me evident in the studies with which I am concerned. First, the matter of class. In England, conventional notions of class status, resting on the traditional socio-economic basis, seem to yield viable results; at least, there appears to be a real correlation between "class" in this sense and the way a voter makes his limited party choice. But in America, ordinary (which is to say, European-oriented) conceptions of class are confusing rather than helpful when applied to voting habits.

Let me deal here quite briefly only with the criterion of "education" which is used in *Voting* as one of the three main measures of

SES. To ask only the quantitative question, "How many years of education?" is to establish a standard so gross that all really interesting distinctions escape it. I have a hunch that in America at the present moment a university education is in the process of becoming so general a cultural possession that it can scarcely be considered a cutting line between classes. The important questions now tend to be: night school or daytime classes? city college or college away from home? agricultural school or arts college? general curriculum or school of education? Ivy League or Big Ten? A real distinction in status now could be established not so much from where a person happens to get his education as from where he is able to imagine getting it. If one insists on turning these things into questionnaires anyone can administer, perhaps the key question should be: Where do you look forward to sending your children to college? It seems to me, at least, that the limitation of ambition, even of imagination in such regards, is the clue to actual class status in the United States, not so much the matter of legally or even economically limited possibilities as of the limitation of aspiration and desire.

It is not, for instance, how much money a man has that fixes him in a certain class (for our classes, as they most effectively function, seem to me clearly "cultural" rather than economic), but what kind of ties, say, he would buy if he had money enough to make a free choice. What kind of clothing, what sort of house, which magazines, what books (if any) would he own? Would he drink beer or Martinis? Would he go to wrestling matches or polo matches? These are the matters that count. Indeed, a distinction closer to that we make in ordinary conversation between "highbrow" and "lowbrow" (in which years of education and income are secondary considerations) would be more to the point than inherited notions of socio-economic class, or even the self-ranking of people who do not really share in this regard the assumptions of the questioner.

At least, if one began with such a standard, he would not produce the really useless and confusing conclusion arrived at by most of this research, namely, that the more educated group votes more Republican. This baffles my own firsthand knowledge, for instance, that university faculties (who are, after all, more educated than anyone) tend to be Democratic—or the special fact that in three English departments with which I have had intimate connections less than 5 per cent of the members voted Republican. What are the operative factors here? I certainly find no hint of them in any of the studies. In what groups does one lose caste by voting Republican? In what groups does he gain status by such a vote? What makes a vote either way *what one does?* The authors of *Voting* make the point quite clearly in one place that the voting decision is parallel in its formation to the formation of taste. I should guess that it is, often at least, precisely like other manifestations of taste, a way of asserting one's belongingness to a particular group, and that it should be studied in respect to the whole syndrome of taste. How many readers of comic books vote for Stevenson? How many people who do not know what an artichoke is prefer the Republicans? What is the connection between wearing hand-painted ties and party choice?

Finally, it seems to me (and here I return to where I began) that there is not in any of these studies sufficient prior speculation on the social meaning of the act of voting as such, opposed to the act of choosing one or another candidate; yet I do not see how one can begin to study the latter until he has distinguished from it and clearly understood the former. In recent years and in direct proportion, I would venture to guess, to the decrease in a really passionate concern with the outcome of elections, there has grown up an increasing public concern with having people *just vote,* no matter whom they vote for. Institutional propaganda in the press and over the radio insists more and more (even at the cost of time for publicity for the competing parties) on everyone's getting out to the polls; so that in the consciousness of the American citizen there is slowly established (of all people, he has been in his freedom of movement and choice relatively immune to this) the notion that not the considered act of deciding on candidates and issues but the mere mechanical act of voting is in itself his essential patriotic duty. To "go to church" (but what church?), to vote (but for whom?), to send his children to college (but what *sort* of college?)—these are the demands on anyone who asks respect from the community.

The whole mythology of voting has been transformed; the vote comes to be regarded as a public act of allegiance to an abstract "democracy" rather than a private decision as to what is good and what bad for the state. The "secrecy of the ballot" becomes an outmoded slogan; what matters is that the act of entering the polling place be *not* secret, known to everyone. That this is merely one symptom of a general drive for *participation* as a good in itself—regardless of its end—should be obvious. It links up closely with the parallel propaganda that nags at us from radio and television: Go to church this Sunday. Not to one church or other, just any church —not to assert your difference but your sameness: everyone the same in different places. It is notorious that we are in the midst of the strangest of all religious revivals, a renewed commitment to the abstract idea of religion rather than to any particular manifestation —in a nation where "man" is any man, "the church" is any church.

On every level of cultural life, this hunger for total participation replaces the older ideal of personal preference and threatens especially the freedom simply to withdraw or hang back. Even school children become subject to such pressures; the coming of Valentine's Day, for instance, no longer means that a boy brings, shyly or boldly, to some girl he has mooned over all year a lacy heart and a declaration of love; but that every kid under pressure brings for every other kid in his entire class some machine-produced greeting remembered the day before at the Five-and-Ten. One does not choose a special Valentine, but celebrates Valentine's Day. I have a hunch that our situation is already far gone in this respect when it comes to voting; but I should be interested in having the problem investigated (as long as the machinery is in motion) by someone with the means and techniques for such research. We seem to be at a critical point; for the abandonment of choice is one of the essential symptoms of a drift toward a totalitarianism of spirit and attitude which can presumably grow even inside a technically open society.

It is well known that in the full-fledged, total state, voting (once sentimentally regarded as the sufficient guarantee of democracy), far from being discouraged, reaches new heights of enthusiasm and participation It is pointless merely to speak of a perversion of the practice; something in the act of voting itself has apparently all along contained the seeds of its present uses. To be sure, in a totalitarian culture, the element of choice, already narrowed for us unredeemably, it seems, to two parties, is further minimized or eliminated altogether; and the whole process becomes purely what it was before only in part, a mass ritual of acceptance and conformity. In what sense and to what degree voting has already become for some of our people such a symbolic gesture of the surrender of personality is a question whose significance cannot be exaggerated. This question, so vital to us at the present moment, I would hope that some future researcher would have the intellectual temerity to ask.

—1954

The Antiwar Novel
and the Good Soldier Schweik

I.

WRITTEN IN Prague in the twenties about the events of 1914 and
1915, *The Good Soldier: Schweik* first reached America with the
Depression, and returns now, after another war and another peace,
strangely involved in history: not only the history of the times it describes, but the history of the times through which it has come
down to us. What shifts of taste and allegiance it has survived!
What collapsed hopes and betrayed dreams!

Perhaps the kind of pacifism it embodies is the sole product of
World War I to have lasted into our era. Certainly the official aims
in whose names that war was fought, and which were theoretically
assured by the Treaty of Versailles, have not come to very much.
The dissolution of the League of Nations, the successes of Stalin
and Hitler, and the outbreak of World War II made clear that the
outward forms of democracy, national self-determination, and international cooperation, imposed by fiat or invoked in piety, had little to do with the inward meaning of the world after 1919. Not
peace and order but terror and instability were the heritage of the
postwar years: an institutionalized terror and a stabilized instability, in whose honor two minutes of silence were observed for the
score of November elevenths between the first Great Armistice and
the second great eruption of violence.

But pacifism, too, was a victim of World War II, which saw
thousands of young men, who earlier had risen in schools and col-

leges to swear that they would never bear arms, march off to battle —as often as not with copies of antiwar books in their packs. Those books were real enough, like the passion that prompted them and the zeal with which they were read; only the promises were illusory. The unofficial war-resisters, who for twenty years had pored over evocations of battlefield atrocities to immunize themselves against the appeals of patriotism, found their own slogans finally as irrelevant as the catch phrases they pretended to despise. To be sure, the end of still another war has seen the upsurge of still another pacifism; but this seems by now part of a familiar pattern, the zig which implies a zag before and after.

Perhaps then, one must content himself with saying more moderately that the chief lasting accomplishment of World War I was the invention of the antiwar novel: a fictional record of the mood out of which the pacifism of between-the-wars was born and of the hopes and fears which sustained it through all the horrors of peace. It is certainly true that before the 1920's that genre did not exist, though it had been prophesied in the first two-thirds of Stephen Crane's *The Red Badge of Courage,* and that since the 1920's, it has become a standard form: both a standard way of responding to combat experience and a standard way of starting a literary career.

In the United States, the examples of Hemingway and Faulkner have ensured the continuing popularity of the genre; the latter struggling as early as *Soldier's Pay* and as late as *A Fable* to give shape to his sense of World War I, and the former providing a classic prototype once and for all in *A Farewell to Arms.* No wonder similar books from abroad have always moved us, from Henri Barbusse's *Le Feu* to *All Quiet on the Western Front,* and notably, of course, *The Good Soldier: Schweik.* And no wonder, too, that the generation of Americans who had broken their pacifist oaths in World War II sought to make amends by keeping faith with the sort of novel that had made war real to them before life itself had gotten around to doing it.

Certainly the flood of antiwar novels that generation has been producing since the forties owes more to certain books that their authors had grown up reading than to the actual fighting that many of them did. A typical case in point is Norman Mailer's *The Naked and the Dead,* begun at Harvard before Mailer had lived through any battles but fictional ones; and quite properly so, since for those of his age *the meanings of their wars had already been established by men twenty and thirty years their senior,* by Hemingway and Faulkner and Jaroslav Hašek, among others.

As a matter of fact, the meaning of their wars has been for most generations established before the fact—in our culture, largely by works of art. The writers of Europe and America who were young enough to fight in World War I were, in this light, unique, endowed with a peculiar freedom their successors have vainly tried to emulate by imitating the forms in which it was expressed. Only the former, however, actually lived in the interval between two conventional ways of understanding war, serving as the gravediggers to one and the midwives to the other.

For a thousand years or so, roughly from the time of Charlemagne to 1914, the wars of Christendom, whether fought against external enemies or strictly within the family, had been felt and celebrated in terms of a single continuous tradition. And those who lived within that tradition assumed without question that some battles at least were not only justifiable but holy, just as they assumed that to die in such battles was not merely a tolerable fate but the most glorious of events. Doubts they may have had, but these could scarcely be confessed to themselves, much less publicly flaunted.

Full of internal contradictions (what, after all, had any military code to do with the teachings of Christ?) and pieced together out of the rag bag of history (tales of Old Testament berserkers like Samson, scholarly recollections of Roman *vertu* and Greek *arete,* popular vestiges of the Germanic combat-religion), nonetheless the Christian heroic tradition proved viable for ten centuries, as viable in the high verse of Dante and Shakespeare and Chaucer as in folk ballads and the sermons of country priests. Yet all the while it lived, of course, it was dying, too, dying with the civilization that had nurtured it, already mourned for by the time of Sir Walter Scott. So slowly did it die, however, that only under the impact of total war were those who fought shocked into admitting that perhaps they no longer believed in what they fought for.

Last to learn that the old tradition had in fact died were the heads of state, kings and emperors, prime ministers and presidents. In their mouths, the shabby slogans For God and Country, For

Christ and King, *Dulce et decorum est pro patria morire*—rang ever less convincingly. But they were not the simple hypocrites their earliest critics took them for; they were merely dupes of history, in whom self-interest conveniently cooperated with confusion. Even more absurd than they, however, seemed the prelates of churches, on whose lips the more bloody battle cries, always a little ironical, appeared suddenly nothing but ironical. Yet it was not the believers who felt the absurdity, only those for whom God was presumably dead.

Small wonder, then, that priest and potentate alike remained unaware that history had rendered them comic, since no one told them except those whose opinions they discounted in advance. Indeed, some to this very day have not realized that the words they speak in all solemnity have been to others for over forty years household jokes. One function of totalitarianism in its manifold forms is precisely to forestall the moment of awakening, imposing by decree the heroic concepts which once flourished by consent. The totalitarian chief counterfeits ever more grotesque versions of the Hero, and in cell and torture chamber attempts to exact from those who dare laugh at him "confessions" that nothing is funny at all. The earliest record of such an attempt, as well as of its gloriously comic failure, is to be found in *The Good Soldier: Schweik*.

Not only in totalitarian societies, however, is the antiheroic spirit assailed by the guardians of the pseudoheroic. In more democratic nations, mass culture is entrusted with the job assigned elsewhere to the secret police; and where those who snicker at pretension are not hauled off to prison, they find it difficult to make themselves heard above the immensely serious clatter of the press and the ponderous voices of official spokesmen, magnified to thunder by P.A. systems. Yet certain writers, like Hašek before them, continue to feel obliged to carry to the world the comic-pathetic news it is reluctant to hear: the Hero is dead. First to know, such writers are the last to forget that ever since World War I they have been called on to celebrate, with due hilarity, the death of the myth of the heroic, even as their predecessors were called on solemnly to celebrate its life.

In the battle front against war, however, there is these days no more possibility of a final victory or defeat than on the battle fronts of war itself. In the former as in the latter, the end is stalemate; for the antiheroic satirists who have carried the day in the libraries and the literary magazines elsewhere seem to have made little impression. The notion of the Christian Hero is no longer viable for the creative imagination, having been destroyed once and for all by the literature of disenchantment that followed World War I; so that no modern Shakespeare could conceive of presenting warriors and kings in the light shed on them by the chronicle plays, nor can we imagine a contemporary Vergil suggesting that death for the fatherland is sweet. Yet we fight wars still, ever vaster and more efficient wars, while senators and commissars alike speak, and are applauded for speaking, in all seriousness the very lines given caricatured senators and commissars in satirical antiwar novels.

Worse still, the antiheroic revolt has itself become in two or three generations a new convention, the source of a new set of fashionably ridiculous clichés. Shameless politicians are as likely to use the slogans of between-the-wars pacifism to launch new wars as they are to refurbish more ancient platitudes. The wild freedom with which the authors of *The Enormous Room* and *Le Feu, The Good Soldier: Schweik* and *A Farewell to Arms,* challenged millennial orthodoxies has been sadly tamed; its fate is symbolized by Picasso's domesticated dove hovering obediently over the rattling spears of the Soviet war camp. Nevertheless, such books still tell us certain truths about the world in which we live, reveal to us certain ways in which men's consciousness of themselves in peace and war was radically altered some four decades ago.

The antiwar novel did not end war, but it memorializes the end of something almost as deeply rooted in the culture of the West: the concept of Honor. It comes into existence at the moment when in the West men, still nominally Christian, come to believe *that the worst thing of all is to die*—more exactly, perhaps, the moment when for the first time in a thousand years it is possible to *admit* that no cause is worth dying for. There are various mitigated forms of this new article of faith: that no cause is worth the death of all humanity, or of a whole nation, or simply of millions of lives; but inevitably it approaches the formulation: no cause is worth the death of a man, no cause is worth the death of *me!*

There are in the traditional literatures of Europe, to be sure, characters who have believed that death was the worst event and honor a figment; but such characters have always belonged to "low comedy," i.e., they have been comic butts set against representatives of quite other ideals, Sancho Panzas who serve Don Quixotes, Falstaffs who tremble before Prince Hals, Leporellos who cower as the Don Giovannis tempt fate. They have been permitted to blaspheme against the courtly codes precisely because those codes have been so secure. And, in any event, their cowardice has always spoken in prose or dialect, worn the garb of a servant or vassal, bowed the knee before an unchallenged master. They represented not a satirical challenge but precisely a "comic relief" from the strain of upholding—against the promptings of our animal nature, the demands of indolence, and greed, and fear—those high values that were once thought to make men fully human. *Non fate fosti viver come bruti, ma perseguir virtute e conoscenza.*

What happens, however, when the Leporellos, the Falstaffs, and the Sancho Panzas begin to inherit the earth? When the remaining masters are in fact more egregious Falstaffs and Leporellos and Sancho Panzas, and all that Don Quixote and Prince Hal and Don Giovanni once stood for is discredited or dead? What happens in a time of democracy, mass culture, and mechanization, a time when war itself is transformed by the industrial revolution? *The Good Soldier: Schweik* addresses itself to answering, precisely and hilariously, this question. And the answer is: what happens is what has been happening to us all ever since 1914, what happens is *us.*

We inhabit for the first time a world in which men begin wars knowing their avowed ends will not be accomplished, a world in which it is more and more difficult to believe that the conflicts we cannot avert are in any sense justified. And in such a world, the draft dodger, the malingerer, the gold brick, the crap-out, all who make what Hemingway was the first to call "a separate peace," all who somehow *survive* the bombardment of shells and cant, become a new kind of antiheroic hero. Of such men, Schweik is the real ancestor. "A great epoch calls for great men," Hašek tell us in a prefatory note. "Today, in the streets of Prague, you can come

across a man who himself does not realize what his significance is
in the history of the great new epoch. . . . If you were to ask him
his name, he would answer . . . 'I am Schweik.' . . . He did not
set fire to the temple of the goddess at Ephesus, like that fool of a
Herostrate, merely in order to get his name into the . . . school
reading books. And that, in itself, is enough."

II.

Not all of Hašek's book, unfortunately, is devoted to portraying
a Falstaff in a world without Hotspurs or Prince Hals. Much of it is
spent in editorializing rather obviously about the horrors of war and
the ironies of being a chaplain, the shortcomings of the Emperor
Franz Joseph and the limitations of the military mind; and toward
the end it becomes rather too literary in a heavy-handed way, especially after the introduction of Volunteer Officer Marek, a figure
obviously intended to speak directly for the author. From time to
time, we feel it as dated, say, as *What Price Glory* or *All Quiet on
the Western Front,* for we have grown by now as weary of the
phrasemongering and self-pity of conventional pacifism as of the at-
titudinizing and pharisaism of conventional patriotism.

It is not Hasek's anticlericalism or anti-Semitism, not his distrust of Magyars or of the long-defunct Austrian Empire, not his
Czech nationalism or his defense of the Czech tongue against German linguistic imperialism that moves us today. The dream of ex-
propriation, too ("After this war, they say, there ain't going to be
any more emperors and they'll help themselves to the big royal es-
tates"), rings hollow for us now, who know how it turned into the
nightmare from which Jan Masaryk leaped to his death two wars
later.

It is only when Hašek turns Schweik loose among scoundrels
quite like himself, the police spy Bretschneider or the atheist Jewish
chaplain, Otto Katz, and permits him to speak his own language—
only, that is to say, when the anarchist intellectual permits himself
to be possessed by his *lumpen* antihero—that the book becomes at
once wonderfully funny and wonderfully true. Schweik is fortu-

nately one of those mythical creations who escape the prejudices of their creators even as they elude our definitions; and he refuses to speak with the voice of the 1920 revolutionary, even as he refuses to speak with the voice of councilors and kings.

He will not be exploited by his author any more than he will by the con men and bullies who inhabit his fictional universe; moving through a society of victimizers, he refuses to become a victim. Though Hašek would persuade us that he is surrounded by Pilates ("The glorious history of the Roman domination of Jerusalem was being enacted all over again"), Schweik certainly does not consider himself a Christ. He is neither innocent nor a claimant to innocence. Charged with political crimes by an absurd police spy, he pleads guilty; and to a fellow prisoner who cries, "I'm innocent, I'm innocent," he remarks blandly, "So was Jesus Christ but they crucified Him for all that. Nobody anywhere at any time has ever cared a damn whether a man's innocent or not."

To Schweik malice is simply one of the facts of life, the inexhaustible evil of man a datum from which all speculation about survival must begin. He neither looks back to a Golden Age nor forward to redemption, secular or heavenly, but knows that if he is to survive it must be in a world quite like the one he has always known. A communicant of no church and a member of no party, he considers that neither intelligence nor charity is likely to ameliorate man's condition. "Anybody can make a mistake," he says at one point, "and the more he thinks about a thing, the more mistakes he's bound to make." And at another, he remarks with a straight-faced nihilism before which we can seek refuge only in laughter, "If all people wanted to do all the others a good turn, they'd be walloping each other in a brace of shakes."

Return evil for evil is Schweik's anti-Golden Rule, though often he assumes the guise of nonresistance, along with the semblance of idiocy, to do it. He is, however, neither a pharisee nor a hypocrite, only a simple conniver—in civil life, a peddler of dogs with forged pedigrees; in war, a soldier who will not fight. His resistance to war is based on no higher principles than his business; both are rooted in the conviction that a man must somehow *live* and, if possible, thrive on the very disasters which surround him. In the end, he is a kind of success, as success goes in a society intent on committing suicide; he eats well, drinks well, sleeps with the mistress of one of his masters, and pummels another mercilessly. But above all, he does not die. What more can a man ask?

He is even promoted from a lowly batman to company orderly, though, of course, the one place he will not go to is the Front. No matter how hard history nudges him, no matter what his orders read, nothing will force him into battle. He marches resolutely backward or in circles, but never forward into the sound of shooting; and by the novel's end, he has managed blessedly to be taken prisoner by his own side. Refusing to recognize the reality of disaster, he turns each apparent defeat into a victory, proving himself in the end no more a *schlemiel* than a Victim, or one of those Little Men so beloved in sentimental protest literature. Yet he seems sometimes all three, for it pleases his native slyness to assume such roles, fooling us as readers, even as he fools his superiors in the fiction they share, and as we suspect he fools the author himself. Indeed, he is fond of speaking of himself as "unlucky," but when he explains what this epithet means, it turns out he is unlucky only to others, especially those unwise enough to entrust him with important commissions.

Schweik's affiliation runs back through all the liars of literature to the father of lies himself, back through Falstaff to the sly parasites of Roman comedy and the Vices, those demidevils of medieval literature. He is, in fact, the spirit that denies, as well as the spirit that deceives: but he plays his part without melodrama, among the clowns, his little finger on the seam of his trousers, and his chin tucked in. So plumb, affable, snub-nosed, and idiotically eager to please does he seem, that we are more inclined to pat his head than to cry, "Get thee behind me!"

Yet on his lips the noblest slogans become mockeries. Let him merely cry, "God save the Emperor" and all who listen are betrayed to laughter; for he speaks in the name of the dark margin of ambivalence in us all—that five or ten per cent of distrust and ridicule that lurks in our hearts in regard even to the cause to which we are most passionately committed. And in the world in which Hašek imagines him, there is none to gainsay him, since the spokesmen for the ninety or ninety-five per cent of ordinary affirmation are corrupted or drunken or dumb.

We cannot help knowing, moreover, that not only the slogans of a distant war and a fallen empire, but those most dear to us now—the battle cries of democracy or socialism—would become in that same mouth equally hilarious; our pledges of allegiance intolerable jokes even to us who affirm them. Surely Schweik is not yet dead, but survives in concentration camps and army barracks, in prison cells and before investigating committees, assuring his interrogators of his feeble-mindedness and his good will as their pretenses to virtue and prudence crumble before his garrulous irrelevancies. "Beg to report, sir," he says, looking us right in the eye, "I'm an idiot, sir." And the idiocy of our definitions of sanity becomes immediately apparent.

It seems appropriate that Jaroslav Hašek and Franz Kafka lived at the same moment in the same city; for, though their politics differed as did the very language in which they chose to write, though one was mildly anti-Semitic and the other a Jew, their visions of the world's absurdity were much the same. Perhaps there was no better place from which to watch the decay of Europe and the values which had nurtured it than Prague; no better place to see how *comic* that catastrophe was.

Jewish legend tells us that precisely in Prague, in the attic of that city's ancient synagogue, the *Golem* waits to be reborn: the sleeping man-made Avenger who will awake only when some terror beyond all the Jews have known threatens the world. And maybe, after all, Schweik is no devil, but only that *Golem* in the uniform of a doomed empire, more comic in his second coming than anyone could have foreseen. "Terribly funny," we say putting down the book, and not taking the adverb seriously enough.

Kafka, we remember, thought himself a humorist, yet we shudder reading him. Hašek, it would appear, believed he wrote a tale of terror and was greeted by laughter. Let us leave the final word to Schweik, who reports, getting the names a little wrong, of course, but making his point all the same, "I once knew a Czech author personally, a chap named Ladislav Hajek. . . . He was a cheerful gentleman, he was, and a good sort, too. He once went to a pub and read a lot of his stories there. They were very sad stories and they made everybody laugh, and then he started crying and stood us drinks all around and—"

The account remains unfinished, like the book in which it appears, for the tale of the Good Soldier Schweik can never really be done; and, in any event, Hašek, who roused him from his long sleep in Prague, died at forty of the T.B. he had contracted in the prison camps of World War I.

Fano, Italy
—1962

FOUR

The Two Memories:
Reflections on Writers and
Writing in the Thirties

To THINK ABOUT the thirties in the second half of the sixties seems not a luxury but a necessity: not one of those acts of reminiscence and nostalgia which are optional, the self-indulgence of a baffled critic, looking, perhaps, for his own lapsed youth (though surely there is something of that in me), but the kind of return to roots and sources so often required for cultural renewal; the re-examination of a past never quite understood—out of an awareness that unless we understand it now we will not understand the present or our own surviving selves. We have barely left behind a decade or so spent in re-evoking and re-evaluating the twenties, reaching back to the years just after World War I in search of a clue to our identity in the post-World War II years; and our own times have been altered as well as illuminated by that search. We have exhumed the Charleston, as well as certain dress styles and hairdos; we have redeemed the fading figure of F. Scott Fitzgerald and revived for a little while memories of Leopold and Loeb; we have even created a magnificent pastiche of the period (its legendary slayings and weary old jokes) in *Some Like It Hot*. And it is the myth of that period, if not the actual fact, which helped make possible a New Jazz Age, a revival of Bohemian Life, complete with Pop Art and what we have agreed recently to call Camp, plus a new sort of Romanticism, utterly without side or solemnity, despite its celebration of feeling over form, and pleasure over piety.

But our hunger for the twenties seems satiated for the moment, as the old-fashioned Beat become the newfangled Hip, and our fantasies demand to be fed with myths of quite another past, for which we ransack the thirties—surrendering nothing, let it be said quickly, of what we have redeemed from the twenties, only seeking to add something other, something more. The way in has been primarily literary so far: a series of studies and reminiscences to begin with —ranging from academic examinations of the past as something dead and therefore fair game for Ph.D dissertations (Walter Rideout's *The Radical Novel,* for instance, and Daniel Aaron's *Writers on the Left,* as well as Allen Guttmann's *The Wound in the Heart*) to more journalistic accounts like Murray Kempton's *Part of Our Time,* or personal memoirs like those of Mary McCarthy and Dwight MacDonald and, most recently, Alfred Kazin's account of "making it" in those bleak years. When the New Establishment remembers its origins (and to become established has always meant to feel obliged to remember) it recalls the thirties.

Even more striking have been the revivals and reprintings of the books which those Establishment figures enjoyed as underground literature in their youth—*not,* be it noticed, those writers whom the official taste of the period itself preferred, Dos Passos, say, or James T. Farrell or even John Steinbeck, despite his almost posthumous Nobel Prize. We tend to agree with the twenties in their adulation of Fitzgerald—grant, in effect, that they understood themselves, or at least chose to celebrate in themselves what we can share; but we correct the thirties even as we revive them—instruct them retrospectively about their own meaning. And we are embarrassed to find European opinion, as expressed by the Nobel Prize Committee, trapped still in the established taste of that much-confused era.

No, it is certain relatively neglected writers of the Depression decade who appeal to us, constitute our mythical thirties—judging at least by what the critics of our age have bullied the paperback publishers into making available once more: Henry Roth's belated best-seller, *Call It Sleep;* the three comic novels of Daniel Fuchs, *Summer in Williamsburg, Homage to Blenholt,* and *Low Company;*

James Agee's *Let Us Now Praise Famous Men;* and especially, of course, the almost lost novels of Nathanael West, *Miss Lonely-hearts* and *Day of the Locust,* in particular, but even his first half-botched piece of Surrealism, *The Dream Life of Balso Snell*—and, *especially* for the cognoscenti, those real hungerers for the thirties, *A Cool Million: or the Dismantling of Lemuel Pitkin.* Latterly, even such indifferent efforts as Tess Slesinger's *The Unpossessed* have been put back into print, and even such egregiously though typically bad prose of the period as Mike Gold's *Jews Without Money* or such correspondingly atrocious poetry as Eli Siegel's "Hot Afternoons Have Been in Montana." Surely there is a certain amount of campy condescension involved in the final two revivals, as well as a certain amount of canniness on the part of publishers to whom it has come through at last: the thirties are in! But there is a kind of vague sense, too, like that which drives the sick dog to consume whatever weeds are nearest by, that the literature of the thirties is good for what ails us.

All the books I have mentioned so far have been American books by urban Jewish Leftists and their fellow travelers, radicals at least of one or another persuasion; but even the works of Southern Agrarians begin to make it onto the supermarket and airport shelves (John Peale Bishop's *Act of Darkness* is about to be republished); and the books of certain European novelists who moved the Depression generation begin to appear again in the hands of the young. Not so long ago, a second edition (revised as thirties books tend to be revised when they are reborn) of Silone's *Fontamara* was issued, and though it has, I fear, won few hearts it had not already won twenty-five years before, the retranslation of Céline's *Death on the Installment Plan* which followed it seems to be moving our younger readers, as the original has already moved a new generation of readers in France.

Besides these revivals on the level of High Style, there have been humbler, more popular rediscoveries, too: sometimes in the form of adaptation, like Clifford Odets' *Golden Boy*—in black-face, with Sammy Davis, Jr. in the title role, straddling the political pieties of two ages; sometimes in the form of remakes, like the long-promised new movie version of *Winterset;* but most often in the form simply of reruns, those twin bills (the very notion of the

Double Feature itself a nostalgic revival) which bring back to the local theater, say, Clark Gable and Greta Garbo, or W. C. Fields and Mae West; after which the real addicts can stagger on home to the Late, Late Show and watch *Grapes of Wrath* or *I Was a Fugitive from a Chain Gang.* One movie face in particular, however, has emerged from the scores called up out of the past, coming to represent the very essence of the period as we redream it: not, oddly enough, Paul Muni or John Garfield who belong to the age completely, but Humphrey Bogart who survived it into the forties and fifties, to the verge of our own era—keeping alive (we are now able to realize) the unshaven cheek and the stiff upper lip of the Depression face through a time when we thought we had forgotten it forever. But there it was all the while, awaiting the moment when we would be able really to see it again, whether worn by Sam Spade in Dashiell Hammett's *The Maltese Falcon,* or the last surviving prospector in *The Treasure of the Sierra Madre,* or Harry Morgan in Hemingway's sole true thirties novel, *To Have and Have Not*— in which, for once, the quite unthirties face of Gary Cooper simply would not do for a Hemingway hero.

And with what astonishment we have lived to discover that face, grown magically young, to be sure, sported again in the sixties by Jean-Paul Belmondo; with what delight learned that we, through Bogey, had been there first. But so, too, were we there first politically; and it is with similar astonishment and delight that we observe the young, on campuses and off, forging once more a Radical Youth Movement, which may be only an analogue of what went on in the thirties rather than a belated offshoot. It hardly matters, however, since, whatever its roots, such a Movement makes possible the kind of dialogue with the past unavailable to those under twenty-five in the forties and fifties. To be sure, there are fundamental differences between their Movement and ours, but precisely this gives us something to talk about, since we are both aware of what divides us as well as of what we have in common—though they, perhaps, tend to be more conscious of the former, and we of the latter.

The Radicalism of the sixties, like that of the thirties, is influenced by the Bohemia which preceded it, and with which it remains uncomfortably entangled; and it differs from its earlier counterpart precisely as the one Bohemia differs from the other. The young radicals of the thirties came out of a world of bootleg and bathtub gin and the tail end of the first Freudian-Laurentian sexual revolution; the young radicals of the Sixties have emerged from the post-1955 world of "pot" and other hallucinogens and that homosexual revolution so inextricably intertwined with the struggle for Civil Rights as well as the quest for "cool." Even in moments of violence, in those demonstrations so satisfactory to the young in any age (and not the young alone), those climaxes of mass action in which the students of the sixties seem to be trying once more—though without full consciousness of the past—to achieve the delusory power felt by the half-million protesters against war on the campuses of the mid-thirties, a new note of almost feminine passivity has entered. Everywhere the desire to *suffer* violence rather than to inflict it seems to possess a generation untouched by the dream of "hard Bolshevism" proper to a world that had not yet learned to detest Stalin and endure Khrushchev—the aspiration to remain innocent even in conflict by playing the role of the raped rather than the rapist, the Jew as opposed to the Cossack.

And more than this, the New Leftist seems oddly, perhaps cripplingly, to *know* that he is indulging in a limited and privileged kind of activity, like joining a fraternity or playing on a team; that after four years or five, or six, he will accommodate to the life around him, run for office, or get a job, in any case, become more like his father than he can really bear quite to acknowledge—unless he leaves politics for drugs, abandons the SDS for LSD; but the real politico cannot abide this way either. But whence, we are driven to ask at this point, the odd passivity and the strange (not cynical but ironic) self-knowledge? And part of the answer lies surely in the thirties and what they have come to mean right now: in the particular way in which the thirties have survived for the activist young, which is to say, in their vicarious memory of that period.

The young have a longer memory than their elders—or even they themselves—are prepared to grant, a memory as long as the imagined lives lived in the books they read; not histories and memoirs and analyses by political scientists, for these seem only dead records of the dead, but fiction and poetry. And the books which have made the mind of this generation turn out to be in large part

the sort of thirties book I referred to earlier, the underground literature loved in their youth by that intermediate generation of Saul
Bellow, Norman Mailer, and James Baldwin, who have also influenced them, since the time of growing up which that intermediate
generation remembers is indistinguishable from the nightmare visions of Nathanael West. West is finally the key figure, at work still
as a living influence in the fiction of writers as young as Jeremy
Larner, whose Dell Prize novel, *Drive, He Said,* may have a title
derived from the poetry of Robert Creeley, but whose vision comes
from *Miss Lonelyhearts* and *Day of the Locust.* But the world of
West, we must never forget for a moment, that "peculiar half-
world," as he called it himself, escaped all the clichés of politics,
even of the left-wing orthodoxy to which he himself subscribed.
Apocalyptics was his special province; and for the sake of a vision
of the End of Things, he was willing to sacrifice what his Communist mentors had taught him was a true picture of society. Once out
of his books, he felt obliged to apologize for his vision (writing to
Jack Conroy, for instance, "If I put into *The Day of the Locust* any
of the sincere, honest people who work here and are making such a
great, progressive fight . . . [he is talking about Hollywood] the
whole fabric of the peculiar half-world which I attempted to create
would be badly torn by them"); but once inside them, he remained
utterly faithful to that vision, however alien it might be to the Stalinist's theoretical America.

No wonder it is even more alien to the version of the thirties
preserved in official histories, or tenderly recollected by the majority of those now over forty whose proudest boast is that they voted
for Franklin Delano Roosevelt three times, or argued over with
endless recriminations and counterrecriminations by the survivors
of the New Deal. There are, mythologically speaking (and we are
in the realm of myth whenever we talk about what survives not in
the archives but in the heads of the young), *two* thirties at least—
two memories of that legendary era, not merely different but competing. And those who walk about possessed by one such set of
memories find it difficult, almost impossible to communicate with
those haunted by the other, or committed, for official reasons, to
evoking and preserving it. I listened recently—at a ceremonial occasion presided over by political scientists—to the movie actor Ed-

ward G. Robinson (himself a survivor of the thirties) not this time playing a gangster role, but reading the documents of *his* thirties: F. D. R.'s First Inaugural Address, topical comments by Will Rogers, etc., etc. And what, I kept asking myself—feeling quite like Saint Augustine crying out, "What has Athens to do with Jerusalem!"—had any of this to do with *my* thirties?

Yet Mr. Robinson's documents illustrated admirably a view of the Depression decade officially sponsored in the golden time of John F. Kennedy, by such court historians as Arthur Schlesinger, Jr.: a view which sees the thirties as a period in which we moved from defeat to triumph—conquering fear and poverty as well as preparing for a victory over the Nazis and Japanese—a time during which Labor came into its own, and the first decisive steps were taken toward the truly Good Society, i.e., the Welfare State. F. D. R. is the hero of this euphoric vision of our not-so-remote past, the true "Happy Warrior," crippled and charismatic, not FDR flanked, perhaps, by Eleanor Roosevelt or Henry Wallace, or some favorite ghost writer, brain truster, trust buster, or whatever. But this vision is embodied in no distinguished work in prose or verse—only in the feeblest sort of pious-commercial plays, the sound tracks of propaganda films prepared by the Department of Agriculture, and the final panels of those wartime comic books showing Roosevelt grasping by the hand Captain America or Superman. Even the elegiac verse occasioned by his death has mercifully faded from the mind.

No, the truly distinguished literature of the time of F. D. R., the books of the period that are preserved in libraries, taught in classes, or—best of all—still passed from hand to hand, scarcely confesses the existence of the New Deal at all; and the figure of Roosevelt, when untypically evoked, signifies irrelevance or impotence, the meaningless world of somewhere else. We can find, if we look hard, an ironical reference or two to his ineffectual legislation in some of the proletarian novels so admired during the period itself: in Clara Weatherwax's *Marching! Marching!*, for instance, first and last winner of the *New Masses* prize for fiction, or in the sort of satirical verse published in that same magazine. Though occasionally, and especially during the early years of his first administration, the Left managed to whip up some public indignation toward Roosevelt, he did not even exist for them as he did for the contemporary extreme Right—as the mythological object of rabid hatred and fear —but only as a subject for condescension and offhand contempt.

Characteristically, *Americana* (an independent left-wing review with which Nathanael West was briefly associated) could manage to say in 1932 only: "As for Mr. Roosevelt personally, we consider him a weak and vacillating politician who will be an apt tool in the hands of his powerful backers." Years later, to be sure, Whittaker Chambers, a literary witness of the era (at least, the period itself had considered him "literary," since certain leading Soviet critics had said kind things about his three published stories; and his play *Can You Hear Their Voices?* produced and directed at Vassar by Hallie Flanagan, had shaken the whole Ivy League) had attributed a somewhat more virulent attitude to his *alter ego* Alger Hiss, reporting of the latter that "the same strange savagery cropped out in a conversation about Franklin Roosevelt." This comment he hastened to explain at some length, in terms oddly reminiscent of D. H. Lawrence's *Lady Chatterley's Lover:* "Hiss's contempt for Franklin Roosevelt as a dabbler in revolution who understood neither revolution or history was profound. It was the common view of Roosevelt among the Communists, which I shared with the rest. But Alger expressed it not only in political terms. He startled me, and deeply shocked my wife, by the obvious pleasure he took in the most simple and brutal references to the President's physical condition as a symbol of the middle-class breakdown." The implicit metaphor is clear enough: F.D.R. as Lady Chatterley's impotent husband, the C. P. as her prepotent lover, and the American working class as Constance herself.

Whether this was, in fact, Hiss's opinion scarcely matters (it is a question for the courts and the kind of journalist who loves correcting the courts, not for literary or social critics); it was, beyond doubt, a prevailing one in the thirties among the Communists and those writers influenced by them. But this means among *most* writers of first-rate talent then functioning in the United States, including certain survivors of the twenties, as well as young men just then rising to prominence, and even younger ones who would have to wait for the forties and fifties for recognition. The only considerable group of gifted artists who then operated completely outside the Communist sphere of influence were the Southern Agrarians—who numbered in their ranks poets like John Crowe Ransom and Allen Tate, novelists like Robert Penn Warren, and who had issued at the very beginning of the thirties their own manifesto, *I'll Take My Stand,* in which they had attempted to define a mythologically resonant and intellectually respectable politics of the Right. But F.D.R. in his anti-mythological Middle seemed as alien to them as to the writers of the Left: an irrelevant, faintly distasteful representative of the hated and feared urban Northeast, who, after T.V.A., was revealed as the Enemy.

I have spoken of the poetic invisibility of Roosevelt so far as if it were merely a historical datum to be researched and recorded; but his mythological irrelevance, in fact, belongs to a literary past with which our present is continuous, to which we still respond. The two most influential literary journals of the forties and fifties, the training ground of the writers who most move us now, or have, at least, until only yesterday (all the way from Saul Bellow to Marshall McLuhan, Karl Shapiro to John Berryman), were *The Kenyon Review,* heir to *The Southern Review,* and *The Partisan Review.* But *The Southern Review* came into existence under the doubtful auspices of Huey Long, redneck rabble rouser and fascist; while *The Partisan Review* was the by-product of the Communist-sponsored John Reed Club in New York, and the imported notions of *agitprop* it had presumably been formed to espouse. To be sure, by the time *The Kenyon Review* itself was being published, the disillusion of the respectable Southern Right with their peasant allies (fictionally recorded in Robert Penn Warren's *All the King's Men)* had already occurred; and *The Partisan Review* moved quickly from Stalinist orthodoxy to Trotskyism and Cold War Liberalism. Eventually, in fact, the two movements coalesced in academic amity, uniting to form the School of Letters, in which another generation of writers and intellectuals were trained. But in their most effective years, both journals reflected the traditions of radical dissent, Right and Left, out of which they had been born.

There has been much idle discussion, pro and con, of late about how "Red" the "Red Decade" really was; but as far as serious writers are concerned, there seems little doubt. In 1932, at any rate, more than fifty writers, among them the best known and most respected of their time, issued a statement called *Culture in Crisis,* in

which they expressed their joint despair over the prospects of our
society surviving its economic collapse, and pledged their support
for the Communist presidential and vice-presidential candidates,
Foster and Ford. Among the signers were Edmund Wilson, Sherwood Anderson, Lincoln Steffens, Langston Hughes, Erskine Caldwell, and John Dos Passos, who were later joined—in the American Writers' Congress, an organization which institutionalized the
attitudes and positions of that first manifesto—by Edward Dahlberg, Katherine Anne Porter, Kenneth Burke, James T. Farrell,
Dashiell Hammett, Richard Wright, Theodore Dreiser, and Ernest
Hemingway. If we add to their number Henry Roth and Nathanael
West, who were deep in the Movement from the start and needed
no large public appeal to recruit them, it seems hard to think of
anyone (with the exception always of the unreconstructed Southerners) not on the list whom one would expect to find included in a
current college course on the literature of the Thirties. And we remember, finally, that a poll of a sample selected from the American
Writers' Congress membership in 1936 showed still 36 voting for
Earl Browder, six for Norman Thomas, only two for Franklin
Roosevelt. How oddly skewed a result as compared with the voting
behavior of the total electorate!

But what had moved the writers on the Left to make a commitment which cut them off from the mainstream of American life in
so spectacular a way, pledging them at one and the same time to
social action and disaffection from the strategies and techniques of
action chosen by the overwhelming majority of their fellow citizens?
If we look at the 1932 manifesto itself, we will find two quite dis-
tinct, though linked, motivations, both operative from the very beginning. The first is a particular brand of self-righteousness, an almost pharisaical smugness in being among the excluded, which
seems an inevitable concomitant of all American radicalism and the
isolation such radicalism implies in the United States: "Very well,
we strike hands with our true comrades. We claim our own and we
reject the disorder, the lunacy spawned by the grabbers."

The second is a vision of disaster and a pleasuring in it—a mas-
ochistic wish-fear that welcomes the End of Days, the Pangs of the
Messiah, the long-awaited Signs of Doom precisely because they

herald terror and annihilation. The writers of *Culture in Crisis* see the world around them as "a house rotting away; the roof leaks, the sills and rafters are crumbling"; but they thrill not to a promise of renovation and renewal, rather to the hope of pulling it down around them, of themselves disappearing under the rubble. How ironically the Rooseveltian phrase about having nothing to fear but fear itself rings in this context, where fear seems the last passion; and how oddly the appeal for hope built into F. D. R.'s speeches by anti-apocalyptic ghost writers contrasts with the cherishing of despair dear to the hearts of the doomsters. For the American writer who signs his own name, terror has been the staple of prose and verse ever since (if, indeed, it was ever anything else, in this land where dissent has always meant the rejection of all official optimisms), and the one thing to fear above all else the failure of fear itself.

And what is present in the manifesto only by implication and nuance is spelled out, fleshed out in the explicit images and fables of a hundred books that followed. Straight autobiographical accounts of what it was like to be alive and responding in this way to the America of the thirties are to be found in works like Malcolm Cowley's *Exile's Return* and Edmund Wilson's *American Jitters*— out of which not the outmoded rhetoric, but a single realized image stays in my mind, Wilson's picture of the just-opened Empire State Building in 1931, the tallest American house of them all, and one born rotting away,

> the pile of stone, brick, nickel and steel, the shell of offices, shafts, windows and steps, that outmultiplies and outstacks them all— that, most purposeless and superfluous of all, is being advertised as a triumph in the hour when the planless competitive society, the dehumanized urban community, of which it represents the culmination, is bankrupt. The big loft is absolutely empty, there is nothing to look at in it—with the exception of one decoration: . . . A large male figure is seen standing upright and fornicating, *Venere aversa,* with a stooping female figure, who has no arms but pendulous breasts. The man is exclaiming, "O, man!" Further along is a gigantic vagina with its name in four large letters under it.

And these books are still in print; *again* in print says it more precisely; yet the reader must be careful, for he will find them disconcertingly altered, bowdlerized, as it were, in Wilson's *American Earthquake* or Cowley's revised edition of *Exile's Return*. The author who survives an apocalypse that never comes, can scarcely believe he waited so breathlessly, so hopefully for the End—and tries to keep us from believing it three decades later.

Another kind of record is to be found in the so-called proletarian novels of the period, with their obsessive accounts of strike after strike defeated, defeated, *defeated* (it was Walter Rideout who first observed their distaste for victory in his acute study, *The Radical Novel in America)*. If the events at Gastonia provide the plot for at least six novels of the era, beginning with Sherwood Anderson's *Beyond Desire* and culminating in poor Miss Weatherwax's *Marching! Marching!,* it is surely because their outcome was satisfactorily disastrous for labor—though the imagination of the time could tailor fact to suit its own needs, as in the case of the strike at Aberdeen, Washington, which actually ended in a triumph for the unions, but in each fictional case was revised into a defeat. It is one more instance of the discrepancies of the Two Memories: the history books assuring us that the thirties were a period of immense gains for organized labor, the era of the Wagner Act and the creation of the C.I.O.; and the more poetic accounts seeing only bloody struggle inevitably debouching in defeat, failure, destruction, utter annihilation—this time in contempt of fact, though perhaps not of deeper truth.

Still, the manifestly proletarian books of the Depression era are its least satisfactory achievements, perhaps in part because of our nagging sense that this is not *really* how things went, our realization that the trade unions succeeded, after all, and that (for us still who are children of that age, as well as for the age itself) nothing fails like success. Certainly, the great causes which moved the thirties were *lost* causes: local miscarriages of justice, small or large, beginning with Sacco and Vanzetti and going on and on to a kind of climax in the Scottsboro boys. And what a shabby history of the exploitation of quite genuine misery for specious political ends it all seems from the vantage point of the present—compounded by our recent knowledge that the victims further victimized by their protectors may not even have been innocent to begin with—not even Sacco, not even Vanzetti. But mere facts matter little in such symbolic cases, tending finally to obscure their mythic significance.

So, too, with the war in Spain, that deep "wound in the heart" (the phrase is Camus', borrowed by Allen Guttmann for the title of a book about the literature created to express the pain born of the Loyalists' defeat): the war, which to those with memories like my own, made World War II seem when it came second-best, too-late, hopelessly impure. It was a war in which the New Deal, the pious Middle, refused—despite much soul searching—to become officially involved; the war in which Roosevelt forbade shipments of supplies to the forces fighting Hitler and Mussolini, but to which thousands of Americans (mostly Communists, largely Jews) went anyhow as volunteers, disowning both reality and their own country as they crossed the borders. But it was especially a war which captured the imagination of writers everywhere, a war which prompted even Hemingway to write four stories (chiefly bad), a play (utterly awful), and an ambitious novel (not quite good enough); and to make what must be the only public speech of his entire career.

Even more incredibly, it brought William Faulkner's signature to a petition, and—working at the deep level of his imagination where his old characters were being continually recast and furnished with new adventures, persuaded him to ship Linda Snopes off to drive an ambulance for the Loyalists. Yet what was for our best writers the chief event of the age—confirming their prescience of Doom—a cause incredibly pure (at least as mythicized) overwhelmed by the Fascists from without, and compromised hopelessly, even before the military defeat, by the maneuverings of the Soviet Union from within: this last, best, lost cause scarcely existed in the world of F.D.R. In James MacGregor Burns' thick and fascinating study of his character, *The Lion and the Fox,* for instance, the whole matter is given apologetic short shrift in three or four pages out of over five hundred: "Roosevelt from the start had favored the Loyalist cause. . . . Publicly, however, the President was adamantly neutral. . . . As the months passed Roosevelt felt increasingly distressed. . . . There were arguments and forces on the other side. . . . But nothing happened. . . . To raise the embargo would mean the loss of every Catholic vote in the coming fall election, Roosevelt said." And anyhow he had other fish to fry, other causes closer to his heart. It was left to the poets to celebrate disaster, and if they sputtered away into sentimentalities over bombed children, who then had the *chutzpah* to criticize, or the insight to point out that such images of desolation and impotence were precisely what the age demanded? Instead, they listened as Harold Rosenberg sang

> *. . . All he knew of life was laughing and growing*
> *Till the iron dropped on him out of the sky.*
> *O gaunt horses of Hades*
> *He has not even one weapon*
> *With which to defend himself.*

and Muriel Rukeyser answered antiphonally,

> *Bomb-day's child will always be dumb,*
> *Cannon-day's child can never quite come,*
> *but the child that's born on Battle-day*
> *is blithe and bonny and rotted away.*

And though they wept publicly, they thrilled a little, in private, too, at the notion of the rotting child. They did not know it was a Marquis de Sade they were all the time demanding, though they had one of their very own close at hand—since every revolution, failing inevitably at all of its ends but terror, produces a laureate of terror: the original Divine Marquis in 1789, Nathanael West in 1935.

West, too, is an expert in the indignities of children. Think, for instance, of the letter from "Desperate" to "Miss Lonelyhearts": "When I was a little girl it was not so bad because I got used to the kids on the block making fun of me, but now I would like to have boy friends like the other girls . . . but no boy will take me out because I was born without a nose—although I am a good dancer and have a nice shape . . . I have a big hole in the middle of my face that scares people even myself so I can't blame the boys." But West is not content with pathos, even when sanctified by a political cause; it is ultimate horror he is after, a kind of final terror which he attains not only in such full-fledged evocations of apocalypse as the often quoted ending of *Day of the Locust,* but more modestly and slyly, as in the "dismantling" scene of *A Cool Million,* rendered in cool idiot English imitating the style of Horatio Alger:

> At this both actors turned on Lem and beat him violently over the head and body with their rolled-up newspapers. Their object was to knock off his toupee or to knock out his teeth and eye. When they had accomplished one or all of these goals, they stopped clubbing him. Then Lem, whose part it was not to move while he was being hit, bent over and with sober dignity took from the box at his feet . . . whatever he needed to replace the things that had been knocked off or out.
>
> . . . For a final curtain, they brought out an enormous wooden mallet labeled "The Works" and with it completely demolished our hero. His toupee flew off, his eye and teeth popped out, and his wooden leg was knocked into the audience.
>
> At the sight of the wooden leg, the presence of which they had not even suspected, the spectators were convulsed with joy. They laughed heartily until the curtain came down and for some time afterwards.

But West is a virtuoso of the macabre, after all, from whom we come to expect such effects as his stock-in-trade. What truly astonishes us is to find a sober-minded apologist for sweet reason and the status quo betrayed by the mood of the time into precisely such grotesque evocations of terror. Certainly, nobody on the Left in the thirties thought of James Gould Cozzens as an ally, and surely no one now associates him (after a series of books pledged to redeeming himself from his temporary lapse) with deep despair, that ultimate *Angst* before the failed possibilities of our civilization—for which Communism once seemed to provide a handy set of formulations, if not a solution. Yet he wrote in the midst of the Depression a little book called *Castaway,* which caught perhaps better than any other single work (being untroubled by ideology) the mood of the times.

Cozzens' book is a modern Gothic novel set in a department store in a large American city, New York perhaps though we cannot be certain. Mr. Lecky, who is the sole character, remains as unsure as we throughout whether he is in Macy's or Gimbels or the May Company or Hell. It is functionally an island, at any rate, the

place on which he wakes to find himself cast away, and he becomes, therefore, a new Robinson Crusoe—even discovering at one
point the print of a bare foot in an aisle between two display counters. But Mr. Lecky is a Crusoe at the end rather than the beginning
of the era of bourgeois free enterprise, a survivor rather than a
founder of the Age of Individualism—a Crusoe lost and starving
not in an unexplored desert, but in the very midst of a world of
Things which he can no longer manipulate or control in his own interest. And when he finally finds (and kills!) the Man Friday,
whose footprint has temporarily lifted up his heart, and whom he
has pursued as much in fear as in hope, it turns out to be only himself, his own terrifying reflection in the glass.

> Mr. Lecky beheld its familiar strangeness—not like a strange-
> er's face, and yet it was no friend's face, nor the face of anyone
> he had ever met. What this could mean held him, he bent closer,
> questioning in the gloom; and suddenly his hand let go the watch,
> for Mr. Lecky knew why he had never seen a man with this
> face. He knew who had been pursued and cruelly killed, who
> was now dead and would never climb more stairs. He knew why
> Mr. Lecky could never have for his own the stock of this great
> store.

But Mr. Lecky—which is to say those of us who came to consciousness in the Thirties—lived on, saved, perhaps, by that very
same Roosevelt in whom we never succeeded in believing. Preserving capitalism, the New Deal also preserved us who had been pre-
dicting its death and our own. And the doom which befell us, quite
as dark in its own way as our blackest vision, turned out to be the
opposite of what we had foreseen. We have moved into the Afflu-
ent, the Great Society (so we are told, and so—in some sense—we
cannot deny); and are assured daily that, Cozzens and the other
melancholy writers of the thirties notwithstanding, we can indeed
have for our own "the stock of this great store." And though we
may protest that, alas, we still do not know how to manipulate or
control the things we inherit, we have been taught at least how to
want and waste them; which means, in effect, that the End for
which so many of us so passionately waited has not come, either
with a bang or a whimper.

Perhaps this is why some of the writers most profoundly possessed by the mood of the period stuttered to silence when new possibilities demanded new responses for which they were not prepared. Henry Roth is the most striking example—the victim surely of personal problems we cannot pretend to know, but in part too, a casualty of the failed apocalypse. The rediscovery of the Thirties has apparently convinced him that he as well as his masterpiece might be reborn; and newspapers stories tell us that he has emerged from hiding and is off in Spain contemplating a second novel, about the fifteenth-century persecution of the Jews and Indians. And maybe he will find a new voice for the new age; though the examples of Dos Passos and Farrell, ghosts haunting their own bodies and their own later books, should give him pause.

Younger men than he, writers whose first efforts never quite appeared in the thirties, have managed to be reborn—like Saul Bellow, for instance, with an abortive thirties-type manuscript stored away for his biographers, or destroyed; and even Nelson Algren, who apparently rewrote his in the form of *A Walk on the Wild Side.* Others, like them approaching their fiftieth year or just leaving it behind, have more disconcertingly produced in the late forties and fifties crypto-thirties works of art, of varying degrees of merit, Bernard Malamud's *The Assistant,* for example, and Arthur Miller's *Death of a Salesman*—in which a kind of secret nostalgia for the Depression underlies all more overt meanings.

Yet with what assurance and authority they move among us, these twice-born younger sons of the thirties: successful authors now welcomed to the pages of *The New Yorker* or *Esquire* or *Playboy,* though at home still in the *Partisan Review,* where they began, and which has become quite as established as they; or, alternatively, successful professors of sociology or political science or American literature, their commitment to poetry and fiction abandoned with other childish things. And what would our universities, much less our magazines, be without them, these astonishing overachievers, blessed with an extra quantum of energy, a demon-on-call left unemployed for a while after the collapse of the politics of the thirties?

But we at least among the twice-born who are writers still—or critics or teachers of writing—though we thrive in post-Depression

America, and, in a certain sense, love our success, cannot love it wholeheartedly. We are still too deeply involved with the persistent memories and defeated expectations I have been trying thus far to define; and like first-century Christians after the failure of the Second Coming, are at our deepest core dead to this world—or convinced anyhow that it is dead to us. It is a hoax, *must* be a hoax (we tell ourselves just before falling asleep, or just after waking up), this depressingly ongoing world with its depressingly immense Gross National Product—all, all illusion. And even at broad noon, we feel ourselves in a kind of interior exile—a comfortable, invisible, but quite real sequestration in the midst of our fellows: profoundly disaffected from everything which our contemporaries with the Other Memory (it scarcely matters whether they be Republicans or Democrats, whether they bless F.D.R. or curse him) consider politics and social action.

For a little while, a vain faith in that eternal loser, Adlai Stevenson, seemed to take us back into the common political arena; and then John F. Kennedy (another loser from the start, though we did not know at first that we knew it) won the allegiance of many of us who had resisted the blandishments of the New Deal—perhaps largely because he created the illusion that if not he, at least his wife, or his wife's sister, read fiction and verse, *our* fiction and verse. But his death produced poetry quite as bad as that which mourned the Happy Warrior before him. And the exacerbation of the situation in Vietnam has completed the process which the intervention in Cuba began (I shall never forget the hippie pickets on that occasion carrying signs which read: *JACQUELINE, VOUS AVEZ PERDU VOS ARTISTES*). The Kennedy *détente* is over; and with what relief we artists and intellectuals—not only veterans of the thirties but our successors as well—have relearned detachment from the great consensus, with what satisfaction settled down to hating L. B. J.

No one as yet has written a great anti-Vietnam poem (as no one, we recall sadly, ever wrote a great anti-Franco one), but those we have are considerably better at least than elegies to middle-of-the-road Presidents—for they draw on *our* memory of the thirties, on a reserve of terror and hopeless protest transmitted via certain poems and books into the creative self-consciousness of the youngest poets and rebels amongst us. There have been a whole series of transitional figures who have tried to straddle the gap between the thirties and the sixties—Norman Mailer, for instance, whose belated flirtation with Trotskyism is recorded in his fascinating if unsuccessful novel, *Barbary Shore.*

Allen Ginsberg, however, is the figure who preeminently represents the link between right now and back then; and in a single remarkable poem called, of course, "America," becomes the living memory of our dying memory of the mythological thirties. He included the poem in his first slim collection, *Howl,* a little book which raised a lot of hell, out of which there emerged finally a new life-style and a new metapolitics that has remained at the center of the cultural scene ever since. There is much that is quite new in "America," testimonies to drugs and fraternal greetings to Jack Kerouac, William Burroughs, and Neal Cassady, names just then beginning to be heard—but there are other names that need footnotes now, which one is tempted to weep composing: Scott Nearing (still alive and very old, an organic food nut these days, somewhere in New England), Israel Amter (does the *Freiheit* still go on, are there survivors still who read *Yiddish* and long for those pristine days?), Mother Bloor (dead, long dead—that wrinkled WASP who used to tie red bandanas around the necks of little Jewish Young Pioneers).

Almost from the start of the poem, we are aware that we are back with our unforgotten past, as the cry, "America when will you be angelic" becomes "When will you be worthy of your million Trotskyites?"; and suddenly the identification is made between "pot" now and Marx then,

> America I feel sentimental about the Wobblies.
> America I used to be a communist when I was a kid I'm not sorry.
> I smoke marijuana every chance I get.
> I sit in my house for days on end and stare at the roses in the closet.
> When I go to Chinatown I get drunk and never get laid.
> My mind is made up there is going to be trouble.
> You should have seen me reading Marx. . . .

But we are not quite prepared, however, when the old ghosts of those endless protests and defeats begin to arise, the wraith of Ginsberg's mother at the very center of them all,

> America free Tom Mooney
> America save the Spanish Loyalists
> Americo Sacco & Vanzetti must not die
> America I am the Scottsboro boys.
> America when I was seven momma took me to Communist Cell
>   meetings they sold us garbanzos a handful per ticket
>   a ticket costs a nickel and the speeches were free
>   everybody was angelic and sentimental about the workers
>   it was all so sincere you have no idea what a good thing
>   the party was in 1835 Scott Nearing was a grand old man
>   a real mensch Mother Bloor made me cry I once saw
>   Israel Amter plain. Everybody must have been a spy.

Irony, of course, plays everywhere in the passage—irony directed not only outward at the smug vilifiers of the Movement, but inward at its own pretensions (the last lovely touch being that almost inadvertent "1835"); but there is pathos, too.

And the source of that pathos is more fully revealed in the title of Ginsberg's next volume, *Kaddish,* which is to say, the Mourner's Prayer of the Jews: the prayer of a surviving queer son for his dead mother and all she represented to him, Newark, Paterson, lost strikes, Communism, madness—that paranoia which is only the apocalyptic vision, the prescience of defeat lived in the darkness of a lonely head, rather than evoked on a printed page. But here is his litany:

> O mother
> farewell
> with a long black shoe
> farewell
> with Communist Party and a broken stocking
>   *
> with your sagging belly
> with your fear of Hitler
>   *
> with your belly of strikes and smokestacks

with your chin of Trotsky and the Spanish War
with your voice singing for the decaying overbroken workers
with your nose of bad lay with your nose of the smell
                                        of the pickles of Newark
with your eyes
with your eyes of Russia

What, after all, could the (after all) good Jews who stood at the center of things in the thirties have asked better than being thus remembered by their children, with pity and fear equal to their own, being thus turned into poems? To be sure, we had thought of ourselves in our blither moments as the fathers of a new society, in our darker ones as the last sons of the world. That we are remembered as Somebody's Mother is a final irony, but somehow a not unattractive one.

John Peale Bishop and the Other Thirties

THE REVIVAL OF the literature of the thirties through which we have recently been living—the republication of novels long out of print, the redemption of reputations long lapsed, the compilation of anthologies long overdue—has been oddly one-sided, a revival of one half only of the literary record of that dark decade: the urban, Marxist, predominantly Jewish half, whose leading journal was the *New Masses* and whose monster-in-chief was Joseph Stalin. And this skewed emphasis, though somewhat misleading, is comprehensible enough; for we live at a moment when a large reading public, educated by a second generation of urban Jewish writers (ex-Marxists, this time around), begins by identifying with certain contemporary literary heroes, like Moses Herzog, whose minds were made by this thirties tradition, and ends by wanting to read the books they read: the fiction of Nathanael West and Daniel Fuchs and Henry Roth, even Mike Gold's *Jews Without Money.*

Some writers, however, who move us just now at least as strongly as Saul Bellow, writers ranging all the way from neo-Gothic journalists like Truman Capote to latterday prophets like Marshall MacLuhan, were nurtured on another, rival tradition which also flourished in the thirties: a provincial, Agrarian, primarily WASP tradition, whose chief journal was the *Southern Review* and whose monster-in-chief was Huey Long. We are less likely to know the basic manifesto of that tradition, a compilation of paeans to the old South called *I'll Take My Stand* by "Twelve Southerners," than such Marxist equivalents as Malcolm Cowley's *Exile's Return* or Edmund Wilson's *American Jitters.*

Yet the former is no more dated, no more alien in its aspirations than the two latter, which, indeed, have been drastically rewritten in later editions, as their authors have changed with the times. All three books are exemplary, useful both for illuminating their own age and tempering our enthusiasm for the unguarded goals and hopes of our own. Just as we find it therapeutic to recall that Cowley and Wilson once looked to the Soviet Union for salvation, we may find it equally so to remember that Robert Penn Warren could once write of the Southern Negro that he "is likely to find in agricultural and domestic pursuits the happiness that his good nature and easy ways incline him to as an ordinary function of his being."

And it is well, too, to come to terms with the hopes for literature which the Southern Conservatives, like the Eastern Radicals, attached to their social and political programs in order to savor the full irony of the fact that both movements did, indeed, produce literary revivals, though, in each case, the most moving books arose out of tension and disillusion rather than allegiance and simple faith. The great writer of the South was already on the scene when the thirties began, but he remained as invisible to the doctrinaire advocates of Southern Agrarianism as Nathanael West and Henry Roth were to be to the doctrinaire Marxist critic. Not until 1939 did George Marion O'Donnell give full recognition to Faulkner in the *Kenyon Review*. In 1930, when *I'll Take My Stand* appeared, Donald Davidson, who was entrusted with commenting on the arts, did not even mention him—concentrating instead on Ellen Glasgow and James Branch Cabell, the latter his leading contender for the laureateship of the South. Yet some of Faulkner's very best work had already been published though, indeed, so embattled and bleak a novel as *The Sound and the Fury* provides little of that "repose" and "continuity" which Davidson hoped for from the Old Dominion—part of his problem being, of course, that it was Virginia and not Mississippi which he had in mind when he spoke generally about the South. Madness, stylistic improvisation, and a radical dislocation of the tradition is what Faulkner was then prepared to offer; and that, Davidson thought, was already being supplied in sufficient quantities by certain despised writers from New York and Chicago.

From our present vantage point, it is easy to see that Glasgow and Cabell, addressing the past as they did in hushed and genteel voices (for all Cabell's vaunted pornography), could evoke from it no promise of a renaissance of letters and that Faulkner alone was capable of providing models for the literature to come that was to celebrate the terrible and elegant death of the South. Not, let us recall, the Faulkner of post-Nobel Prize banalities about dignity and endurance, but the shrill and despairing Faulkner, who mocked the world of the mid-thirties with *Sanctuary,* and was able still to write as late as 1944 (in the course of asserting that his real subject matter had never been the South at all): " . . . life is a phenomenon but not a novelty, the same frantic steeplechase toward nothing everywhere and man stinks the same stink no matter where in time."

Before any other Southern writer of distinction, John Peale Bishop seems to have sensed the value and significance of what *this* Faulkner was doing—not merely going on record in praise of his double vision, his capacity to appreciate simultaneously the myth of the Sartorises and the fact of the Snopeses, but imitating his techniques as well, in, for instance, a story called "Toadstools Are Poison," which he published in 1932 in emulation of Faulkner's "That Evening Sun." We are more likely to be aware of such later heirs of the dark Faulkner as Robert Penn Warren and Eudora Welty, Carson McCullers and Truman Capote, even so belated a continuer of the line as Flannery O'Connor. Yet Bishop was there first in picking up the cues for a fiction Gothic, as the fiction of the South has always been since the days of Edgar Poe, but fully aware at last of what before had only been hinted: that the blackness of darkness which haunts it is not merely embodied in the Negro, but quite simply *is* the Negro—that nightmare creature born of the contempt for manual labor and the fear of the sexuality of their own women which had so paradoxically made the White masters of the South heroes but not quite men.

Such a fiction is by definition even further from the possibility of "repose" than that of the industrial North and East; for if the latter is torn between the terrible fact of the present and the dream of a barely possible pure future, the latter is pulled apart between an equally dismal actuality and the dream of a manifestly unreal pure past. Nonetheless, the manifestos of the Agrarians tell the kind of lie which illuminates the truth of the fiction of Faulkner and Warren and Bishop, even as the Marxist manifestos tell the kind of lie which illuminates the truth of the novels of Nathanael West and Henry Roth. If we would recapture the past of three decades ago, we need to relive both the elation of the beautiful lies which nurtured it, and the discomfiture of the grim truths spoken from the heart of those lies. It would, therefore, be a special shame if Bishop's single completed novel, *Act of Darkness,* remained unavailable a moment longer, since in it one committed by birth and temperament to the myth of the South both rehearses it and—passionately as well as tenderly—gives it the lie.

We must, then, if we are to understand Bishop and his age, learn to think of him as perhaps the most important Southern novelist of the thirties* despite the slimness of his production. Yet if we bring him to mind at all these days, we are likely to associate him with a different genre, a different decade, even a different region. Certainly we tend to remember him first as a poet, second as a critic—and only last, if at all, as a writer of fiction. And though this emphasis is, on the one hand, a function of the way in which his influential friends (Scott Fitzgerald, Edmund Wilson, Allen Tate, among others) have chosen to mythicize and preserve him; on the other, it is a result of the way in which his writing career actually developed.

True enough, Bishop may have first captured the imagination of a large audience as the semi-fictional highbrow poet, Tom d'Invilliers, who moves through the pages of Fitzgerald's *This Side of Paradise;* but his verse had already appeared in print under his own name even before the publication of that novel in 1920—in fact, three years before the start of World War I, which is to say, a year before the initiation of Harriet Monroe's *Poetry* and the official beginnings of modernism in American verse. And he continued to

---

* Carson McCullers is his chief rival; but though her first and best book, *The Heart Is A Lonely Hunter,* which appeared in 1936, is a true thirties book, adapting the terror of the Depression to a world of freaks reflected in a child's eye, her reputation belongs to the forties into which she lived, and to which she provided a bridge.

write poems until his death in 1944, publishing four volumes in his lifetime and leaving enough uncollected poetry to justify Tate's putting together a *Collected Poems* in 1948, as well as a special selection for English readers in 1960.

In his preface to the latter volume, Tate celebrated Bishop's achievement as a poet, paid a passing compliment to his fiction, then went on to give the highest praise to his criticism—recording a belief that his dead friend had been "one of the best literary critics of the twenties and thirties." And in this opinion, Edmund Wilson (perhaps even better qualified to judge) had seemed to concur, when he had earlier gathered Bishop's scattered criticism into book form for the first time. But Bishop's critical writing, collected in a single volume, disconcertingly adds up to less than one would have expected from the impressions created by individual pieces; just as his verse, however elegant and accomplished, seems in retrospect too much a fading echo of styles already obsolescent before he had perfected his skills.

No, it is only in Bishop's fiction that I, at any rate, hear an authentic and original voice, only in his one successful novel and a handful of short stories, that I come on rhythms and phrases, images and myths that live on in my head. But he does not seem at first glance a *thirties* writer even in this area of his greatest achievement; for he began to write fiction, too, long before the collapse of post-World War I prosperity had made the thirties possible—publishing his very first stories when the twenties had barely started: one of them, characteristically elegant and unconnected with things to come, in *The Undertaker's Garland,* a volume on which he had collaborated with Edmund Wilson.

Wilson and Fitzgerald, Fitzgerald and Wilson: how inextricably Bishop's life as a writer is involved with theirs, and how inevitably we are tempted to see him through what we know more securely about them. But the clues they seem to offer are likely to lead us astray, suggesting that Bishop's spiritual home was Princeton (where he had met his two friends); that not *The Sound and the Fury* but *The Great Gatsby* provided him with a model for his fiction; and, finally, that he is a twenties writer in his deepest heart. Wilson, to be sure, who began as a true child of that earlier decade, was reborn as a leading spokesman for the radical thirties and survived to become a kind of elder statesman for the generation of the forties and fifties; but Fitzgerald we think of as having belonged so utterly to the era which learned in large part its very life-style from him, that he could not survive its disappearance. And Bishop seems, after all, much more like the latter than the former.

Why not, then, regard him simply as a twenties writer, who, living too long without accommodating to a new era, found himself quite out of fashion. Certain of his allegiances, surely, like a great deal of his rhetoric, he shared with those older writers, who—having barely found their voices before World War I—were bereft by that War of subjects appropriate to those voices; and insisted forever after on regarding its horrors as a personal affront rather than a universal catastrophe. Like many of his contemporaries, too, Bishop subscribed with equal fervor to the cult of self-pity and the religion of art, which seemed for a while—until the coming of more fashionable political faiths—to fill quite satisfactorily the vacuum left by the vanishing of older pieties. And like most of them, he espoused a righteous contempt for the vulgarities of American culture and a yearning for old world charm which, combined with a favorable exchange rate, led to expatriation in the Holy City of Paris.

It was the War which took him to France for the first time; and returning briefly to America, he did not cease to remember it, writing at the close of an essay on his alma mater, which he published in 1921: "If I had a son who was an ordinarily healthy, not too intelligent youth I should certainly send him to Princeton. But if ever I find myself the father of an extraordinary youth I shall not send him to college at all. I shall lock him up in a library until he is old enough to go to Paris." Shortly thereafter he made his first post-War removal to Europe, then a second much longer one, which lasted until 1933, and during which three sons were born to him on the continent to which he had dreamed of sending them if they proved themselves "extraordinary" enough.

And what does all this shuttling between Princeton and New York and Paris have to do with the thirties, which turned from New York and Princeton, as well as Detroit or Sauk City or Newark, New Jersey, toward the Holy City of Moscow (to which only a few were foolish enough to venture in fact)—or alternatively, to the Holy Anti-City of Jefferson's Monticello (to which none, however foolish, could manage to return)? Little enough in fact; indeed, so little that we are not surprised when Bishop, in quest of a setting for his one finished novel, moves backward in time, out of the mid-thirties which saw the publication of the book to the pre-World War I years of his own childhood. And in that relatively remote era, he rehearses—or rather lets his boy hero with whom he shares the almost anonymous name of John rehearse—a familiar tale, not less indebted to certain prevailing modes of the twenties for being so palpably autobiographical. The commonplace which reminds us that life often imitates art, does not make sufficiently clear that it is inevitably yesterday's art, outmoded art, i.e., a cliché, which today's life is likely to repeat.

In *Act of Darkness,* at any rate, we find Bishop, though apparently convinced he is recreating his own early experience, recreating instead fictional patterns already well established by his predecessors and contemporaries at home and abroad. On the one hand, we encounter such standard American plots as the belated flight from mama; or the boy vicariously inducted into maturity by witnessing the fall to woman of an older man on whom he has a homosexual crush. On the other, we are confronted by such fashionable European imports as the direct initiation into manhood at the hands of a whore (fumbled the first time, achieved the second); and especially the fable of conversion popularized by Joyce's *Portrait of the Artist as a Young Man,* in which a baffled youngster—realizing after many wrong turnings that only Art gives meaning to Life— goes forth to write his first novel.

All this familiar stuff is transformed in *Act of Darkness,* however, not only by the subtlety of language and delicacy of cadence which Bishop somehow redeemed from mere elegance by transferring it from verse to prose; but also by the typical thirties tone and voice in which he renders it. It is not finally a social message which gives to the fiction of the Depression years its special character, though the critics of that age once liked to think so. Horace Gregory, who was willing to hail Bishop's book when it first appeared as "one of the few memorable novels of the decade . . .", hastened to add, almost apologetically, that it had "no pretensions of being a 'social document.' " No matter; since the hallmark of the thirties is rather a certain panic shrillness, a sense of apocalypse, yearning to become religious but held by the mode to secular metaphors.

This we find everywhere in the period: in those atypical novels produced then by writers out of another decade—in Faulkner's *Sanctuary,* for instance, or Hemingway's *To Have and Have Not* or James Gould Cozzens' *Castaway;* as well as in the most characteristic work of writers who belong entirely to that dark decade—in Nathanael West's *Miss Lonelyhearts,* say, or Henry Roth's *Call It Sleep.* They are *mad* books all of them, even more disturbingly than they are crypto-religious ones: sometimes actual projections of madness, sometimes accounts of long flirtations with insanity, ending in not quite credible escapes back into reason and peace—as if the political debates which occupied the age were finally mere analogues, leftover nineteenth-century metaphors called on to express a crisis of consciousness for which the times had not yet found a new language.

And of all the books of the period, *Act of Darkness* (along with *Call It Sleep)* comes closest to revealing that not-quite secret. How different its panic mood is from the more theatrical despair typical of the twenties (think of Fitzgerald's *All the Sad Young Men),* which, after all, was never incompatible with euphoria. A comparison of the two types of book reveals how—though the Great War may have been felt chiefly as a personal affront, the Great Depression seemed Armageddon itself, a kind of end of the world. It is odd and maybe even a little degrading to realize how we Americans (not only our writers, finally, but all of us) were driven to ultimate despair not by contemplating the destruction of fabled cities abroad or even the prospect of our own deaths in foreign lands, but by a confrontation at home with the Crash, the end of prosperity and fun and games. The colloquial phrase says it exactly: the Depression struck *home* to us as the War had not; and the image of the desolated American city seemed an image also of our own devastated souls, whereas that of the ravaged European capital had signified only the death of that Culture with which we had never been quite at ease.

Most Depression novels, therefore, played out their fables against the background of the ruined American city, making the native urban landscape for the first time the chief symbolic setting for our kind of Gothic. Not so in Bishop's case, however, despite his commitment after his college years to the Princeton-New York-Paris circuit, despite his father's northern city origins, despite his own final retreat to New England to die. Faulkner himself may have been driven in the Depression years from Jefferson to Memphis, out of whose backalleys Popeye emerges to stalk the pages of *Sanctuary,* that other inverted parable of rape and the Southern Lady. But Bishop turns back, in the midst of the general panic that was possessing the land, to where his own personal panic had begun, to precisely the sort of small Southern community in a farm setting which the Agrarians celebrated; but which for him (despite the kind things he had to say of the South in his more abstract commentary) is the place of horror from which, at the end of his book, he is escaping, even as he escapes the "soft torture" of his mother's love and the temptation to madness.

His poems, on the other hand, do have a kind of urban setting; since in them he imagined himself and his friends (Edmund Wilson, for example, turned not so improbably into an antique Senator) moving through an imaginary city clearly intended to remind us of Rome. But his is *not* the Rome—however much Allen Tate would like us to believe it—created in the fantasy of Southern neo-Classicists like George Washington Custis, delivering his annual Fourth of July oration dressed in a toga, or Thomas Jefferson dreaming the University of Virginia. Bishop's is rather a doomed and decadent city—much like the "unreal City" of T. S. Eliot's *The Waste Land,* or even more like Cavafy's Alexandria: an imperial capital whose great Caesars are all dead, and which is assailed from without by barbarians and Christians, from within by doubt; a city whose inhabitants are waiting—as so many so variously but so nearly unanimously waited in the thirties—for the End:

> We did not know the end was coming: nor why
> It came; only that long before the end
> Were many wanted to die . . .

So, too, his first and unfinished novel, *The Huntsmen Are Up in America,* is set in legendary dying cities—this time called Venice and New York. But that novel stutters away before its intended close in the most legendary part of New York (doubly strange and wonderful for the Southerner), which is to say, in Harlem, where Bishop tries to bring to the surface the underground theme that obsessed him: the idyll which turns nightmare of a sacred union of White and Negro, the pale virgin and black stud. The idyllic names for the partners in that union are Venetian, of course, Desdemona and Othello; but to do justice to its nightmare aspects, Bishop had to take it back to where, in his troubled mind, it really belongs: back to his own birthplace of Charles Town, West Virginia, called in his fiction "Mordington"; though its actual name is distributed to the two leading characters of his completed novel, to the Charlie and Virginia who were for him the prototypes of Othello and Desdemona.

"Mordington" is, at any rate, the background not only for *Act of Darkness,* which he published in 1935, but also for the collection of stories called *Many Thousands Gone,* which had appeared four years earlier. It was apparently Bishop's aim in the five stories which make up the book, as well as in the novel, to create a mythical equivalent of the small town he knew best: his own Yoknapatawpha County, which is to say, a microcosm of the South, true both to its sociological facts and its legendary meanings. Sociologically, Bishop is not nearly so successful as Faulkner; for despite his patent determination to write the sort of "realistic" book his age had convinced itself it admired, his data keeps incandescing (at best) into poetry, or dissolving (at worst) into self-conscious symbolism. Yet in the course of his failed attempt at recording history, he does succeed in releasing from himself and what of the past lives on in his memory their essential myth.

In an extraordinary little story called "If Only," a pair of genteel Southern spinsters known as "the Sabine Sisters," who have survived the Civil War only to confront indigence, find themselves one day possessed of a Negro servant called "Bones." The allegorical import of the names is not less important for being self-evident: the evocation of Rome and rape in the first, of death and the Minstrel Show in the second. Bones, at any rate, almost miraculously restores the decayed household of the sisters to an elegance which they perhaps only dreamed of having had before; but simultaneously begins to appear before them in darkly sinister, though inconclusively sexual manifestations—winking out at them in naked insolence from their bathtub, asleep on one of their beds, "terrible and tall . . . and very black." Dismayed and horrified, the two women find themselves incapable of telling whether their ambiguous servant is a madman, or a figment of their own madness: and they cannot, in any event, disengage themselves from their "nigger," since "with him they lived in terror, but in the tradition."

Act of Darkness, which is concerned with the escape from both the terror and the tradition, is less perfectly achieved; but by the same token, it seems richer, less a bare parable. And we are finally more deeply moved and illuminated by it, for all its obtrusive faults: its two halves which fall apart in tone and tempo, its point of view which shifts without clear motivation or redeeming grace, etc. etc. Any teacher of composition could tick off its flaws; yet the tale it tells survives its technical ineptitude: the story of a boy early bereft of his father, almost swallowed up by his mother's love and dogged through his lonely house by a Negro homosexual of his own age, who at last finds a kind of salvation by attaching himself, purely and passionately, to his young Uncle Charlie. Uncle Charlie, however, first seduces a young farm girl whom the boy is prepared to love though not possess; then takes him to a whorehouse in an unsuccessful attempt at inducting him into guilt and manhood; finally rapes a not-so-young Southern lady, a friend of and surrogate for the boy's mother, called by the twice symbolic name of Virginia.

The climax of the book's action and the heart of its meaning is contained in a long courtroom scene, during which Charlie is, at the lady's instigation, tried for having assaulted her; and ends by claiming that not he—dandy and bully and restless seducer—but the woman herself—intellectual and freethinker and virgin—had been the effective rapist: that "he shamelessly allowed her to complete his animal rapture," maintaining the whole time "only a passive prowess." And young John is undone by the confession, pushed over the brink of a breakdown by what seems to him the ultimate affront to his own dubious masculinity: "What I could not forgive was his denying his domination over what had been done in the darkness of the woods. . . ." But John is not alone in his dismay at this comic-tragic denouement; for the reader finds himself shaken as he is shaken only when some inadequate but long-lived arche-typal version of the way things are is inverted and extended, an ulter-ior, and uncomfortable, significance made clear.

I should suppose that the Southern reader especially would be discomfited; for though rape is the subject *par excellence* of South-ern literature in the nineteenth and twentieth centuries—a concern as obsessive as that with seduction in eighteenth-century England —it is typically the rape of a white woman by a black man, real or fancied, which lies at the center of the plot. Bishop's novel, how-ever, tells no nightmare tale of a black man grossly offending or falsely accused; though there is an attenuated and dislocated echo of the standard fable in the subplot of the black fairy with whom the white boy narrator flirts in horrified attraction, and who is fin-ally killed off-scene by being pushed out of a window by somebody else. In the main action, a white man, a gentleman—in fact, just such a gentleman farmer as the Agrarians were then making the focus of their hopes for social reform—is responsible, at least pas-sively, for the act of darkness which the color of his skin seems to belie.

But *why,* the book insists that we ask, why such a total inversion of the archetype? Surely not just because it happens to have hap-pened so in some series of actual events from which Bishop may have made his fiction. So easy an answer the novel itself will not let us accept, evoking as a clue toward its close the pair of ill-fated Shakespearian lovers who had already begun to haunt Bishop, as we have seen. Desdemona and Othello appear again and again dur-ing the thirties in all of Bishop's work, whether in verse or prose, the first explicit reference, as we might expect, in the book whose protagonist is called "Brakespeare," *The Huntsmen Are Up in America.* Describing the city of Venice, Bishop writes, as if by the way, "it was only there, I am sure, that the ceremony could have been found that would have wed Desdemona to her black Moor." And a gloss on the metaphor is to be found in one of his best poems, a kind of epigraph to the body of his work, which he called "Speaking of Poetry":

> The ceremony must be found
> that will wed Desdemona to the huge Moor.

It is not enough—
to win the approval of the Senator . . .
                For then,
though she may pant again in his black arms
(his weight resilient as a Barbary stallion's)
She will be found
when the ambassadors of the Venetian state arrive
again smothered . . .
                (Tupping is still tupping
though that particular word is obsolete . . .)

The allegorical meanings are clear enough: elegance must be
married to force, art to magic, the mind to the body—*married,* not
merely yielded up to the kind of unceremonious possession which
turns inevitably into destruction. It is ritual, "ceremony" which
makes of passionate attachment a true marriage, as it makes of
passionate perception a true poem: which is to say, the marriage of
Desdemona and Othello becomes a metaphor for the poetic act.
Equally clear is the nature of the appeal of that metaphor to the
race-obsessed, sexually queasy Southern mind: the image of black
"tupping" white, a miscegenation, which—lacking appropriate cer-
emonials—is no more than a rape.

Fair enough, then, that after Charlie's trial and conviction, his
unnerved nephew—who had earlier found satisfaction in simpler
boys' books, idyllic like Audubon or sinister like *Oliver Twist*—
should have turned to Bishop's favorite play to learn for himself
how the poet can confer order and beauty and significance on what
otherwise must remain heartbreakingly chaotic and sordid and
meaningless. "Had the actual murderer of Desdemona . . . "
Bishop reports him as thinking, "been brought into a Venetian
court, his trial would have made no more sense than Charlie's had
done in the Mordington courthouse."

But there is no "huge Moor" in the Mordington affair, we want
to cry out at this point, no black man at all, only Uncle Charlie. To
which Bishop responds through his narrator, evoking for the first
time relevant Shakespearian criticism as well as the text: *neither
was Othello a "huge Moor" really—only a Venetian nobleman,
neither blacker nor whiter than the farmer from West Virginia.*

"The Venetian gentleman," Bishop's John explains to us, "who wore mulberries on his shield, since his name was Il Moro, had, in the repetition of the story of the murder of his wife, been mistaken for a Moor. In time, passing to the North, he had become a black-skinned barbarian, Othello."

The blackness of Othello is, then, *Act of Darkness* insists, a misconception, a mistake; or more precisely, the rapist of white women is black only as the dream of revenge against their emasculating Ladies is black inside the darkness of the white heads of Southern males. The Prosecuting Attorney, pressing for Charlie's conviction, underlines this when he so oddly repeats in his own language the burden of the scholarship on *Othello:* " . . . once more the cry of rape is heard in the land and . . . this heinous and horrible crime, has been committed, not by a man of the colored race . . . but is imputed to one whose former education, training and fair tradition should have predisposed him to a career of honor and worthy actions."

There is another turn of the screw beyond this, however, as we already know; a second and even more terrifying inversion implicit in Charlie's plea that it was he who had been raped, that the true Othello is Desdemona: the pale virgin dreaming her own dark violation, and projecting that dream outward upon the white male who resents her—at the cost of his manhood and honor, and at the risk of his life. But the end of the illusion which concealed this truth from a defeated nation, which survived only by imagining itself the last home of chivalry, means the beginning of the end of that nation's myth and its very existence. Intuiting this, *Act of Darkness* becomes a work of prophecy, a parable of that death of the South which all of us are living through in agony right now.

Its protagonist, at any rate, having been deprived of that illusion by his uncle and Shakespeare, is preparing at the book's end to leave not only the small lies of his mother, but the larger lies of the sweet land which seemed for a while to sustain them, to go North. First, however, he has to return to the whorehouse to which his uncle had earlier taken him in vain, where, this time, he musters up enough "passive power" to accomplish his own deflowering. "It was when her hands were on me," he tells us, "that I knew what was

again being accomplished was the act in the woods, that all its ges-
tures must be repeated and forever repeated, the rape of the mind
by the body."

But at this point, we are no longer sure (and how did we ever
deceive ourselves that we were, even in deepest Dixie?) about
which is mind, which body, which White, which Black, who Desdemona, who Othello, who the virgin and who the whore. The mythical marriage which Bishop imagined in his verse has, in fact, been
accomplished, the archetypal opposites united in a confusion that
begins in madness and ends in poetry.

Buffalo, New York
—1966

Henry Roth's Neglected Masterpiece

IT WOULD NOT BE quite true to say that Henry Roth's *Call It Sleep* went unnoticed when it appeared in 1935. One contemporary reviewer at least was willing to call it "a great novel" and to hope that it might win the Pulitzer Prize, "which," that reviewer added mournfully, "it never will." It never did, the prize going instead to H. L. Davis's *Honey in the Horn,* which was also the Harper Prize Novel of the year and was even touted by Robert Penn Warren in the *Southern Review*—then still being subsidized by Huey Long. Not only the Southern Agrarians were looking elsewhere, however, when Roth's single book was published; almost everyone seemed to have his eye on his own preferred horizon, on which he was pretending to find his own preferred rising star.

The official "proletarian" party was busy hailing Clara Weatherwax for a desolately enthusiastic tract disguised as fiction and called *Marching! Marching! "Marching! Marching!"*—runs the jacket blurb—"is the winner of *The New Masses* contest for a novel on an American Proletarian theme, conducted jointly by *The New Masses* and the John Day Company—the first contest of the kind ever held." It was also the last such contest, partly, one hopes, because of the flagrant badness of the winner (the climax of Miss Weatherwax's book runs as follows: ". . . some of us thinking *Jeez! Bayonets! Machine Guns! They got gas masks on those bags around their necks on their chests—gas!* and others *For God's sake, you guys, don't shoot us! Come over to our side. Why should you kill us? We are your brothers")*—but chiefly, one suspects, because a basic change in the political line of the Comintern instituted in 1936 led to the substitution of the Popular Front novel for the Proletarian one.

John Steinbeck, the most sensitive recorder of that shift, was to publish his resolutely proletarian *In Dubious Battle* in 1936, but this reflects a lag demanded by the exigencies of publishing. *The Grapes of Wrath,* which represents the full-scale political-sentimental novel of the last half of the thirties, did not reach print until 1939. Meanwhile, Dos Passos and Farrell, the most ambitious talents of the first part of the decade, were closing out their accounts by putting between the covers of single volumes those fat trilogies *(Studs Lonigan* actually appeared in 1935; *U.S.A.* was that year in its last stages) which seemed for a while to the literary historians the great achievements of the period. And at the same time, Hemingway was preparing for his own brief fling at being a "proletarian" author, improbably publishing a section of *To Have and Have Not* in *Cosmopolitan* magazine during 1934.

To the more dogged proletarian critics, Henry Roth seemed beside Weatherwax or Dos Passos, Farrell or even Hemingway woefully "poetic" and uncommitted. "He pleads [prefers?] diffuse poetry to the social light . . ." the reviewer for the *New Republic* complained, adding rather obscurely but surely unfavorably that Roth "pinkly through the flesh sees the angry sunset." Actually, there was some point in chiding Roth for not writing a "socially conscious" book, since his dedication to Eda Lou Walton (his teacher, sponsor, and friend, who had identified herself clearly enough with the proletarian cause) indicated a declaration if not of allegiance at least of general sympathy. Certainly Roth did not take his stand outside of the world bounded by the *New Masses,* the *Nation,* and the *New Republic,* as, say, did John Peale Bishop, whose *Act of Darkness* was also published in 1935, or Thomas Wolfe, whose *Of Time and the River* was just then thrilling the adolescent audience for whom he had rediscovered *Weltschmerz* in *Look Homeward, Angel.* Nor was Roth willing to launch the sort of satirical attack on social commitment undertaken only a year later by another young Jewish writer, Daniel Fuchs, in *Homage to Blenholt.*

He was ideologically in much the same position as Nathanael West, whose *A Cool Million* appeared in the same year with *Call It*

Sleep, and whose technique, different as it was, also baffled the official "proletarians." Both had reached intellectual maturity inside a world of beliefs which they felt no impulse to deny but which they did not find viable in their art. West died inside that world and Roth apparently still inhabits it insofar as he retains any connection with literary life at all. At any rate, looking back from 1960 and the poultry farm in Maine to which he has finally withdrawn, that is the world he remembers. "Is Yaddo still functioning?" he recently asked an interviewer. "Whatever happened to Horace Gregory and Ben Belitt?" There is a half-comic pathos in the questions and the continuing faith from which they spring that a literary movement to which Roth never quite belonged must still somehow be going on.

But in Roth's novel itself there is little enough manifest social consciousness. Though his scene is Brownsville and the East Side of New York just after the turn of the century and his protagonists are a working-class Jewish immigrant family, there is small sense of an economic struggle. Jobs are gotten and lost because of psychological quirks and dark inner compulsions; money does not corrupt nor does poverty redeem; no one wants to rise like David Levinsky or fears to fall like the harried protagonists of Theodore Dreiser. If there is a class struggle and a revolutionary movement, these are revealed only in an overheard scrap of soapbox oratory at the climax of the novel, where they seem singularly irrelevant to the passion and suffering of Roth's child hero who is living through that climax.

> "In 1789, in 1848, in 1871, in 1905, he who has anything to save will enslave us anew! Or if not enslave will desert us when the red cock crows! Only the laboring poor, only the masses embittered, bewildered, betrayed, in the day the red cock crows, can free us!"

But even this prophecy uttered out of a "pale, gilt-spectacled, fanatic face," is turned into a brutal sexual jest, recast in light of the obsession which rides the book, its protagonist, and its author. "How many times'll your red cock crow, Pete, befaw y'gives up? T'ree?" asks a mocking Irish voice from the sidelines.

Perhaps it is this obsessive transformation of all experience into equivocations based on a hated and feared sexuality which put off the kind of reader who might have been expected to hail the kind of book Roth actually wrote. That the *New Masses* critics deplored him and the Southern Agrarians scarcely registered his existence is, after all, to be expected; nor is it proper to feel dismay over the yellowing lists of best-sellers in old newspapers, carefully documented testimony to what the largest audience was reading in 1935 *instead* of Roth. For some the whimsy, Anglophile or pseudo-Oriental, of James Hilton (both *Goodbye, Mr. Chips* and *Lost Horizon* topped the lists) seemed the specific demanded by the pangs of the Great Depression, while others found tranquillity in the religiosity of *The Forty Days of Musa Dagh* or in Mary Pickford's *Why Not Try God?* For those less serious or more chic, there was the eunuchoid malice and sentimentality of Alexander Woollcott's *While Rome Burns;* and the most nearly invisible audience of all (furtive high school boys standing at the circulating library racks in candy stores and their older sisters behind the closed doors of their bedrooms) were reading Donald Henderson Clarke's *Millie* and *Louis Beretti* —the demi-pornography which no library would think of stocking twenty-five years later.

But what of those specifically interested in Jewish literature in the United States, those who, picking up a first novel by a twenty-seven-year-old New Yorker, thought of Mary Antin's *The Promised Land* or remembered Abraham Cahan's breakthrough to the rich disorderly material of Jewish-American life? There is surely no more Jewish book among American novels. Though its young hero, David Schearl, for instance, goes to public school, that Gentile area of experience is left shadowy, unrealized. Only his home and the *cheder* and the streets between become real places, as only Yiddish and Hebrew and the poor dialects of those to whom English is an alien tongue are rendered as real languages. And yet those presumably looking for the flowering of a rich and satisfactory Jewish-American literature were not moved to applaud.

Some of them, on the contrary, protested against the unloveliness of Roth's ghetto images, the vulgarity and poverty of the speech he recorded—as if he had invented them maliciously. "Doggedly smeared with verbal filthiness," one such critic wrote.

"*Call It Sleep* is by far the foulest picture of the East Side that has yet appeared." It is, of course, the typical, the expected response to the serious writer by the official spokesmen of the community out of which he comes. Yet there was in Roth a special kind of offensiveness, capable of stirring a more than conventional reaction; for the real foulness of his book is rendered not directly but through the consciousness of an extraordinarily acute and sensitive boy of seven or eight. Its vulgarity, that is to say, is presented as *felt* vulgarity, grossness assailing a sensibility with no defenses against it.

The technique of *Call It Sleep* is contrived to make manifest at every moment that its real subject is not so much abomination in the streets as that abomination in the mind. Aside from a prelude, in which the arrival of David and his mother in America is objectively narrated, and a section toward the book's end which blends into a Joycean rhapsody the sounds of a score of city voices as overheard by some omniscient Listener—the whole substance of the novel is presented as what happens inside the small haunted head of David. It is only through him that we know the dark cellar swarming with rats whose door he must pass on his way in or out of the warm sanctuary of his home; the rage and guilt of his paranoid father or that father's impotence and fantasies of being cuckolded; his mother's melancholy, and her soft, unfulfilled sexuality; the promise of her body and the way in which it is ogled by others; the fact of sex in general as pollution, the very opposite of love. For David, the act by which he was generated is an unmitigated horror (in a dark closet, reeking of mothballs, he is initiated by a crippled girl, her braces creaking as she embraces him, "Between the legs. Who puts id in is de poppa. De poppa's god de petzel. You de poppa"); and he longs for a purity he cannot find in his world, a fire, a flame to purify him from his iniquity as he has learned in *cheder* Isaiah was once purified.

No book insists more on the distance between the foulness man lives and the purity he dreams; but none makes more clear how deeply rooted that dream is in the existence which seems to contradict it. It is, perhaps, this double insight which gives to Roth's book a Jewish character, quite independent of the subject matter with which he happens to deal. Certainly, it reveals his kinship to Nathanael West, also a novelist of the thirties, whose relationship to his own Jewishness is much more equivocal than Roth's, but who quotes in his earliest book an observation of Doughty's about the nature of Semites in general which illuminates his own work as well as Roth's: the Semite stands in dung up to his eyes, but his brow touches the heavens. Indeed, in Jewish American fiction from Abraham Cahan to Philip Roth, that polarity and tension are present everywhere, the Jew mediating between dung and God, as if his eternal function were to prove that man is most himself not when he turns first to one then to the other—but when he touches both at once. And who can project the awareness of this more intensely and dramatically than the child, the Jewish child?

It is possible to imagine many reasons for Roth's retreating to childhood from adult experience; for retreat it does seem in the light of his second withdrawal, after the publication of a single book, into the silence in which he has persisted until now. To have written such a book and no other is to betray some deep trouble not only in finding words but in loving the life one has lived enough to *want* to find words for it. A retreat from all that 1935 meant to Roth: from the exigencies of adult sexuality and political commitment alike—this is what *Call It Sleep* seems to the retrospective insight of 1960. The book begins in 1907, and though it jumps quickly some five years, never quite reaches the year of the Russian Revolution (the roster of splendid betrayals listed by the street-corner speaker stops at 1905) and the vagaries of Leninism-Stalinism; just as in coming to a close in a boy's eighth year it stops safely short of the point where "playing bad" becomes an act that can end in deflowering or pregnancy. In its world before the falls of puberty and the October Revolution, one can remember 1905 and Mama —play out the dream of the apocalypse and the Oedipal triangle in all naïveté.

Cued by whatever fears, Roth's turning to childhood enables him to render his story as dream and nightmare, fantasy and myth—to escape the limits of that realism which makes of other accounts of ghetto childhood documents rather than poetry. In its own time *Call It Sleep* was occasionally compared to Farrell's *Young Lonigan,* but one cannot conceive of such a foreword to Roth's book as that written for Farrell's by "Frederic M. Thrasher, Associate Professor of Education, New York University, Author of *The Gang.*" Roth's book aspires not to sociology but to theology; it is finally and astonishingly a religious book, though this fact even its latest admiring critics tend to ignore or underplay. Only in the account of a child's experience could a protégé of Eda Lou Walton (it would have been another matter if he had been sponsored by Mary Pickford) have gotten away with a religious resolution to a serious novel about ghetto life; and it was to a child's experience that he was canny enough to turn. An evasion of responsibility? A strategic device of great subtlety? It is not necessary to decide.

David Schearl, at any rate, is portrayed not only as a small boy and a Jew but also as a "mystic," a naïve adept visited by visions he scarcely understands until a phrase from the sixth chapter of Isaiah illuminates for him his own improbable prophetic initiation. Having just burned the leaven of the year in preparation for the Passover ("All burned black. See God, I was good? Now only white Matzohs are left"), David sits watching the play of light on the river and is transported ("His spirit yielded, melted into light. . . . Brighter than day . . . Brighter"). But he is awakened from his ecstasy by the tooting of a barge ("Funny little lights all gone. Like when you squeeze too hard on a toilet . . ."), thrust back into darkness until two Gentile hoodlums persuade him to drop a strip of zinc down into the third rail of a trolley line and he feels that in the dark bowels of the earth he has discovered the source of all light ("And light, unleashed, terrific light bellowed out of iron lips"). This light he identifies with the burning coal that cleansed the unclean lips of Isaiah, though his rabbi mocks him ("Fool! Go beat your head on a wall! God's light is not between car-tracks")—and in his joy he wets his pants.

For better or worse, the prophetic poetry reduced to an exercise learned by rote and beaten into unwilling boys has come alive in David, delivered him from fear so that he can climb the darkest stairway untroubled. ("Gee! Look! Look! Is a light . . . Ain't really there. Inside my head. Better is inside. . . .") Released a little from the warm bondage that binds him to his mother, he can climb now even to the roof of his house, where he meets for the first time the Gentile boy, Leo, a twelve-year-old seducer and eater

of forbidden foods, beside whose absolute freedom David's limited
release seems slavery still. And in Leo's house he finds new images
for the inner light, the purifying flame, in a portrait of Jesus with
the Burning Heart and a box bearing the symbolic fish, the name
GOD. For the rosary that box contains, he agrees to introduce Leo
to his sluttish cousin Esther, whose grimy favors Leo finally wins in
the cellar beneath her mother's candy store.

As Leo and Esther squeal and pant in the darkness of one cellar shed, David crouches in another trying to exact light from the
holy beads for which he has betrayed his family, his Jewishness, his
very desire for cleanliness.

> Past drifting bubbles of grey and icy needles of grey, below a
> mousetrap, a cogwheel, below a step and a dwarf with a sack
> upon his back . . . sank the beads, gold figure on a cross
> swinging slowly . . . . At the floor of the vast pit of silence
> glimmered the round light, pulsed and glimmered like a coin.
> —Touch it! Touch it! Drop!

But the light eludes his efforts; and the other two, who have per-
formed the act of darkness at the very moment he sought the light,
emerge blaming each other as they are discovered by Esther's sister. "Tell 'er wut I wuz doin', kid," Leo blusters. "Yuh jew hewhs!
We wuz hidin' de balonee—Yaa! Sheenee!"

AFTER such a denouement, nothing is possible for David but a
plunge into hysteria, a hysteria which overcomes him as he is rereading the passage about the calling of Isaiah, betrays him into
telling to his *rebbe* a story compounded half of his father's delu-
sions, dimly perceived, and half of certain reminiscences of his
mother, ill understood: his mother is not his *real* mother, he is a
bastard, son of a goyish organist in an old country church, etc., etc.
This fantasy the *rebbe* hastens to carry to David's home, arriving a
moment before the horrified parents of Esther appear with their
own scandal. And David, overwhelmed by guilt and fear, offers to
his father a whip, grovels at his feet, the rosary falling from his
pocket as if to testify to the truth of his illegitimacy, his contami-
nated blood. At this point, he must run for his life, his father's long
rage at last fulfilled, presumably justified; and he runs where he

must, toward God in the dark cleft, to the third rail, the coal of fire that can take away iniquity.

He snatches a ladle from beside a milk pail and flees to an obbligato of city voices, which from the girders of a half-finished building, a warehouse, a bar, a poker table speak with unclean lips of lust and greed, hatred and vengefulness. Only David dreams of a consummation that will transcend and redeem the flesh, finally thrusts the metal he bears between the black lips of the tracks and the awful lightning is released, his body shaken by ineffable power, and his consciousness all but obliterated. Yet his intended sacrifice redeems no one, merely adds a new range of ambiguity to the chorus in which one voice blasphemes against the faith of another and all against love. Himself dazzled, the reader hears again certain phrases he has before only half understood, listens again, for instance, to the barroom voice that mocked the street-corner orator, "How many times'll your red cock crow, Pete, befaw y'gives up? T'ree?"—notices the "three," the name "Pete," and remembers the other Peter who, three times before the cock crow, denied his Rabbi.

In the interplay of ironies and evasions the final meaning of the failed sacrifice, the private apocalypse (the boy does not die; the world is not made clean; only his parents are rejoined more in weariness than affection over his bed) is never made quite clear, only the transcendence of that meaning, its more than natural character. Turning the final pages of Roth's book, one realizes suddenly how in the time of the Great Depression all the more serious fictionists yearned in secret to touch a religious note, toying with the messianic and the apocalyptic but refusing to call them by names not honored in the left-wing journals of the time. The final honesty of Roth's book lies in its refusal to call by any fashionable honorific name its child hero's bafflement as he learns the special beauty of a world which remains stubbornly unredeemed: "Not pain, not terror, but strangest triumph, strangest acquiescence. One might as well call it sleep."

—1960

SEVEN

Our Country and Our Culture

THE END OF the American artist's pilgrimage to Europe is the discovery of America. That this discovery is unintended hardly matters; ever since Columbus it has been traditional to discover America by mistake. Even in the days when it was still fashionable to talk about "expatriation," the American writer was rediscovering the Michigan woods in the Pyrenees, or coming upon St. Paul in Antibes. How much more so now when the departing intellectual does not take flight under cover of a barrage of manifestos, but is sent abroad on a Fulbright grant or is sustained by the G.I. Bill. The new American abroad finds a Europe racked by self-pity and nostalgia (except where sustained by the manufactured enthusiasms of Stalinism), and as alienated from its own traditions as Sauk City; he finds a Europe reading in its ruins *Moby Dick,* a Europe haunted by the idea of America.

The American writer soon learns that for the European intellectual, as for him, there are two Americas. The first is the America of ECA and NATO, a political lesser evil, hated with a kind of helpless fury by those who cannot afford to reject its aid; the second is the America invented by European Romanticism—the last humanistic religion of the West, a faith become strangely confused with a political fact. To the European, the literature of America is inevitably purer, *realer* than America itself. Finding it impossible to reject the reality of death, and difficult to believe in anything else, the European is perpetually astonished at the actual existence of a land where only death is denied and everything else considered possible. Overwhelmed by a conviction of human impotence, he regards with horrified admiration a people who, because they are too naïve to understand theory, achieve what he can demonstrate to be theoretically impossible.

From Europe it is easy to understand the religious nature of the American belief in innocence and achievement; to see how even the most vulgar products of "mass culture," movies, comic books, subliterary novels are the scriptures of this post-Christian faith—a faith that has already built up in Western Europe a sizable underground sect which worships in the catacombs of the movie theaters and bows before the images of its saints on the newsstands. A hundred years after the *Manifesto,* the specter that is haunting Europe is— Gary Cooper! Vulgar, gross, sentimental, impoverished in style— our popular subart presents a dream of human possibilities to starved imaginations everywhere. It is a wry joke that what for us are the most embarrassing by-products of a democratic culture are, in countries like Italy, the only democracy there is.

It seems to me that it has become absurd to ask whether a democratic society is worthwhile if it entails a vulgarization and leveling of taste. Such a leveling the whole world is bound to endure, with or without political guarantees of freedom; and the serious writer must envision his own work in such a context, realize that his own final meanings will arise out of a dialectical interplay between what he makes and a given world of "mass culture." Even the Stalinists, though they thunder against American jazz and cowboy suits for children, can in the end only kidnap our vulgar mythology for their own purposes. The sense of an immortality here and now, so important to American culture and parodied in Forest Lawn Cemetery, finds its Soviet counterpart in the mummification of Lenin or the touting of Bogomolets; while our faith in progress and achievement finds an ersatz in the Five Year Plans and the statistics doctored to assist belief. In its Russian form, what is possible in America has become compulsory, an unofficial rite has been made an orthodoxy. And even in our own country there have been occasional attempts to impose optimism (and eventually, one can only suppose, youth and naïveté) by law.

Yet for us, hope has never become just official, a mere camouflage for actual exploitation, though indeed two generations of writers just before us believed so; and it was their sense of having alone penetrated our hoax of prosperity and happiness that nourished their feelings of alienation. The error of such writers was double (such errors, naturally, do not preclude good writing; being *right* is, thank God, optional for the writer). Not only was the American *mythos* real and effective, the very opposite of the hypocritical and barren materialism is seemed; but also everywhere, down to the last layer of babbitry, there existed beside this belief its complement: an unspoken realization of the guilt and terror involved in the American experience. In his sense of lonely horror, the writer was most one with everyone else.

Precisely the uncompromising optimism of Americans makes every inevitable failure to accomplish what can only be dreamed an unredeemable torment. Among us, nothing is winked at or shrugged away; we are being eternally horrified at dope addiction or bribery or war, at things accepted in older civilizations as the facts of life, scarcely worth a tired joke. Even tax evasion dismays us! We are forever feeling our own pulses, collecting statistics to demonstrate the plight of the Negro, the prevalence of divorce, the failure of the female orgasm, the decline of family Bible reading, because we feel, we *know* that a little while ago it was in our power, new men in a new world (and even yet there is hope), to make all perfect. How absurd of our writers to have believed that only they were pained at the failure of love and justice in the United States! What did they think our pulp literature of violence and drunkenness and flight was trying symbolically to declare? Why did they suppose that the most widely read fiction in America asks endlessly, "Whodunnit? Where is the guilt?"

I think we are in the position now to understand that the concept of the "alienated artist" itself was as much a creation of the popular mind as of the artist. It is no accident that Edgar Allen Poe is both the prototype of the American Poet as Despised Dandy, and the inventor of the most popular genres of "mass culture." The image of the drunken, dope-ridden, sexually impotent, poverty-oppressed Poe is as native to the American mind as the image of the worker driving his new Ford into the garage beside the Cape Cod cottage; together they are the American's image of himself. Poe, Crane, Fitzgerald—each generation provides itself with its own lost artist—and their biographies are inevitable best-sellers.

I do not mean to imply that the role of scapegoat is not actually painful for the artist; his exclusion and scourging is the psychodrama of us all, but it is played out in earnest. Poe was in a certain sense a poseur, but he died of his pose; and the end of Fitzgerald was real terror. I want only to insist that the melancholy and rebellious artist has always been a collaborator in American culture—that it is only when he accepts the political or sentimental halftruths of democracy, when he says *yes* too soon, that he betrays his role and his countrymen—and that the popular mind at its deepest level is well aware of this.

Of all peoples of the world, we hunger most deeply for tragedy; and perhaps in America alone the emergence of a tragic literature is still possible. The masterpieces of our nineteenth-century literature have captured the imagination of readers everywhere, precisely because their tragic sense of life renews vicariously the exhausted spirit. In Western Europe, the tragic tension no longer exists; it is too easy to despair and to fall in love with one's despair. Melodrama, *comédie larmoyante,* learned irony and serious parody—these are the forms proper to the contemporary European mind. In the orbit of Stalinism, on the other hand, despair has been legislated away; justice triumphs and the wicked suffer—there is no evil except in the other. Some lies are the very stuff of literature, but this is not among them; it breeds police forces rather than poetry.

Only where there is a real and advancing prosperity, a constant effort to push beyond all accidental, curable ills, all easy cynicism and premature despair toward the irreducible residuum of human weakness, sloth, self-love, and fear; only where the sense of the inevitability of man's failure does not cancel out the realization of the splendor of his vision, nor the splendor of his vision conceal the reality and beauty of his failure, can tragedy be touched. It is toward this tragic margin that the American artist is impelled by the neglect and love of his public. If he can resist the vulgar temptation to turn a quick profit by making yet one more best-selling parody of hope, and the snobbish temptation to burnish chic versions of elegant despair, the American writer will find that he has, after all, a real function.

Indeed, he is needed in a naked and terrible way, perhaps unprecedented in the history of Western culture—not as an entertainer, or the sustainer of a "tradition," or a recruit to a distinguished guild, but as the recorder of the encounter of the dream of innocence and the fact of guilt, in the only part of the world where the reality of that conflict can still be recognized. If it is a use he is after and not a reward, there is no better place for the artist than America.

—1952

EIGHT

Caliban or Hamlet:
A Study in Literary Anthropology

THERE IS A peculiar paradox—the Caliban-Hamlet Paradox, I have chosen to call it—which resides at the heart of American Literature, and which is so intricately bound up with a basic ambiguity at the heart of European-American cultural relations, our endlessly baffled attempt to understand each other, that to study one means inevitably to deal with the other. Yet the first problem seems clearly an aesthetic one, amenable to formalistic or, at any rate, conventional literary approaches; while the other belongs just as clearly to the realm of sociology or social anthropology, which (as any college catalogue will testify) is a realm utterly alien to that of the arts. How, then, to deal with one world without betraying the other, or with both without falsifying both?

I should like tentatively, though not too much so (since I have been working along these lines for a couple of decades now), to attempt here an approach, perhaps best called literary-anthropological, that seems to me to satisfy the difficult conditions I have just defined. To one practising this approach, it scarcely matters whether he begins with the sociological aspect of the problem or the literary one. Indeed, it seemed to me at first best to introduce the subject I have chosen to confront with a consideration of the assassination of President Kennedy—or more specifically, with a pair of quotations extracted from a review that appeared in *Encounter* for June 1964 of Thomas G. Buchanan's odd and unconvincing study, *Who Killed Kennedy?*

"What Mr. Buchanan is trying to establish," the reviewer writes, "is that . . . this pattern [of Kennedy's assassination] does not accord with the popular [American] belief that the murder of a President is necessarily the irrational act of a lonely and isolated individual who is diseased or deranged in mind." But precisely this belief is what the official Warren Commission report has ended by endorsing, drawing for us the portrait of an utterly alienated mama's boy prompted to a revenge whose motives he never quite understood by all the forces of heaven and hell that possessed him. That portrait, I have tried to indicate with certain deliberate echoes of Shakespearian language, assumes or implies a prototype which presumably failed to come to the reviewer's mind: the image, however vulgarized and degraded, of Hamlet.

What does occur to him is a quite different, though equally authentic Shakespearian prototype, appropriate to the political-plot version of Kennedy's death sponsored by Mr. Buchanan and particularly appealing to Europeans. "Mr. Buchanan uses the murder of the President," the reviewer writes in another place, "to hold up a mirror to America which reflects such a Caliban image of brutishness and corruption that her enemies can only view it with glee. . . ." But why the second rather than the first prototype moves men on the other side of the Atlantic, why they continue to search for a millionaire Caliban behind the scenes, while we are content with a *lumpen* Hamlet front and center, cannot be explained as long as we remain on the political or sociological level. Even to begin, we must answer a prior—and more properly literary —question: what do Caliban and Hamlet, which is to say the myths they embody, represent to the deep imagination of both worlds?

Such an answer is found, however, not in newspapers or the transcripts of police interrogations but in novels and plays and poems, and especially in the deep images that lie at their hearts. Let me, then, make a new start by asking a pair of purely literary questions, which may seem at first quite beside the point, but which will eventually lead us toward the kind of explanation we are seeking. First, why did T. S. Eliot at the moment of his recent death, why does he now seem so irrelevant to young readers and writers of poetry? And second, why does Walt Whitman, so long deceased, seem so living a model at the moment—living as he has not been for some three or four decades?

Simply to ask these questions, to recognize that they can, even must be asked, is to suggest that American writers, old as well as young, are turning away after nearly half a century from sophisticated literary cosmopolitanism; and that they are returning—with extraordinary ferocity and what can only be called a willing suspension of intelligence—to the crassest kind of nationalism, nativism, and primitivism: back to Caliban, in short. We hear once more these days (as we have not heard since the triumph of Whitman) of the necessity for exploiting American themes, using the native American language, and inventing—or restoring—native American meters. In this Calibanistic program, the school of poetry once centered at Black Mountain College joins with that once centered in San Francisco—bohemian academies joining extra-academic bohemians to rescue poetry from the Anglophile universities and recreate it in the Anglophobe cafes.

We have lived, consequently, to see not only Walt Whitman himself, but more recent Whitmanizers like Henry Miller, William Carlos Williams and Louis Zukofsky move from the periphery to the center of literary interest; while poets of the generation of Allen Ginsberg do variations on themes from *Leaves of Grass,* and the old Poundian cry, "Break the iambic!" (i.e., the European heritage, the tradition, the accent of *Hamlet)* is echoed and re-echoed, as if from the barricades. "But what does it mean?" one asks further, "What is really at stake?" And the immediate answer at least is that the cultural situation responds to, even perhaps prophetically anticipates, a political and social one: that we have been preparing for an era in which it will become possible for Negro writers (relatively unsophisticated, and culturally—as we like to say—deprived) to act as the principal spokesmen for the American people; and for the life they share to seem the archetypal life of us all, the language in which they communicate our archetypal tongue. The relationship of Whitman to this revolution Garcia Lorca intuitively grasped long ago, writing in *The Poet in New York:* "Sleep, Walt, and let a black boy announce to the golden Whites the arrival of the reign of an ear of corn." But it is desirable, perhaps, to come to terms with that relationship less metaphorically.

As is well known, we Americans are forever re-inventing ourselves in terms of the experience and values, the attitudes and idioms of one or another ethnic and cultural group out of the many which constitute our community. When the elected archetypal group is of one kind (genteel, university-educated, Atlantic Seaboard Anglo-Saxons, for example, as in the second half of the nineteenth century; or New York and Chicago Jews, with vestigial Marxist and Freudian vocabularies, as just before and after World War II), we are likely to think of ourselves as participating in a common cultural enterprise with Europe or the whole Western world. When, however, small-town boys from the Midwest or South —their various inherited cultures, chiefly North European, boiled away in the melting pot—emerge at the center of our culture, as they did just before and after World War I, they tend to think of their art as made against the total European-Mediterranean tradition, in despite or contempt of their cultural heritage. Walt Whitman composed their manifesto long before they were born:

> Come Muse migrate from Greece and Ionia,
> Cross out please those immensely overpaid accounts,
> That matter of Troy and Achilles' wrath, and Aeneas',
>   Odysseus' wanderings,
> Place ' Removed" and "To Let" on the rocks of your snowy
>   Parnassus . . .

How much more the Negroes (and following their example, the Negro-izers, Beat and Hip) tend in the sixties to create for us—and reflect from us—a desire to re-establish our culture on a denial of that Western cosmopolitanism whose political face is White Imperialism. Once we have granted that the nationalist-nativist-primitivist strain in our life and art is our most authentic expression, we are compelled to see the Negro as the ultimate, the absolute American —rivaled only by the Indian, to whose image he is assimilated in our classic books. Certainly, he is no transplanted European, but no more is he a displaced African after three hundred years on our soil; he is a new man, made in the U.S.A., a pure product of the New World.

Another way to say this is that the Negro is totally what all other Americans are only in part: the living embodiment of that absolute Other dreamed by Europeans—sometimes sympathetically, more often in fascinated horror—before they had ever dragged an actual Black from Africa to slavery in America. To be sure, that dream was prompted by self-hatred and a reversion from culture, and nurtured by a despair of reason and a yearning for the natural past, which existed only in myth; but it has, nonetheless, vexed Europe ever since the eighteenth century or earlier, eventuating in poems on the one hand, and emigration on the other. And here, of course, is the source of the paradox to which I began by alluding: the reason why the native American when he glories in his naïveté, and thinks he is most anticosmopolitan—is in fact most abjectly submitting to Old World tradition.

In this sense, Walt Whitman and Mark Twain are the most European of our writers, assuming masks and poses with which the reader abroad can be at ease, as we never can be at home; for such writers strive to seem what the European eternally demands we make ourselves for his sake: the mythological anti-European he has defined in his literary tradition. In that tradition, Mediterranean and German and Englishman, rationalist and Romantic and pragmatist find themselves oddly at one. And it is, perhaps, possible to say that Europeans can be aware of their own world as a single cultural unit only against a clearly identified cultural other: Islam once, American more recently. But this is another paradox, for another day and another sort of writer—one looking from rather than toward that Old World, in which the New was invented.

Let me return to my main concern by asking instead: when, then, are American artists most deeply and truly selves of their own contriving, as opposed to the selves Europeans so eagerly foist on them? And let me suggest by way of an answer: when they are permitted, permit themselves rather, freely to ransack their whole cultural heritage (Hebraic-Hellenistic-Renaissance-Romantic, all that they share with Europe); and when they end choosing, not what was already chosen for them before they existed as a people, but at first hand whatever they will. Or, to insist once more on the paradox, our writers are most themselves when they are able to see themselves precisely in borrowed images, images long used for their own purposes by our European forebears.

What images our writers do in fact choose to portray their sense of themselves and of us are fascinatingly various. I shall, however, pass over here all but one: omitting, for instance, the American artist's vision of himself and his people in the guise of Christ—as the Suffering Servant by whose stripes the European Gentiles are healed. Yet this image is of critical importance both in Hemingway and Faulkner and recurs on the edge of unconscious parody in Arthur Miller's *After the Fall,* from which I once heard a baffled lady spectator emerge muttering to herself, "Why, that son-of-a-bitch thinks he's Jesus Christ." Nor shall I deal with the Ulysses image in its peculiarly American form: that non-Homeric, romanticized figure out of Dante by way of Tennyson which so spectacularly haunts the imagination of Ezra Pound.

I prefer instead to concentrate on Hamlet, once more as revised by the Romantic imagination: the peculiarly American Hamlet seen backward through Goethe's young Werther. I choose this figure not only because it makes such a neatly illustrative Shakespearian pair with Caliban, but also because the Hamlet image seems to me the one that has most obsessively concerned our writers, all the way from *The Power of Sympathy,* whose appearance coincided with our birth as a nation, to *The Hamlet of A. MacLeish* or even Hyam Plutzik's Horatio poems. The central document in the history of American Hamletism is surely Melville's *Pierre,* a novel unparalleled until Mailer's *An American Dream* for the unguarded way in which it projects deep fantasies shared by the author and his culture; and the *locus classicus* is the passage in which Pierre stands before his bookshelf:

> His mind was wandering and vague; his arm wandered and was vague. Some moments passed, and he found the open *Hamlet* in his hand, and his eyes met the following lines: 'The time is out of joint, Oh cursed spite,/ That ever I was born to set it right.' He dropped the true volume from his hand; his petrifying heart dropped hollowly within him. . . .

But though it is Pierre who finds the key lines for Americans in *Hamlet,* he is no more Werther-Hamlet-like, after all, than, say,

Poe's Roderick Usher, or any of the Dimmesdale-Coverdale melancholics of Hawthorne, or Faulkner's Quentin Compson, or Saul Bellow's Herzog, for that matter; or, to leave literature for life and remember the place from which we began, than Lee Harvey Oswald. We must understand, at any rate, the long background of convention and expectation against which Prufrock cries out, "No! I am not Prince Hamlet, nor was meant to be," the sense in which simply rejecting that tragic role in favor of the comic Polonius one is in our land a revolutionary gesture, a break with tradition.

What, then, is the special appeal of *Hamlet* to the American imagination; of the plot, on the one hand, with the obligation to revenge fumbled and fumbled, then suicidally achieved; and of the character, on the other, with an anguish and melancholy disproportionate (as Eliot once more has insisted) to the events? Surely, that very anguish and melancholy to begin with; for we inhabit a country where the required optimism of the ruling majority breeds a compulsory *angst* in the writing minority, the drunken revelry of fathers a withdrawn brooding on the part of their sons. And the notion of suicide itself titillates even more, suggesting the possibility of an irrepressible, an unanswerable revolt against inherited obligations. Also, I think, American writers have tended to take the Prince of Denmark at his word when he speaks of his coward-making conscience; for we are experts on the inhibitory nature of conscience, as even Eliot, for all his theoretical anti-Hamletism, testifies:

> Between the conception
> And the creation
> Between the emotion
> And the response
> Falls the Shadow

Finally, however, I am tempted to believe that on some level of consciousness many American intellectuals have found (as I have found certainly) in the Romantics' favorite Shakespearian play, Melville's "form book," an oddly apt parable of our relationship to Europe. While Europeans tend to think of us mythologically as rebellious slaves, which is to say, politically and in the context of society, we need to regard ourselves as wronged sons, which is to say, psychologically and in the context of the family. Both the Christ

image and the Hamlet one cater to this inner necessity; for arche-
typally speaking, Hamlet is Christ after the death of God, a Son of
the Father whose progenitor survives only as a dubious ghost and
whose single surviving prayer is: *My God, my God* (or, *Father,
Father) why hast thou forsaken me?* The Hamlet image is, however, more unequivocally Oedipal and therefore more congenial to
us: the figure of a son, who is a university graduate and intellectual
as well as a Prince, loving still the soiled mother who has (perhaps)
bereft him of his real, i.e., his good, father and put him at the
mercy of his bad one: a drunken murderer and usurper whom that
son should overthrow, and, indeed, might, were he not robbed of all
power except that over words by the monstrous love that ties him
more to his whored mama than to any paternal ghost.

The troubled cry of Hamlet when he first realizes his mission
and his disability is, at any rate, a peculiarly American one, which
we need no Pierre to discover for us:

> The time is out of joint; O cursed spite,
> That ever I was born to set it right.

Here in a couplet is summed up the attitude toward the Old World
and all in the New which comes to resemble it (resplendent pomp
and established power and presumed injustice) that motivates not
only such private vengeances as Oswald's, but also such public ven-
tures as our current campaign in Vietnam, or the often-proposed,
often-delayed plan to "liberate Eastern Europe." But while the
American, in Saigon or Dallas or Budapest, is imagining himself as
Hamlet, the European may well be seeing him as Caliban.

Indeed, Shakespeare, who was not at all thinking about America, of course, when he wrote *Hamlet,* was precisely concerned with
the New World when he was conceiving *The Tempest* and inventing Caliban. Despite his perfunctory effort to suggest a non-Ameri-
can setting for *The Tempest,* it is reasonably clear that Shakespeare
had been reading accounts of an expedition to the Bermudas, ·as
well as Montaigne's essay on cannibals, while the fable of the play
(one of the very few for which no model has been found) was
forming in his mind. And it is highly probable that "Caliban" is a
deliberate anagram of "cannibal," itself in all likelihood a corrup-

tion of "Carib," which is to say, a native of the Caribbean or a Red Indian.

At any rate, we can profitably think of Caliban as one of the earlier European portraits of the indigenous American, *l'homme sauvage* of an already existing mythology transplanted to the New World: part-Indian, part-Negro, all subhuman—indeed, as Shakespeare fancies him (remembering doubtlessly the medieval notion of the Western hemisphere as a watery world), part-fish. Caliban is, however, not only a sketch of the dark-skinned peoples in whose presence white Europeans have attempted to work out their destinies on our continent; he is also the model according to which such transplanted white Europeans have sometimes tried to remake themselves. D. H. Lawrence, as a matter of fact, believed that willy-nilly Americans of European origin do become assimilated to Indians and Negroes, being appropriately "fugitive slaves" to begin with; and he quotes, in the introductory chapter to *Studies in Classic American Literature,* a tag from *The Tempest* as appropriate to all inhabitants of the United States, whatever their origin.

> 'Ban, 'Ban, Ca— Caliban,
> Has a new master— Get a new man.

But what finally does this Calibanistic view of America mean, this vision of the archetypal American not as the son of a usurping false-father and a sullied mother, but as a deformed slave, rebelling against legitimate authority at the instigation of certain European turncoats (more fools even than knaves) who have plied him with liquor? What follows when we have identified the mythological American with the drunken offspring of a witch and the Devil, bent on raping female innocence and overthrowing a mastery imposed in utter reason and benevolence? What can follow except condescension and contempt? Yet there is a qualifying note already present in Shakespeare, in the lines he gives Prospero reflecting Europe's sense of responsibility for America, for the institution of slavery, which was its first gift to us, and for the blackness of darkness embodied in slavery. "This thing of darkness I," Prospero says (and the personal pronoun hangs at the end of the line, confessing Caliban to be the responsibility not of that arrant evil he had presumably left behind in the Old World, but of the best he had been able to bring to the New), "Acknowledge mine."

It is a fascinating dialogue which the Shakespearian analogues suggest to us: the voice that Americans have claimed as their own crying, "O cursed spite. . ."; and the voice which Europeans have preferred answering, with a dying fall, ". . . Acknowledge mine." It does not even matter that certain Europeans later switch sides, i.e., support Caliban against the Master of Arts whose creature he is—hail Whitman, praise John Steinbeck, make a cult of Dashiell Hammett or of those ultimate imaginary Americans, those Calibans thrice removed, the Beatles. Occasions for misunderstanding still arise, opportunities for pathos and comedy—not only in literature but in life, in the councils of the U.N. or on the established routes of tourism—as the American, who is sure that he is Hamlet, confronts the European, who is convinced that he is Caliban.

Even funnier and more pathetic, however, is the confusion of certain American Hamlets attempting to persuade themselves, as the fashion changes at home, that they are in fact Calibans, have been secret sea monsters all along. Karl Shapiro is a case in point, for instance, with his boasted shift from the Eliotic style of his earlier poems to the Whitmanian stance of "The Bourgeois Poet"; and Norman Mailer another, self-transformed into what he calls a White Negro, i.e., Caliban, from the Harvard boy dreaming of combat on the banks of the Charles.

> . . . Rightly to be great
> Is not to stir without great argument,
> But greatly to find quarrel in a straw . . .

Most moving and most significant at the moment, however, is the case of James Baldwin, who, beginning with the delicate and scrupulous examination of conscience in *Go Tell it On the Mountain, Notes of a Native Son* and *Giovanni's Room,* has been impelled to move on toward the brutal histrionics of *Another Country* and *Blues for Mr. Charlie.*

> . . . Examples gross as earth exhort me.

I would suppose that to a Negro (or an Indian) the notion of playing Caliban has a special attraction, since not only most Europeans but many of their white brethren (eager to keep the number of Hamlets down) have thrust the role of rapist-rebel-slave upon them; and it must seem, at any rate, preferable to the alternative role of Uncle Tom. Even this is more farcical than tragic, however, deserving not the Hamlet cry I find trembling on my lips ("O cursed spite. . ." once more) but almost any Calibanistic vaunt: perhaps best of all those astonishingly chic verses Shakespeare put into Caliban's mouth, a Beat American poem before its time:

Freedom, high-day! high-day, freedom! freedom!
high-day, freedom!

Buffalo, New York
—1965

NINE

Toward a Centennial:
Notes on *Innocents Abroad*

IT IS NOW nearly a hundred years since Mark Twain embarked on "the first organized pleasure party ever assembled for a transatlantic voyage," and began making the notes which were to become that occasionally mad, often tedious, but somehow eminently satisfactory travel book, *The Innocents Abroad or the New Pilgrim's Progress: Being Some Account of the Steamship QUAKER CITY's Pleasure Excursion to Europe and the Holy Land*. A century later, we find it perfectly natural that Twain should have been present as a kind of laureate-*ex-officio* at the initiation of mass tourism in the United States—his way, to the tune of $1,250, paid by a California newspaper; for we know now that with the publication of his "New Pilgrim's Progress," he was launching a literary career marked by an almost obsessive concern with Europe and the quest for American identity.

No one, however, had any sense of this on June 8, 1867, when the *Quaker City* sailed, since—though Twain had already done some newspaper pieces about a voyage to Hawaii—his sole published volume, *The Celebrated Jumping Frog and Other Sketches*, suggested an exclusive concern with quite other, much more parochial material. Yet, over and over, he was to return to the themes of *The Innocents Abroad*: not only in other self-declared travel books like *A Tramp Abroad* or *Following the Equator*, but in such fictions as *The Prince and the Pauper*, *A Connecticut Yankee in King Arthur's Court*, *Personal Recollections of Joan of Arc*, *Tom Sawyer Abroad*, *The Mysterious Stranger*. Even in his greatest

104

work, *Huckleberry Finn,* the encounter with Europe is represented, despite the exclusively American scene, in the ill-fated meeting between Jim and Huck, on the one hand, and the Duke and the Dauphin, on the other. To be sure, those two self-styled Europeans are arrant frauds; but precisely insofar as they are fraudulent, they embody what Twain took to be the essential nature of Old World aristocracy.

At any rate, Twain's participation in the excursion seems to have been more suffered than welcomed, the representatives of the Plymouth Church (apparently the moving spirit behind the whole enterprise) preferring to advertise such better known prospective passengers as Henry Ward Beecher and General Sherman, neither of whom finally went along. Mark Twain, however, was there on schedule, along with "tnree ministers of the gospel, eight doctors, sixteen or eighteen ladies, several military and naval chieftains," and other similarly undistinguished but pious fellow-adventurers. "The whole affair," Bret Harte was acute enough to point out in 1870, "was a huge practical joke, of which not the least amusing feature was the fact that 'Mark Twain' had embarked on it." Yet this joke eventuated in a classic work which, without ceasing to be amusing, marks a critical point in the development of our literature, and especially in our attempt through literature to find out who we Americans are.

We have always been aware that ours is a country which has had to be invented as well as discovered: invented even before its discovery (as Atlantis, Ultima Thule, a western world beyond the waves) and re-invented again and again both by the European imagination—from, say, Chateaubriand to D. H. Lawrence or Graham Greene—and by the deep fantasy of its own people, once these existed in fact. Europeans, however, begin always with their own world, the Old World, as *given* and define the New World in contrast to it, as nature versus culture, the naïve versus the sophisticated, the primitive versus the artificial. We Americans, on the other hand, are plagued by the need to invent a mythological version of Europe first, something against which we can then define ourselves, since for us neither the Old nor the New World seems ever given and we tend to see ourselves not directly but reflexively: as the Other's Other. Only when the two worlds become one, as they seem now on the verge of doing, will Europeans and Americans alike be delivered from the obligation of writing "travel books" about each other, i.e., books whose chief point is to define our archetypal differences and prepare for our historical assimilation.

In the past, certainly, most American writers have, either in avowed fictions or presumed factual accounts, created myths of the two worlds and their relationship; from Washington Irving and James Fenimore Cooper, through Poe and Hawthorne and Melville to James and Hemingway, Eliot, and Pound, scarcely any of our major authors have failed to face up to this task. Those few who have rejected it—Thoreau and Whitman come first to mind—have felt their refusal in itself as somehow heroic and if not quite a sufficient *raison d'être,* at least a satisfactory *raison d'écrire.* For a long time, however, the general American obligation to accommodate to each other the myths of Europeans and ex-Europeans was oddly parochialized by being entrusted to the small group of highly educated White Anglo-Saxon Protestants from a few Atlantic seaboard cities, who remained for decades the sole public spokesmen of the United States.

It was that group, in any case, who first undertook the archetypal voyage to Europe (Dr. Franklin, in his disguise as a good, gray Quaker, being the mythological forerunner of them all), defining it in letters, articles and books as simultaneously a Descent into Hell and an Ascent to Olympus. The inferno into which the earlier travelers thought of themselves as descending was the Hell of surviving Medievalism, which is to say, of oppression, class distinction, "immorality" (belated vestiges of Courtly Love), and, especially, Roman Catholicism; while the Olympian heights they fancied themselves as scaling were represented by the preserved monuments of antiquity, the reconstructed cathedrals of the Middle Ages and the artistic achievements of the Renaissance as displayed in museums. Unfortunately for their peace of mind, the works of art which such WASP travelers admired to the point almost of worship were hopelessly involved with the values, religious and political, which such travelers most despised. The benign culture-religion into which the faith of their mothers was, by slow and imperceptible degrees, lapsing came into inescapable conflict with the violent anti-Catholicism to which the fiercer faith of their fathers had, just as gradually, shrunk. And though they did not often confess the disease bred by that conflict, they were surely troubled by it.

A little later, their direct descendants, Henry James and Henry Adams, were to suggest a solution, fully achieved only later still by their remoter heirs, T. S. Eliot and Ezra Pound (in whom anti-Semitism tended anyhow to replace anti-Catholicism): the total abandonment of the negative vestiges of Protestantism in favor of the culture-religion and whatever fashionable cults were best adapted to it. But so drastic an accommodation was achieved only at the risk of expatriation and apostasy, which is to say, the surrender of essential "Americanism," as defined in the WASP tradition. How different the Old World was to look to such recusant Puritans only the twentieth century was able to reveal; yet that century revealed, too, how like one half of the older view, at least, their revision of it remained.

One need only contrast their point of view with the versions of Europe and Americans in Europe produced by the quite different kinds of writers to whom the task of re-inventing the two worlds was transferred in the new century: with those birthright Roman Catholics, for instance, like F. Scott Fitzgerald in *Tender Is the Night;* or with those post-Jamesian urban Jews, like H. J. Kaplan in *The Plenipotentiaries* or Bernard Malamud in his Italian stories. The ultimate contrast, however, is with myths of Americans abroad imagined by those absolutely non-European Americans, the Negroes, best represented, perhaps, by James Baldwin in his novel *Giovanni's Room* or his pioneering essay "A Stranger in the Village." We have had to travel far, indeed, on a journey for which the only maps are precisely the books we have been discussing, to get from the Old World of Irving or Longfellow or Hawthorne or Melville, even of James or Eliot, to stand in the Europe Baldwin experiences and overhear his musing, as he watches a group of Swiss villagers: "The most illiterate among them is related in a way I am not to Dante, Shakespeare, Michelangelo . . . the Cathedral of Chartres says to them what it cannot say to me. . . ."

But this is also true of the most illiterate among the Western Americans of the mid-nineteenth century, in whose name Mark Twain pretended to speak; for Twain represents merely the other side of the old WASP ambivalence, its secular Puritanism—that fear of High Art and High Church worship which the followers of Henry Adams had rejected in favor of the religion of Art. Twain may refuse the Virgin and choose the Dynamo, but he remains immeasurably closer to the first American travelers in Europe than any latterday American Catholic or Negro or Jew. Whatever sense of alienation he may feel from Dante, Shakespeare, and Michelangelo, to Shakespeare at least he is bound by a kinship of blood and tradition he can never quite disavow. To be sure, his relationship to Michelangelo is more than a little ambivalent, for Michelangelo was a Mediterranean and a lackey of Cardinals and Popes. "I used to worship the great genius of Michael Angelo," he tells us, " . . . but I do not want Michael Angelo for breakfast—for luncheon—for dinner—for tea. . . . I never felt so fervently thankful, so soothed, so tranquil, so filled with a blessed peace, as I did yesterday when I learned that Michael Angelo was dead."

Yet even here, Twain's is no more the utterly alienated view of a James Baldwin than it is, say, the tormentedly involved response of a second-generation Italo-American, the son of an illiterate peasant from the Abruzzi who has grown rich and returns to confront the world his father had fled. Twain stands on precisely the Protestant Anglo-Saxon middle ground, from which Mediterranean Europe was being surveyed in his time by such more genteel exploiters of experience abroad as William Dean Howells and Bayard Taylor. As a matter of fact, by the time Twain was beginning to write, Taylor himself had decided that Europe was pretty well used up as a literary subject; and in *By-Ways of Europe* (a book about spots off the main lines of travel, published in the same year as *The Innocents Abroad),* had vowed that he would produce no more such essays. Twain, however, being the spokesman for the lowbrow tourism which succeeded the upper middlebrow variety in whose name Taylor had written, follows the old routes with no sense that they have suffered from literary overexposure, or that, indeed, there are any others.

He was, to be sure, the prisoner of a tour plan laid out by organizers for whom the world worth seeing had been defined once and for all by the genteel essayists of the generations before and the writers of guidebooks, who were their degenerate heirs; but he, who protested so much else, does not protest the limits thus imposed on him. Bret Harte, in his otherwise extremely laudatory review, complains of precisely this, "Yet, with all his independence, 'Mark Twain' seems to have followed his guide and guidebooks with a simple, unconscious fidelity. He was quite content to see only that which everybody else sees, even if he was not content to see it with the same eyes. . . ." In one sense, the case can be made even stronger; for more often than anyone seems ever quite to remember, Twain saw those "same sights" with exactly the "same eyes" as those who had gone the same route before him.

He shares especially the bad taste of his generation and its immediate predecessors: admiring extravagantly, for instance, the mediocre Cathedral of Milan ("a poem in marble"), the gross funeral statuary in the cemetery of Genoa, the inferior sculptures exhumed at Pompeii, and even—despite his general contempt for "old paintings"—the Guido Reni "Saint Michael Conquering the Dragon," which the pale heroine of Hawthorne's *The Marble Faun* had also overesteemed. But he shares also their sentimental, hypocritical politics and morality: combining a theoretical hatred of royalty, for instance, with an actual willingness to submit to the charms of emperors, if they are efficient (like Louis Napoleon) or kind to their pretty young daughters (like the Czar of all the Russias); and complementing a theoretical abhorrence for European frankness about sex with an actual eagerness for seeking out occasions to put that abhorrence to work.

Like many of the contemporaries he affected to despise, he wants to have it both ways—to attend unashamedly a performance of the can-can ("I placed my hands before my face for very shame. But I looked through my fingers"), but to be morally offended at the presence beside him of "staid, respectable, aged people." ("There were a good many such people present. I suppose French morality is not of that strait-laced description which is shocked at trifles.") As long as it is understood that sex is for the consumption of men only, and especially of young bachelors, Twain is not morally troubled. He even manages to admire certain pictures "which no pen could have the hardihood to describe," drawn on the walls of what he calls delicately "the only building in Pompeii which no woman is allowed to enter," and barely manages to work up in a dutiful climax, a vision of the wrath of Heaven being visited upon its long-dead clients.

Only when sex threatens the purity of women, or, more precisely, I suppose, of ladies, is his Puritan indignation genuinely stirred; and that indignation is doubled, of course, when a Churchman is involved in the dubious proceedings. Surely, one of the most extraordinary passages in *The Innocents Abroad* (the feeling invoked absurdly out of proportion with the declared occasion) is the long digression on the seduction of Eloise by Abelard and the consequent decline of Abelard's fortunes. With what prurient relish Twain recounts the disasters which overwhelmed "the dastardly Abelard," summing up his downfall finally with that Protestant, bourgeois, American phrase of utter contempt: "He died a nobody. . . ."

But on the way to that climax, he lingers with especial pleasure over Abelard's castration, which he does not name, falling back on a quotation from an anonymous "historian" to hint at it: " 'Ruffians, hired by Fulbert, fell upon Abelard by night, and inflicted upon him a terrible nameless mutilation.' " To which Twain adds: "I am seeking the last resting place of those 'ruffians.' When I find it I shall shed some tears on it . . . and cart away from it some gravel whereby to remember that howsoever besotted by crime their lives may have been, those ruffians did one just deed. . . ."

The notion of an adulterous passion committed and generous enough to be redemptive seems to Twain only "nauseous sentimentality"; for he is as immune to the continental tradition of Courtly Love as any Anglo-American lady novelist. Even in its most attenuated and spiritualized form, as celebrated for instance in the poems of Petrarch to Laura, the Medieval love code finds no sympathetic response in Twain, who only cries by way of protest, "Who glorifies poor Mr. Laura?" Not that he ever blames the young ladies involved, considering them, by definition, innocent victims. "I have not a word to say against the misused, faithful girl," he comments of Eloise herself, taking her side as instinctively as Harriet

Beecher Stowe had taken that of Mrs. Byron, in an article printed in the very issue of *The Atlantic Monthly* in which Howells had reviewed Twain's travel book; for, like Mrs. Stowe, Mark Twain believed that a "reverence for pure womanhood is . . . a national characteristic of the American. . . ."

Certainly, it was a characteristic of those genteel vestigial Puritans to whose company Twain aspired; and whenever he found a living example of that "pure womanhood" ready to hand—as he did in Mary Mason Fairbanks aboard the *Quaker City*—he submitted to her censorship in an act of guilt-ridden hypocrisy, which he apparently took for virtue. "I was never what she thought me," he wrote on the occasion of 'Mother' Fairbanks' death in 1899, "but I was glad to seem to her to be it." Such submission to conscience as embodied in a surrogate mamma of genteel taste and sentimental Christian principles appeared to Twain, at any rate, a way into the cultured WASP world; and this conviction seemed to him justified when the book which had taken final shape under Mrs. Fairbanks's supervision was hailed by William Dean Howells, spokesman-in-chief for that world.

His spontaneous expression of pleasure at that review is, however, a giveaway, not only in its unguarded vulgarity, but in the implications of its metaphor. He had felt reading it, Twain said, like the woman whose baby had come white; and, indeed, with the acceptance of *The Innocents Abroad,* he had been accepted as fully "white," in the sense that the Anglo-Saxon first settlers of America had given that mythological adjective.

But he was not, finally, quite one of them, as was to become embarrassingly evident to his genteel defenders at the infamous Whittier Birthday Dinner, a decade or so after his voyage on the *Quaker City.* Confronting what Stuart P. Sherman would still be able to call as late as 1910, "the leading geniuses of New England," i.e., the most proper literary Bostonians, Twain told into the "black frost" of their disapproval an utterly irreverent, pseudo-Western yarn involving "Mr. Longfellow, Mr. Emerson, Mr. Oliver Wendell Holmes—confound the lot. . . ." Twain was never able really to understand why his homely anecdote had failed to tickle his auditors; but Mr. Sherman, last apologist for the values he had unwittingly challenged, is in no doubt. "I know very well," he asserts, "that Congreve or Addison or George Meredith would have agreed . . . that Mark Twain's reminiscence was a piece of crude, heavy intellectual horseplay—an impudent affront offered to Puritan aristocracy by a rough-handed plebeian jester from Missouri."

But why, Twain must have wondered, was his Whittier's birthday speech rejected by the sort of men who had accepted his European travel book, much of which was precisely the same sort of "crude, heavy, intellectual horseplay," presented through exactly the same sort of *persona,* "a rough-handed plebeian jester from Missouri." Stuart Sherman himself, as a matter of fact, is quite as ready to condemn the book as the speech, and on similar grounds: "The Mississippi pilot, homely, naïve, arrogantly conceited . . . turns the Old World into a laughing stock by shearing it of its humanity —simply because there is nothing in him to respond to the glory that was Greece, to the grandeur that was Rome—simply because nothing is holier to him than a joke." William Dean Howells, however, had not been nearly so severe in his review of the book by the man he kept referring to as "Mr. Clements"—only a little condescending, perhaps: "It is no business of ours to fix his rank among the humorists California has given us, but we think he is, in an entirely different way from all the others, quite worthy of the company of the best."

Finally, however, Howells is willing to exempt the "California humorist" from charges of *lèse-majesté* in the realm of culture: " . . . it is always good-humored humor, too, that he lavishes on his reader, and even its impudence is charming; we do not remember where . . . it is insolent, with all its sauciness and irreverence." Even here the descriptive phrases remain condescending, though they are apt enough, after all, in defining a writer who composed his book to shock (a little) and mollify (a lot) the woman whom he had appointed his shipboard "mother." Charming . . . impudence," "insolent," "sauciness"—these are terms suitable not so much to a man as to a boy, one of those naughty boys who are not in the final analysis downright "bad." And, indeed, Twain himself uses the word "boys" constantly to describe his closest associates among the Pilgrims, the lively few who, with him, constantly sought to flee the more aged and grim members of what he likes to call the "synagogue." Already at the very beginning of his career, he is beginning to trade on that "boyishness" which he never willingly surrendered, in order to get away with what would have been counted sacrilege in a full-fledged man. And a sufficiently perspicuous critic might well have predicted at that point, that the hero in whom Twain was to embody his most mature definition of the American character would necessarily be a juvenile, just one more boy in a cast of boys.

But the "Mark Twain" of *The Innocents Abroad* is a bigger boy than Huck Finn: a boy full-grown enough to regret that his fellow voyagers scanted whist and dancing and love-making in favor of prayers and the singing of hymns, and to wander the streets of Europe in search of good cigars, a decent shave, and an authentic pool table—yet one not too mature to steal bunches of grapes on his way down from the Acropolis, and to torment his guides with childish horseplay. The "Mark Twain" of 1867 was, in short, the kind of boy-man we think of referring to as a "Westerner," one in whom the power of adulthood and the irresponsibility of childhood ideally combine. Twain, however, did not consider himself quite such a "Westerner" as he was later to describe in *Roughing It,* "stalwart, muscular, dauntless, young braves . . . erect, bright-eyed, quick-moving, strong-handed young giants. . . ."; for these exist only as legend, i.e., as someone else.

The character called "Mark Twain" in *The Innocents Abroad* is a comic version of these heroic types, a *schlemiel*—or clown-Westerner—a wandering jester who has learned among the "young braves" (to whom, of course, he had always been a butt) to hate cant, despise sentimentality, distrust sophistication, and who has picked up from them a new vocabulary—a native American diction —in which that hatred, despite and distrust can become a kind of humor acceptable to the New England Brahmins themselves: a way of discharging in laughter the nagging doubts about high art and European civilization that troubled their social inferiors if not them. Moreover, "Mark Twain" had lived in a landscape so terrifyingly beautiful in its aloofness from man's small necessities, so awe-

somely magnificent in its antihuman scale, that beside it the scenery of the Old World was bound to seem pallid, domesticated,
dwarfed.

"Como? Pshaw! See Lake Tahoe," one of his chapter headlines
reads; and in a footnote to another, this time concerned with the
Sea of Galilee, Twain notes: "I measure all lakes by Tahoe, partly
because I am far more familiar with it than with any other, and
partly because I have such a high admiration for it. . . ." Yet each
time he begins by evoking the peaceful splendor of that Western
lake, he ends in rage—rage at the rest of the world, which he considers somehow betrays its mythical splendor. On the shores of the
Sea of Galilee, for instance, he remembers dreamily how on Tahoe
"the tranquil interest that was born with the morning deepens and
deepens, by sure degrees, until it culminates at last in resistless fas-
cination!" But an instant later he is near hysteria, scolding the Pal-
estinian landscape, as it were, for failing him and his memories:
"these unpeopled deserts, these rusty mounds of barrenness . . .
that melancholy ruin of Capernaum; this stupid village of Tiberias
. . . yonder desolate declivity where the swine of the miracle ran
down into the sea, and doubtless thought it was better to swallow a
devil or two and get drowned into the bargain than to have to live
longer in such a place. . . ."

Earlier, taking off from a comparison with Lake Como, he had
been even more extravagant in his praise of Tahoe: "a sea whose
every aspect is impressive, whose belongings are all beautiful,
whose lovely majesty types the Deity!" But he subsides quickly
from the high level banality of such schoolroom English prose, into
pure barroom American—and once more into the rage, which
seems as appropriate to the latter, as platitudes to the former style.
This time, however, his rage is directed, quite unexpectedly, against
the American Indians.

> Tahoe means grasshoppers. It means grasshopper soup. It is
> Indian, and suggestive of Indians . . . . People say that Tahoe
> means "Silver Lake"—"Limpid Water"—"Falling Leaf." Bosh!
> It means grasshopper soup, the favorite dish of the Digger
> tribe . . . . It isn't worthwhile in these practical times, for
> people to talk about Indian poetry—there never was any in

them—except in the Fenimore Cooper Indians. But *they* are an extinct tribe that never existed. I know the Noble Red Man. I have camped with the Indians; I have been on the war-path with them, taken part in the chase with them—for grasshoppers; helped them steal cattle; I have roamed with them, scalped them, had them for breakfast. I would gladly eat the whole race if I had a chance.

It is an astonishing performance, which begins by puzzling us, ends by sending us back to a novel published more than a decade before —to Melville's *The Confidence Man,* a book which Mark Twain doubtless never read, but one whose twenty-sixth chapter, "Containing the metaphysics of Indian-Hating, according to the views of one evidently not so prepossessed as Rousseau in Favor of Savages," serves as a gloss to his meditations beside Como.

Attempting to answer, via a series of shadowy spokesman characters, the question: "Why the backwoodsman still regards the red man in much the same spirit that a jury does a murderer, or a trapper a wild cat," Melville finds himself impelled to define the essential nature of the "backwoodsman," which is to say, precisely the kind of man through whose mask Twain has chosen to comment on Europe in *The Innocents Abroad.* "Though held as a sort of barbarian," Melville tells us, "the backwoodsman would seem to Americans what Alexander was to Asia—captain in the vanguard of a conquering civilization. . . . The tide of emigration, let it roll as it will, never overwhelms the backwoodsman into itself; he rides upon the advance, as the Polynesian upon the comb of the surf. Thus though he keep moving on through life, he maintains with respect to nature much the same unaltered relation throughout; with her creatures, too, including panthers and Indians." And more generally, Melville observes, "the backwoodsman is a lonely man. . . . Impulsive, he is what some might call unprincipled. At any rate, he is self-willed; being one who less harkens to what others may say about things, than looks for himself, to see what are things themselves."

But what does the backwoodsman see, when he "looks for himself, to see what are things themselves" in respect to culture rather than nature, Europe rather than the wilderness, when he becomes an "innocent abroad"? The Westerner's bleak vision of the Old World was recorded much later by Ezra Pound, who was born properly enough in Hailey, Idaho—rendered in verse at the moment of America's entry into World War I, itself, in a sense, the continuation of tourism by other means.

> There died a myriad,
> And of the best, among them,
> For an old bitch gone in the teeth,
> For a botched civilization,
>
> Charm, smiling at the good mouth,
> Quick eyes gone under the earth's lid,
>
> For two gross of broken statues,
> For a few thousand battered books.

Two major American talents had begun to wrestle with the problem, however, long before the nineteenth century was over: the two writers of their generation by whom Europe was most obsessively felt as an enigma to be endlessly attacked, precisely because it could never be entirely solved—Samuel Clemens and Henry James. Both, at any rate, were the authors of novels in which a Western American, defined as pristine Protestant and incorruptible democrat, tries to come to terms with a Europe seen as essentially aristocratic and Roman Catholic.

James's *The American* was not published until 1877, eight years after the appearance of Twain's *The Innocents Abroad,* but in terms of fictional time, their protagonists missed meeting each other in the museums of France by less than a year; for it was, James tells us, "On a brilliant day in May, in the year 1868," that *his* gentleman from San Francisco—called with obvious symbolic intent Christopher Newman—was lounging in the Louvre. Like that other San Franciscan, "Mark Twain," Newman, we learn, was suffering from an "aesthetic headache" in the presence of all those masterpieces; and like his improbable opposite number, he was convinced from the start that the fresh copies of the Old Masters being made by various young ladies right before his eyes were superior to the dim and dusty originals.

It is easy enough to surmise what Newman is supposed to represent, but a certain Mrs. Tristram (who most nearly speaks for James in the book) makes Newman's meaning explicit, by explaining to him, " 'You are the great Western Barbarian stepping forth in his innocence and might, gazing a while at this poor effete Old World, and then swooping down on it.' " At that point, however, the "great Western Barbarian"—whom James never quite understood, in fact—demurs, crying out, "I am a highly civilized man"; and spends the rest of the novel trying to prove it, at considerable cost not only to himself but to his author, who loses thereafter the comic tone on which he has opened in melancholy and melodrama. But if one chronicler of the New Barbarian in the Old World failed because of his distance from the character he was attempting to portray, the other continually risks disaster because of his uncomfortable closeness to the *persona* he has assumed.

Neither the reader nor the author of *The Innocents Abroad* is ever quite sure where Samuel Clemens stops and "Mark Twain" begins, how far Clemens is in fact what Stuart Sherman described as "the kind of traveling companion that makes you wonder why you went abroad" (in more contemporary terms, the kind of American consumer for whom Europe is just one more item on the menu of Mass Culture), and how far he is the satirist of that kind of traveler. There is no doubt, in any case, that his book is primarily about such travelers rather than about the Old World itself; that it is consequently not a "travel book" at all in the traditional sense, but a chronicle of tourism at the precise point when the Puritan aristocrat abroad is giving way to the Puritan plebeian on tour.

What the plebeian—that unforeseen new man—finds wrong with the Old World, the Old Masters, the land of the Old Testament is precisely that they are all *old,* i.e., worn out, shabby, dirty, decaying, down at the heels. This abject prejudice against seediness, however ennobled by time, both Clemens and "Twain" share with their fellow travelers. To be sure, there is ambivalence aplenty in *The Innocents Abroad,* most spectacularly exemplified in the chapters on Venice, where the wary Westerner, the man resolved at all costs not to be had, begins by asserting point-blank, "This famed gondola and this gorgeous gondolier!—the one an inky, rusty old canoe with a sable hearse-body clapped onto the middle of it, and the other a mangy, bare-footed guttersnipe with a portion of his raiment on exhibition which should have been sacred from public scrutiny." But a few pages later, he has apparently changed his mind, observing in conventional panegyric tones, "The Venetian gondola is as free and graceful, in its gliding movement, as a serpent. . . . The Gondolier *is* a picturesque rascal for all he wears no satin harness, no plumed bonnet, no silken tights."

This doubleness of vision, however, this alternation between daytime debunking and nighttime subscription to a dream ("In the glare of day, there is little poetry about Venice, but under the charitable moon her stained palaces are white again. . . .") does not arise out of the dialogue between Clemens the artist and "Twain" the comic innocent; it has lain deep in the heart of every run-of-the-mill tourist ever since that memorable year of 1867, when, for the first time on record at least, "Everybody was going to Europe. . . ." Occasionally, of course, Twain moves from echoing the Americans abroad to mocking them, but never for their vulgarity, their grossness of perception, their smug contempt for culture. What stirs his satirical impulse is rather their pretentiousness, their pitiful attempts at culture climbing: their signing hotel registers in French, or claiming loudly never to have eaten a meal without the proper wine—or, especially, their mouthing of high-flown phrases out of guidebooks in the presence of works of art they do not really understand.

When he is recounting the playful desecration of revered cultural sites, his tone is bafflingly equivocal—as in the episode in the crater of Mount Vesuvius which so infuriated Stuart Sherman. "Some of the boys thrust lone slips of paper down into holes and set them on fire, and so achieved the glory of lighting their cigars by the flames of Vesuvius, and others cooked their eggs over fissures in the rocks and were happy." Surely, there is a note of friendly mockery here, but none of that cold fury with which Twain reports, say, the credulity of Europeans in the face of holy "relics" and "miracles," or the gushing response of some of his fellow Americans to such utterly ruined pictures as da Vinci's *Last Supper*. ("Maybe the originals were handsome when they were new, but they are not now.")

Only at the climax of the book, when the author-protagonist stands face to face with the oldest monument he has encountered, with, that is to say, an ultimate incarnation of the persistence of the past, toward which he has been as ambivalent as any other ignorant American, are his last scruples overcome, his final equivocation resolved. It is the Sphinx that conquers him: "After years of waiting, it was before me at last. . . . There was a dignity not of earth in its mien. . . . It was gazing out over the ocean of Time—. . . . It was MEMORY—RETROSPECTION—wrought into visible, tangible form. . . . And there is that in the overshadowing majesty of this eternal figure of stone . . . which reveals to one something of what he shall feel when he shall stand at last in the awful presence of God." But at this point, when he has been converted, however temporarily, to the religion of culture, Twain looks up and sees on the jaw of the Sphinx "a wart, or an excrescence of some kind," which turns out to be, of course, a fellow American, a companion on the tour—in search of a souvenir.

"We heard," Twain tell us, abandoning himself finally to total rage against just such an "innocent" as he had all along pretended to be, "the familiar clink of a hammer, and understood the case at once. One of our well-meaning reptiles—I mean relic-hunters—had crawled up there and was trying to break a 'specimen' from the face of this, the most majestic creation the hand of man has wrought." Confronted with such absolute sacrilege, however, all Twain can conceive of doing is to call a cop, i.e., a sheik, whom he urges to warn the intruder that his offense is "punishable with imprisonment or the bastinado." A hundred years later, it has become clear just how ineffectual such sanctions are against the American tourist's irrepressible need to chip away piece by piece the Old World he does not quite dare confess bores him; but what else was there then for Twain to do in response—except, of course, to write a book.

The Shape of *Moby Dick*

THAT *Moby Dick* is something more or less than a well-made novel no critic has ever doubted. Had Henry James taken the trouble to classify it, he would surely have put it in the category of "loose and baggy monsters," which, considering its overt themes and secret obsessions is fair enough. But not quite good enough for me, I fear. "*How* loose, and *why* baggy?"—these are the questions which have concerned me for some years now, and to which I have not yet found quite satisfactory answers; for which reason, I worry them again this evening, beginning with what is most obvious and moving on—hopefully—to what is most obscure.

But surely the most obvious thing about *Moby Dick* is the fact that it describes a voyage, *is*—in its mythological essence—a Voyage, or, as we would put it these days, a Trip: a venture There and Back, temporarily out of this world, away from terra firma into worlds more fantastic, or to use Melville's preferred metaphor, more watery. He typically dissolves or dives into vision, rather than taking off or flipping out as we children of a Space Age would have it. Nonetheless, he moves on out of here and now, which is to say out of civilization and sanity, as classic American writers—through their books, at least, and their imagined surrogates—tend almost universally to do.

Not only Americans, however, have imagined the Voyage or the Trip as the essential poetic experience. From the time of the *Odyssey* on, heroes have been set in motion, often through or into worlds quite as watery as Melville's, since until the mythologizing of Outer Space the Sea was the reigning image for Otherwhere. Yet there is something singular about American versions of the Voyage, which are typically for us, aberrantly for the Western tradition in general, neither quests nor homecomings. Our heroes do not fare forth in search of the Golden Fleece or the Golden Girl who goes with it, nor do they end in the connubial bed of home, rooted like a tree into deepest earth. No, the protagonists we admire and who set in motion our classic books flee *from* home; they are escapees, refugees, men in flight, whose direction is not toward but away: like Ishmael himself or Natty Bumppo before him or Huck Finn to come.

Yet the prototype of them all is Odysseus, though Homer did not know it, Odysseus beyond the point to which the Greek imagination could take him, Dante's Odysseus—or as he, beneficiary of Roman rather than Hellenic sources, prefers to call him: Ulysses. It is in the twenty-sixth canto of the *Inferno* that America is invented for the European mind, as well as the myth of the West and the Western, which is to say, the westering Hero. When Dante makes his Ulysses cry to his "brothers," the shipmates "who through a hundred thousand dangers have reached the West" an appeal to attempt an even more ultimate West, the forbidden watery world, he puts in his mouth words eminently American: "Do not reject the experience—following the course of the sun—of the unpeopled world." After which, of course, only disaster can follow; for when land is sighted in the Western Hemisphere, the God of Europe, who has declared it taboo, sucks Ulysses and his crew down into the bottom of the ocean, whirling them about three times, and then a fourth "until the sea closed over us again."

That Dantesque cadence and image recur again and again in our literature, as our latterday refugees from home, from what Dante had called "the sweetness of having a son, the obligation to an aging father and the legitimate love that should have made Penelope rejoice," head for similar fates at the ends of utterly alien worlds: Gordon Pym, for instance (in the final paragraphs of Edgar Allen Poe's *The Narrative of A. Gordon Pym*) on the verge of his whirlpool, remarking, "And now we rushed into the embraces of the cataract, where a chasm threw itself open to receive us." Thus Melville, speaking in the voice of Ishmael and responding to some recent reading surely of both Dante and Poe, recreates almost exactly the feel of the close of Ulysses' speech: "And now, concentric circles seized the lone boat itself, and all its crew, and. . .spinning, animate and inanimate, all round and round in one vortex, carried the smallest chip of the *Pequod* out of sight. . .then all collapsed, and the great shroud of the sea rolled on as it rolled five thousand years ago."

But it is the relationship between myth and form, archetype and structure that I am interested in this evening. For it seems to me that the structure of our classic books is fugal—of *Moby Dick* preeminently, but also, say, of *Huckleberry Finn*—repeated themes pursuing each other and themselves, overlapping, echoing, inverting —not so much telling a tale as recording the reverberations of the taleteller's voice; and that the reason for this is, quite simply, that form follows myth—an archetypal account of a flight from reason and control and civilization demanding a mode of narration that eschews the rationality of plot, the return home of a well-made fiction. Formally as well as thematically, our authors are always suggesting to us the shape of the wilderness and a longing to light out for the unexplored territory ahead, the next *mondo senza gente,* which is to say, Dante's "unpeopled world."

If all this sounds like "the fallacy of imitative form," it is meant to, since almost all American writers of distinction have subscribed to this fallacy, this peculiarly American literary heresy. In light of all this, it is interesting to reflect that the single great book of our nineteenth century which achieves an orderly structure, a form almost classical in its grace and stability, is Hawthorne's *The Scarlet Letter,* which is the sole classic American book about the rejection of flight, Dimmesdale's refusal in the forest of Hester's suggestion that he flee the established community either to seek (in the image of Fenimore Cooper) a more ultimate Western wilderness, or (in anticipation of Henry James) the once-abandoned corruption of Europe. Correspondingly, the most flagrant of our nineteenth-century nonnovels or antinovels is *Moby Dick,* which begins with Ishmael already in flight and already aware that his taking to sea means an abandonment of ordered reality as well as the homeland: "By reason of these things, then," Melville has him confide in us, "the whaling voyage was welcome; the great floodgates of the wonder-world swung open. . . ."

Nonetheless, even if Ishmael knew himself from the first to be embarked on a dream-fugue, Melville seems to have thought for a while that he was about to write, in some conventional sense, a novel; and in its first chapters, there survive fragments of a failed novel in the realistic mode, "a continuous narrative." At least this was how Melville spoke of the book to others (perhaps thought of it himself) in the early stages, insisting "I mean to give the truth" —as opposed, apparently to the free fantasy of *Mardi*—with perhaps "a little fancy to cook the thing up." But the "continuous narrative"—the account, it can be presumed, of a struggle between a monomaniac Captain and a virtuous sailor, an irresistible demonic force and an immovable angelic obstacle (just such a story as Melville finally got down in *Billy Budd*)—was never written, or rather barely begun. Bulkington, the Handsome Sailor, obviously intended to play protagonist to Captain Ahab's antagonist, is introduced, forgotten, suddenly remembered at the start of Chapter XXIII ("Some chapters back," he writes, "one Bulkington was spoken of, a tall, new-landed mariner. . .") and as quickly hurried out of sight ("Let me only say," he concludes, "that it fared with him as with the storm-tossed ship. . . this six-inch chapter is the stoneless grave of Bulkington. . .").

Something obviously had happened in Melville's mind between Chapter III and Chapter XXXIII, some deep change in purpose and direction overtaken him; and much of the writing about *Moby Dick* in our own time has concerned itself with a quest for the causes of this change—in Melville's rereading of Shakespeare, for instance, and his encounter with Hawthorne, whom he was to love so ill-fatedly forever after. And doubtless, both of these external events helped to make Melville aware of what the internal logic (more properly, illogic, I suppose) of his fugal tale had been all the time demanding: to bury Bulkington, for instance, rather than praise him, to leave only Ahab and Ishmael finally, which is to say, two parts of his duplicitous self, to confront each other in the howling watery wilderness, which is to say, the region of nightmare common to both.

Melville did not, could not, resist the voice of his demon, writing finally the book he had to, rather than the one he thought it wise to do. But the need for money and the pressure of time were on him when he saw his way clear at last; and he attempted to remake his novel without destroying any of the pages already written. To have altered the ironic tone of the opening to accord with the tragic climax to which he felt driven would have taken too long; to have eliminated Bulkington completely would have required tiresome revisions (and besides he was extraordinarily fond of him); to have cut down the sheer bulk of the Queequeg-Ishmael story would have demanded starting all over again. And so, as ever, Melville settled for what he thought of as a "botch." "All my books are botches," he once wrote, and explained, "Dollars damn me." Damned by dollars, saved by his demon; it is the story of his writing life.

But it is not the whole story; for if an account of the Voyage into the World of Myth and Wonder defies, finally destroys, the novel form, invented precisely (as Samuel Richardson himself once boasted) to drive the "marvelous" and "wonderful" from the realm of prose fiction—such Voyage literature suits admirably the older and more honorable form of the Epic. And, indeed, it is toward the Epic that Melville aspired all his life long, an Epic Poem in Prose which he finally wrote in *Moby Dick*. Whitman, with similar ambitions driving him, was to equivocate between prose and verse in *Leaves of Grass;* but Melville seems never to have doubted that a Democratic Epic, the Epic of uncommon common men, must be cast in the humbler and homelier form. Perhaps, after all, it was the chief value of his deceiving himself into thinking that he was writing a novel, that this confusion kept him from the temptation to verse. Consider what grief he came to later on when he did turn to verse in *Clarel,* an epic attempt which fails as notably as *Moby Dick* succeeds.

Moby Dick is, however, not merely a Democratic Epic but also a Romantic or Erotic one; and in this sense, too, it owes a debt to the tradition of the novel, which in so many other ways it betrayed. The proper subject of the Epic is War and the Return from War; while the subject *par excellence* of the Novel is love. To be sure, we modern readers, conditioned by two centuries of the post-Richardsonian novel, eagerly seek out in the *Iliad* the story of Briseis and Chryseis, which is to say, the erotic; just as we choose to recall out of all the grim events of the *Aeneid* the sentimental episode of

Dido. But this is a matter of our eccentric taste and should not deceive us. The God of the Epic Poets is Ares not Aphrodite; and in writing of a love which triumphs over death Melville is of the tribe of Richardson rather than of Homer—or, indeed, even of Shakespeare who is so much on Melville's mind as he writes *Moby Dick*.

What misleads us a little at first in *Moby Dick* is the fact that its great love story involves two men, one white and one colored, rather than a man and a woman; but this, after all, is the traditional American way, the deepest of all our native myths of love. When Ishmael arises out of the sea at the book's close (in the epilogue which manages to get past the catastrophic ending that was for Dante a final word), he is clinging to a coffin which has been marked with the patterns originally tattooed on the body of his dearly beloved Queequeg, clinging, in fact (in the metaphor which is poetic fact), to all that is immortal in his dead friend.

It is a strange unheroic Happy Ending for an Epic Hero; but, then, Ishmael is a strange unheroic hero to begin with—one who does nothing after his original feat of running away, except to watch (as one watches in a dream the exploits of all he most fears and adores in his deepest self) the self-destruction of Ahab, the fatal encounter of the Killer and the Beast from the Depths, the mad Yankee Captain and Moby Dick who has castrated him. It is, of course, Ahab rather than Ishmael who seems like the traditional heroic figure of ancient legend: the man with a mission, who raises his lance against the most formidable monsters and conquers them; except that for Melville the ancients' unequivocal Hero is himself a monster who must be destroyed, and who therefore lifts his lance in vain. And why not, after all, since Moby Dick, unlike those pests destroyed by Theseus and Perseus and all the classic rest, is somehow divine: not God himself, perhaps, since there is no God; but a symbol at least of the vacuous mystery which resides at the center of the universe once thought to be filled with the plenitude of God.

Ahab cannot be, then, the real hero of Melville's tale—only the hero-villain of a tale within his tale, or, more precisely, a *play* within his tale (complete with stage-directions and asides), since for Melville all nightmare aspires to Shakespearian form. And this hero-villain, this maimed half-hero is watched by Melville's other half-hero, Ishmael, a character who tends (like Hamlet himself at the moment of *his* play within a play) to fall out of the plot into the audience.

But exactly here is the final clue to the complex form of *Moby Dick,* which embodies at once envelope and enveloped, the dreamer and the dreamed: a Democratic Romantic Epic, pretending to be a novel, which encloses a nightmare pretending to be a lost play by Shakespeare. But it is, however, the pseudonovel, the secret epic which contains the pseudodrama; even as the drama's half-hero, the Warrior turned monomaniac killer, is contained in the epic's half-hero, the runaway who in his flight from reality and death represents the author in his flight from form.

—1967

The Pleasures of John Hawkes

EVERYONE KNOWS THAT in our literature an age of experimentalism
is over and an age of recapitulation has begun; and few of us, I suspect, really regret it. How comfortable it is to be interested in literature in a time of standard acceptance and standard dissent—when
the only thing more conventionalized than convention is revolt.
How reassuring to pick up the latest book of the latest young novelist and to discover there familiar themes, familiar techniques—ac-
companied often by the order of skill available to the beginner
when he is able (sometimes even with passionate conviction) to
embrace received ideas, exploit established forms. Not only is the
writing of really new books a perilous pursuit, but even the reading
of such books is beset with dangers; and it is for this reason, I suppose, that readers are secretly grateful to authors content to rewrite
the dangerous books of the past. A sense of *déjà vu* takes the curse
off the whole ticklish enterprise in which the writer engages, miti-
gates the terror and truth which we seek in his art at the same time
we cravenly hope that it is not there.

John Hawkes neither rewrites nor recapitulates, and, therefore,
spares us neither terror nor truth. It is, indeed, in the interests of
the latter that he endures seeming in 1960 that unfashionable and
suspect stereotype, the "experimental writer." Hawkes' "experimentalism" is, however, his own rather than that of yesterday's *avant-
garde* rehashed; he is no more an echoer of other men's revolts than
he is a subscriber to the recent drift toward neo-middlebrow sentimentality. He is a lonely eccentric, a genuine unique—a not
uncommon American case, or at least one that used to be not un-

common; though now, I fear, loneliness has become as difficult to maintain among us as failure. Yet John Hawkes has managed both, is perhaps (after the publication of three books and on the verge of that of the fourth) the least read novelist of substantial merit in the United States. I recall a year or so ago coming across an ad in the *Partisan Review* in which Mr. Hawkes' publisher was decrying one of those exclusions which have typically plagued him. "Is *Partisan,*" that publisher asked, "doing right by its readers when it consistently excludes from its pages the work of such writers as Edward Dahlberg, Kenneth Patchen, Henry Miller, John Hawkes and Kenneth Rexroth?"

But God knows that of all that list only Hawkes really *needs* the help of the *Partisan Review.* Miller has come to seem grandpa to a large part of a generation; while the two Kenneths are surely not without appropriate honors and even Dahlberg has his impassioned exponents. Who, however, reads John Hawkes? Only a few of us, I fear, tempted to pride by our fewness, and ready in that pride to believe that the recalcitrant rest of the world doesn't deserve Hawkes, that we would do well to keep his pleasures our little secret. To tout him too widely would be the equivalent of an article in *Holiday,* a note in the travel section of the *Sunday Times,* might turn a private delight into an attraction for everybody. Hordes of the idly curious might descend on him and us, gaping, pointing— and bringing with them the Coca-Cola sign, the hot-dog stand. They've got Ischia now and Majorca and Walden Pond. Let them leave us Hawkes! But, of course, the tourists would never really come; and who would be foolish enough in any case to deny to anyone daylight access to those waste places of the mind from which no one can be barred at night, which the least subtle visit in darkness and unknowing. Hawkes may be an unpopular writer, but he is not an esoteric one; for the places he defines are the places in which we all live between sleeping and waking, and the pleasures he affords are the pleasures of returning to those places between waking and sleeping.

He is, in short, a Gothic novelist; but this means one who makes terror rather than love the center of his work, knowing all the while, of course, that there can be no terror without the hope for love and love's defeat. In *The Cannibal, The Beetle Leg,* and *The Goose on the Grave* he has pursued through certain lunar landscapes (called variously Germany or the American West or Italy) his vision of horror and baffled passion; nor has his failure to reach a wide audience shaken his faith in his themes. In *The Lime Twig* he takes up the Gothic pursuit once more, though this time his lunar landscape is called England; and the nightmare through which his terrified protagonists flee reaches its climax at a race meeting, where gangsters and cops and a stolen horse bring to Michael Banks and his wife the spectacular doom which others of us dream and wake from, relieved, but which they, improbably, live.

It is all, on one level, a little like a thriller, a story, say, by Graham Greene; and, indeed, there is a tension in *The Lime Twig* absent from Hawkes' earlier work: a pull between the aspiration toward popular narrative (vulgar, humorous, suspenseful) and the dedication to the austerities of highbrow horror. Yet Hawkes' new novel finally avoids the treacherous lucidity of the ordinary shocker, the kind of clarity intended to assure a reader that the violence he relives destroys only certain characters in a book, not the fabric of the world he inhabits. In a culture where even terror has been so vulgarized by mass entertainers that we can scarcely believe in it any longer, we hunger to be persuaded that, after all, it really counts. For unless the horror we live is real, there is no point to our lives; and it is to writers like Hawkes that we turn from the wholesale slaughter on T.V. to be convinced of the reality of what we most fear. If *The Lime Twig* reminds us of *Brighton Rock,* which in turn reminds us of a movie by Hitchcock, it is of *Brighton Rock* recalled in a delirium or by a drowning man—*Brighton Rock* rewritten by Djuna Barnes. Hawkes, however, shares the effeteness of Djuna Barnes's vision of evil no more than he does the piety of Greene's vision of sin. His view avoids the aesthetic and the theological alike, since it deals with the mysteries neither of the world of art nor of the spirit—but only with the immitigable mystery of the world of common experience. It is not so much the fact that love succumbs to terror which obsesses Hawkes as the fact that love breeding terror is itself the final terror. This he neither denies nor conceals, being incapable of the evasions of sentimentality: the writer's capitulation before his audience's desire to be deceived, his own to be approved. Hawkes' novel makes painfully clear how William Hencher's love for his mother, dead in the fire-bombings of London, brings him back years later to the lodgings they once shared—a fat man with elastic sleeves on his thighs, in whom the encysted small boy cannot leave off remembering and suffering. But in those lodgings he discovers Banks and his wife Margaret, yearns toward them with a second love verging on madness, serves them tea in bed and prowls their apartment during their occasional absences, searching for some way to bind them, his memories, and his self together. "I found," he reports of one such occasion, "her small tube of cosmetic for the lips and, in the lavatory, drew a red circle with it round each of my eyes. I had their bed to myself while they were gone." It is, however, Hencher's absurd and fetishistic passion which draws Michael Banks out of the safe routine of his life into crime, helps, that is, to turn a lifetime of erotic daydreaming about horses into the act of stealing a real race horse called Rock Castle.

And the end of it all is sheer terror: Hencher kicked to a pulp in a stable; Margaret Banks naked beneath the shreds of a hospital gown and lovingly beaten to death; Michael, screwed silly by all his nympholeptic dreams become flesh, throwing himself under the hooves of a field of horses bunched for the final turn and the stretch! What each of Hawkes' doomed lovers has proposed to himself in fantasy—atrocious pleasure or half-desired indignity—he endures in fact. But each lover, under cover of whatever images, has ultimately yearned for his own death and consequently dies; while the antilovers, the killers, whose fall guys and victims the lovers become, having wished only for the death of others, survive: Syb, the come-on girl, tart and teaser; Little Dora, huge and aseptically cruel behind her aging schoolmarm's face; and Larry, gangster-in-chief and cock-of-the-house, who stands stripped toward the novel's end, indestructible in the midst of the destruction he has willed, a phallic god in brass knuckles and bulletproof vest.

> They cheered, slapping the oxen arms, slapping the flesh, and cheered when the metal vest was returned to him—steel and skin—and the holster was settled again but in an armpit naked now and smelling of scented freshener.
>
> Larry turned slowly round so they could see, and there was the gun's blue butt, the dazzling links of steel, the hairless and swarthy torso. . . .

"For twenty years," shouted Dora again through the smoke opaque as ice, "for twenty years I've admired that! Does anybody blame me." Banks listened and . . . for a moment met the eyes of Sybilline, his Syb, eyes in a lovely face pressed hard against the smoothest portion of Larry's arm, which—her face with auburn hair was just below his shoulder—could take the punches . . .

And even these are bound together in something like love.

Of all the book's protagonists, only Sidney Slyter is without love; half dopester of the races, half amateur detective, Sidney is at once a spokesman for the novelist and a parody of the novelist's role, providing a choral commentary on the action, which his own curiosity spurs toward its end. Each section of the novel opens with a quotation from his newspaper column, *Sidney Slyter says,* in which the jargon of the sports page merges into a kind of surrealistic poetry, the matter of fact threatens continually to become hallucination. But precisely here is the clue to the final achievement of Hawkes' art, his detachment from that long literary tradition which assumes that consciousness is continuous, that experience reaches us in a series of framed and unified scenes, and that—in life as well as books—we are aware simultaneously of details and the context in which we confront them.

Such a set of assumptions seems scarcely tenable in a post-Freudian, post-Einsteinian world; and we cling to it more, perhaps, out of piety toward the literature of the past than out of respect for life in the present. In the world of Hawkes' fiction, however, we are forced to abandon such traditional presumptions and the security we find in hanging on to them. His characters move not from scene to scene but in and out of focus; for they float in a space whose essence is indistinctness, endure in a time which refuses either to begin or end. To be sure, certain details are rendered with a more than normal, an almost painful, clarity (quite suddenly a white horse dangles in mid-air before us, vividly defined, or we are gazing, close up, at a pair of speckled buttocks), but the contexts which give them meaning and location are blurred by fog or alcohol, by darkness or weariness or the failure of attention. It is all, in short, quite like the consciousness we live by but do not record in books —untidy, half-focused, disarrayed.

The order which retrospectively we *impose* on our awareness of events (by an effort of the will and imagination so unflagging that we are no more conscious of it than of our breathing) Hawkes decomposes. For the sake of art and the truth, he dissolves the rational universe which we are driven, for the sake of sanity and peace, to manufacture out of the chaos of memory, impression, reflex and fantasy that threatens eternally to engulf us. Yet he does not abandon all form in his quest for the illusion of formlessness; in the random conjunction of reason and madness, blur and focus, he finds occasions for wit and grace. Counterfeits of insanity (automatic writing, the scrawls of the drunk and doped) are finally boring; while the compositions of the actually insane are in the end merely documents, terrible and depressing. Hawkes gives us neither of these surrenders to unreason but rather reason's last desperate attempt to know what unreason is; and in such knowledge there are possibilities not only for poetry and power but for pleasure as well.

Goshen, Vermont
—1960

John Barth: An Eccentric Genius

NINETEEN-SIXTY WAS a year in which two American eccentrics of great integrity and power produced ambitious books which (once more!) have received neither the acclaim nor, I suspect, the kind of reading they deserve. The first is Wright Morris whose *Ceremony in Lone Tree* was received generally with the stony respect it has become customary to accord his work. His latest book is the thirteenth he has published, and at this point the response to him has become ritualized: the small sales, the impassioned pitches of a few critics, the baffled sense that now, *now* he must surely be on the verge of popularity (he has finally one book in paperback, *Love Among the Cannibals*). Certainly, he has become the best-known little-known author in the civilized world—a "case" we would all be loath to surrender; but even this indignity Wright Morris will doubtless endure as he has endured all the others visited on him in his exemplary career.

To be, like Morris, a really American writer these days— doggedly provincial and incorruptibly lonely—requires a special sort of obtuseness, with which Morris is lucky enough to be blessed; and John Barth, who is my second eccentric, shares this obtuseness. In his case, however, I feel somehow that it is an obtuseness chosen rather than given; for Barth is not only a younger man than Morris, but is also, unlike Morris, an academic—with proper degrees and a job in a university. All of which means, it seems reasonable to assume, that Barth approaches each of his inevitable publishing failures with an awareness of their inevitability; while Morris, one surmises, launches each new book with an embittered but unbroken hope. I see the first of these American types as a character played by W. C. Fields and the second as one played by Buster Keaton: comics both of them; though reflecting on the one hand the absurdity of great expectations eternally frustrated, and on the other that of foregone defeat accepted with a kind of deadpan pleasure.

John Barth's *The Sot-Weed Factor*—the title is early American for a tobacco merchant—is his third novel, set like his first two in Maryland, or more precisely in the single country of Maryland which he knows best—his America. (Only such a European-oriented writer as Whitmen at his worst believes that to portray America one must encompass its imaginary vastness, its blurred continental totality.) Barth works his corner of our land, reconstructs it with all the intensity of Morris re-imagining Nebraska, Hemingway Upper Michigan, Faulkner Northern Mississippi, or Whitman (in his less cosmic moments) Brooklyn; though Barth is surely aware that the territory he explores has less ready-made mythic import for other Americans than almost any region to which he might have been born. It does not represent the moral miasma we identify with the Deep South, nor the well-armed innocence of the East, nor the frigid isolation of New England, nor the niggling Know-Nothingism of the small-town Midwest, nor the urban horrors of the industrialized East.

Maryland, in fact, is not yet invented for our imaginations; and the invention of the place he knows is the continuing task Barth has set himself, the continuing interest that binds together his three books. His is not, of course, the interest of the pious antiquary or local colorist; what he discovers is scandal and terror and disreputable joy—which is to say, the human condition, the disconcerting sameness of human particularity. Yet John Barth is, on one level, a historical scholar; and his books, even when they deal with contemporary or nearly contemporary events (like *The Floating Opera* or *End of the Road)* give the odd effect of being worked up from documents, carefully consulted and irreverently interpreted. He finds in history not merely the truth, not really the truth at all—for each of his novels exploits the ambiguities of facts and motives— but absurdity. He is first of all a philosopher, and knows not only what Marx knew (that if history does, indeed, repeat itself, the second time is always comic) but also what Heraclitus knew (that

there is only a second time). He is, in short, an existentialist comedian suffering history, not just because it happens to be *à la mode*
to be comic and existentialist, but because, born in Maryland in his
generation and reborn in graduate school, he can scarcely afford to
be anything else. He has, moreover, talent enough to be what he
has to be, against all the odds, *unfashionably.*

Granted all this, it was predictable enough that Barth would
eventually try what looks like a full-scale historical novel and is in
fact a travesty of the form. And the probabilities were all along that
when he attempted such a book he would produce one not slim
(like the *tour de force* of Lampedusa's "The Leopard") but traditionally, depressingly fat. This is in fact so.

The Sot-Weed Factor is a volume of over eight hundred pages,
dealing with the adventures of a rather unprepossessing male virgin
called Ebenezer Cooke, who in the declining years of the seventeenth
century came to America—equipped with a doubtful patent as
"Poet and Laureate of Maryland" which somehow involved him
not only in the cultural life of his time but also in political and religious struggles, Indian warfare and the miseries of love. That the
book is too long is obvious—*i.e.,* it is too long for most reviewers to
read through so that, though they are respectful, they are also cau-
tiously brief and non-committal. For fifty pages at a time it can
even be boring or confusing or both; but what are fifty pages in so
immense a text, and what do a little boredom and confusion matter
in the midst of so dazzling a demonstration of virtuosity, ambition
and sheer courage?

To have settled for less than eight hundred pages would have
been to accept timidly the unwritten edict that in our time only bad
books can be long, only the best-seller can risk dullness. Why
should the antihistorical novel not be equal as well as opposite to
the standard received historical romance in fullest bloat? Why
should it not also contain *everything,* though everything hilariously
transformed? Though Barth's antihistory does not end as mere parody, it begins as such: the reconstruction of a Good Old Time in
which Sir Isaac Newton, with buggery in his heart, pursues his students across the quad; and the portrait of Lord Baltimore, a disguised master spy, who is not even really the spy he claims to be
but a more devious counteragent impersonating the impersonator.

Similarly, Barth's antinovelistic form distorts the recognitions and reversals of popular literature, first in the direction of travesty and then of nightmare: brother and sister recognize each other on the verge of rape; Indian and white man find they possess a common father when they confess a common genital inadequacy; the tomahawked and drowned corpses in one chapter revive in the next. Yet somehow the parody remains utterly serious, the farce and melodrama evoke terror and pity, and the flagrant mockery of a happy ending constricts the heart. And all the while one *laughs,* at a pitch somewhere between hysteria and sheer delight.

The book is a joke book, an endless series of gags. But the biggest joke of all is that Barth seems finally to have written something closer to the "Great American Novel" than any other book of the last decade. In *The Sot-Weed Factor* he recapitulates (not by way of imitation but out of a sensitivity to the dark forces that have always compelled such concerns in our fiction) all the obsessive themes common to our classic novels: the comradeship of males, white and colored, always teetering perilously close to, but never quite falling over into, blatant homosexuality; sentimentalized brother-sister incest or quasi-incest; the antiheroic dreams of evasion and innocence; the fear of the failed erection.

And the madness of the scene he calls up strikes us as a familiar madness, no recent surrealist import but that old disjunction of sense and order expected in American books, the homely insanity we scarcely notice in the work of Brockden Brown, Edgar Poe or John Neal. Indeed, in a way delightfully unforeseen, Barth's novel more closely resembles the horrendous farrago of John Neal's *Logan* (first published in 1822) than any more recent fiction, middlebrow or beat; though for the influence of *Werther* and Ossian, Barth has substituted that of Rabelais, Sterne, Sir Thomas Browne, and the Marquis de Sade. No real American book, after all, can be born without some recognizable European ancestors.

The very styles of Barth's novel are based on Baroque and Mannerist models, and one of the charms of *The Sot-Weed Factor* is the insouciance with which it moves in and out of its counterfeits of seventeenth century diction. It is, however, no mere pastiche, but a piece of ingenious linguistic play, a joyous series of raids on half-forgotten resources of the language, largely obscene. If anyone has forgotten how many kennings there are in English for copulation, Barth's book will refresh his memory as it runs the gamut of unions, routine and recherché, between man and woman, man and man, man and beast. One important element of *The Sot-Weed Factor* is pornography, comic and serious; and in the book within a book (a secret diary of Captain John Smith which is discovered piece by piece throughout the action) Barth has succeeded in writing the kind of subversive erotic tale with historic trimmings which Mark Twain tried and failed at in *1601*. The point is that Barth—here parting company with his American predecessors—sees the world he renders primarily in terms of sex, and manages somehow to believe that even in America passion is central to the human enterprise.

He is, in the fullest and most satisfactory sense, a "dirty" writer; and this is one reason for his earlier books having dismayed critics, who want their sex programmatic (as in Lawrence, Miller, Durrell, Mailer, etc.), and the public, which wants it sniggering and sentimental (as in almost all best-sellers). Barth gives us sex straight, gay or vicious but never moralized, the literary equivalent of the painfully hand-copied erotica passed from cell to cell in the men's block of prisons; and since American literature has long lived in a jail labeled "For Men Only," he could not have found a more appropriate model.

The Sot-Weed Factor is, finally, not only a book about sex and society, but also one about art, a long commentary on the plight of the artist in the United States by a writer already initiated into contempt and misunderstanding, but preferring still irony to self-pity. After noticing in great detail the difficult relations of the poet with church, state and the opposite sex, the illusions of recognition and the reality of neglect, Barth entrusts his last word to a verse epigraph, presumably composed for his own gravestone by his antiheroic poet, and, of course, left off by his heirs in the interests of piety:

> *Labour not for Earthly Glory:*
> Fame's *a fickly Slut and whory.*
> *From the* Fancy's *chast Couch drive her:*
> *He's a Fool who'll strive to swive her!*

And Barth adds, alluding wryly to the place he himself was born, that his warning must have got about, for the marches of Dorchester in Maryland "have spawned no other poet since Ebenezer Cooke, Gentleman, Poet and Laureate of the Province."

—1961

THIRTEEN

Montana: P. S.

ONE BECOMES A Montanan in strange ways. I made my own peculiar kind of peace with this state by writing the article reprinted below. Not that I knew I was sealing a permanent relationship when I wrote it—far from it; or that a good many of my readers accepted it in that sense—even farther from it! Much resentment and hostility boiled up immediately, not only in the breasts of local readers (after all, how many people in Montana read the *Partisan Review,* where the piece originally appeared?), but also of those who had heard about it from the readers, or even those who had heard about it from those who had heard about it from the readers. People who never, I am sure, read *anything,* have approached me imbued with honest indignation and only the vaguest notion of what my infamous article on "The Montana Face" was about. It was not merely that I was biting (they thought) the fine, generous Western hand that was feeding me; but that I had not even been born in the state I chose to criticize. Montanans have a special distrust of those who come here by free choice rather than by the accident of birth. In my more bitter moments, I suspect that the native Montanan cannot really understand why anyone from outside would choose to settle in such a place of his own free will—without some dark and dirty secret purpose.

I will not say that I have ever actually suffered for what I have written—or even for having chosen rather than endured becoming a Montanan. One is protected in Montana (can I make this point now that I am the father of three children born in the state?) by a vast intellectual indolence, an indifference to ideas, which Montanans sometimes confuse with tolerance or courtesy. I am sure that no one will ever be lynched in this state again, not so much because we have become more law-abiding or less brutal, as because it would take too damned much effort! Nevertheless, I have been annoyed in little ways: once blackballed as a speaker at a religious conference for being "too controversial" a person, though at the last minute I made it, thanks to the burst appendix of a more orthodox participant; and more than once, rather inefficiently slandered. The slander in itself is interesting. I remember one University Freshman, who had been forced to read my essay (not by me, let me add quickly!), telling his teacher that he knew all about the author of this lying "story," an Easterner who considered himself too good to talk to anyone and who made his children call him "sir"! This, for the record, is what one Montanan at least considered the final depths to which a man might sink.

Even more embarrassing to me are the responses of some of those who like the essay: both those, usually disaffected Westerners, who consider me a fellow "debunker," and pluck me by the sleeve to tell me in whispers how many men Calamity Jane slept with and what she charged—or just how sordidly some Great Montanan came to his drunken end—and those, usually self-satisfied Easterners, who are shocked to discover that I still live in Montana, and look at me with pity and admiration for daring to live among the surly natives I have offended. It is only an unworthy desire to stay in character as a hero that keeps me from crying out that I did not write my article to prove Montana blacker than any place else, but only to describe its particular shade of black. This, I know, upsets those who feel their prosperity depends upon pretending that it is white and delights those who take its blackness as a proof of the whiteness of Peoria or Santa Barbara or Hoboken. But such are the risks of telling even the smallest part of the truth one sees.

Reading over my own article now after seven or eight years, I find in it a note of passionate engagement that indicates a *family* quarrel, perhaps the peculiar bitterness of an adopted son. A man has, if not a special right, at least a special obligation to reveal with brutal candor the failures of his own household; and it is beside the point to protest, "But things are as bad everywhere else!" What matters is what is bad about one's own affairs. Maybe I have fallen into local pride and am well on the way to becoming a booster, but it seems to me that in certain areas at least we can assert without boasting that we are even worse than everyone else! At any rate, my criticisms of Montana strike me now not as those of a snide outsider, but as the perplexed reactions of one accepting a fate and a home. A writer, whether native or adopted, is a dangerous citizen at best, since he is a citizen, first of all, of the Republic of Letters, and he tends to seem (before he is safely dead and schools have been named after him) to give aid and comfort to the enemy.

I have heard Montanans sometimes idly wishing, at the appropriate conferences on the arts, that a "great writer" might emerge from their midst—forgetting as they dream the bitter image of Florence left behind by Dante or the terrible portrait of Dublin preserved in the works of Joyce. I would recommend to those who consider their state most justly represented in the literature of Chamber of Commerce bulletins or Northern Pacific ads, to pray nightly that Montana *never* produce a first-rate writer. There is no use being sentimental about such matters. I remember the after-dinner comment of an eminent novelist from the South who was visiting in Missoula. To the young lady who asked him whether he didn't think So-and-So might someday write the Great Montana Novel, since "he loved the state so much!" The Southerner answered: "To write about a place well, you must *hate* it!" And after a pause, he added, "The way a man hates his wife."

There is nothing I would want to change in my original piece, and, barring some stylistic revision, I reprint it as I wrote it. I do not mean that I still see everything the same way, but that I still find truth in that fresher, naïver reaction. Though I have since learned more things about the state and its people that I resent and want to change, I have also become more inured to them. I know them rather than feel them passionately. The prevailing contempt for intellectual achievement and the adulation of mediocrity (the school principals who ask for "C" students as teachers, because "they'll fit in better"); the paralyzing ancestor-worship that wants to fake history rather than investigate it; the brutal drunkenness and W. C. T. U. gentility with only a railroad track to separate them; the self-righteous reproaches against the South for "prejudice," in a state where until recently there was a law against miscegenation and where a Negro can still scarcely find a place to get his hair cut; the uneasy, hypocritical relationship with the Indian; the "cultural" organizations whose yearly elections are bloody battles for social prestige; the mummery and dressing up to attract tourists (with hired Indians wearily parodying their tribal dances)—and the privately expressed contempt for those tourists for being taken in; the smug assumption that the God-given glories of our landscape somehow redeem the gross inefficiency of men who can't keep their streets in good repair or support a decent newspaper—all these have become as familiar to me as the scenery itself.

I sometimes pass weeks without being aware of them, as I sometimes go for weeks without seeing "The Montana Face," my description of which has brought me so much abuse. I am now willing to admit that native Montanans do not see that face, the visible sign of an inner inarticulateness which some of them at least are quite prepared to grant. At first, when they shouted their unawareness at me, fire in every eye, I thought they were lying, engaged in a vast conspiracy of deceit. They see the "Eastern Face," "The New York Face," all right, dark, nervous, over-expressive to their eyes; but their own is to them (and why not?) the face *par excellence,* the face in the Garden that was made in God's image. I did not intend to offend anyone's physical pride, even though I had not yet clearly realized how body-centered pride is in a land where ball teams are subsidized before museums are built or orchestras founded; and I think that now I should try to find a new strategy for saying what I mean that would not send people hurt and puzzled to the mirror. Perhaps, I might call it the "Gary Cooper Face," which would say what I was after, and leave everyone feeling flattered! Having raised this ticklish issue, however, I feel obliged to finish it by confessing that more and more rarely (but not less strongly) my old vision returns to me—and suddenly I see before me faces that have not only been starved of richness and subtlety of experience, but are proud of it! For their deprivation one feels pity, but for the smugness, rage!

"And is there, then, Mr. Critic, nothing good to be said for us?" "And do you really feel, Mr. Holier-than-thou, as superior to everyone else as you sometimes seem to imply?" God forbid! It is only that too many people are only too willing to advertise the good aspects of Montana in bad prose; and that I have (put it down to bad toilet-training or unfortunate prenatal influences) the irreverent desire to tell the other side of the whole truth. I have never felt holier than anyone else—only a little louder, a little less inhibited!

It is vexing to have to say it, but I might as well make clear some place that it is only because I like Montana, after all, that I consider it worth raising my voice over its more flagrant weaknesses. Indeed, it is for and not in spite of those weaknesses that I like it—because there is so much to gripe about, and it is so hard to get anyone to listen; because in the beauty of its natural setting, man, when he is vile (and when is he not?), seems viler than elsewhere. Montana seems to me the hardest place in the world to be a hypocrite, though, indeed, I have neighbors who succeed quite well at that difficult task. For myself I can say that at least I do not try.

When I feel the enervating effect of the mountains overcoming me, and I have no desire to revile my fellow-men for their weaknesses, but want only to lie on a riverbank and hear with closed eyes the noise of the water that tells me: *nothing matters—nothing matters—nothing matters—this is the real Montana,* I leap to my feet and drive, past the rusty beer cans and the white roadside crosses, back to town. To restore myself to my senses it is enough to go to the Monday night meeting of the P.T.A. where some local candidate for the legislature is lying in semi-literate periods about what he intends to do for the underpaid schoolteachers, or to the Thursday night wrestling matches, where the girl in fringed buckskin is screaming, "Break his lousy arm! Break it off! Kill him!" Or best of all, if it is Saturday, I go back to that saloon I wrote about in my original article, with its once-new neon lights beginning to flicker and its linoleum a little scarred. Nothing has changed much, though. The whores have gone for good from the rooms upstairs, but there are the bargirls, fat and seedy enough for anyone; and the poker game on the green table is still going, the same dealer looking gravely through his rimless glasses under the ten-gallon hat. There is a "Western Combo," complete with tenor, the guitars electrified and stepped up so that "Sixteen Tons" sounds like an artillery barrage and no one is tempted to waste good drink-

ing time by attempting conversation. The boss, a little more bat-
tered around the ears, is still grinning from behind the bar under
the same old fly-specked sign reading, "Yes, we serve crabs. Sit
down."

But the boss has a new lieutenant, a younger version of himself,
with a beat-up pug's head, too, though less punchy looking; and the
two of them take turns setting up drinks on the house. "Haven't
seen *you* for a hell of a long time." The lieutenant is wearing new
cowboy boots, though he is only two years away from the Near
North Side of Chicago; he has just dropped out of the journalism
school at the University. "Worth thirty-five bucks," he says
proudly, indicating the boots. "I got 'em from a wine-o just off the
freights for half a gallon of muscatel. Christ, he needed it bad.
Walked next door to drink it *(we* don't let 'em drink from bottles at
the tables here, but next door they don't give a damn). Walked out
barefoot—*barefoot*—and it was snowing, too. 'Take it or leave it,' I
told him, 'half a gallon for the boots.' They were red with yellow
threads but I had them dyed black. Look pretty good, don't they?
Thirty-five bucks." The band begins to play "You are my Sunshine," good and loud and I can't hear any more, but I get it. I'm
home. Montana or the end of you know who.

Missoula, Montana
—1956

FOURTEEN

Montana: P. P. S.

I RETURNED TO Montana in 1969 after an absence of five years—
not to live there for another little while, as I had after trips elsewhere before, but just to visit, like one more tourist from the East.
I was disconcerted to discover, however, that I didn't feel like a
tourist at all, only oddly, disturbingly at home; so that I found myself growing annoyed, for instance, when a trio of obvious first-time
Easterners sitting across the aisle from me in the plane kept nudg-
ing each other as we circled down into Hellgate Canyon, crying out,
"Are those really the Rocky Mountains? Hey, those are *really* the
Rockies." "Those are actually the Bitterroots," I wanted to say,
though of course I didn't, except in the silence of my own head,
"and in their icy shadow I used to walk, shivering, on winter morn-
ings from my home to my office. Those are *my* Bitterroots."

And yet for nearly thirty years before that moment, I had believed, needed to believe that my relationship to those mountains,
to the whole place and its people depended on my feeling myself an
eternal stranger in an eternally strange land. I should have known,
of course (I had actually come close to saying it, though not, it
would seem, really imagining it), that precisely the sense of being
alienated from the landscape and all the others who moved through
it was what had made me, and would keep me forever—present or
absent, waking or sleeping—a true Montanan, which is to say, just
such an Eternal Stranger in a land that will, must, remain eternally
strange to all white ex-Europeans, no matter what games they play
at the Rodeo or on pack trips into the remoter "Primitive Areas."

But it was the surface familiarity of it all that struck me first—
not the habitual feeling of alienation, but the sense of having re-

turned to, perhaps of having never really left that accustomed scene. There were the same wooden faces under the broad-brimmed Stetsons and the bright colored headscarves bulging over half-concealed curlers; and I found myself wondering if my face had not through the years come imperceptibly to look more like theirs than those of the dudes who came to buy two weeks of wilderness, frozen into that noncommital mask which had seemed to me at first so hopelessly, almost terrifyingly foreign. In a short time, at any rate, I was no longer looking at the Face but at faces, in search of old friends and enemies who have never ceased, and never will, I suppose, to occupy my dreams.

How odd to be back among those who, by accident as it were, mere chance, know as much of your own private life as anyone outside your skin ever can, and with whose own private lives you are equally familiar; so that you and they are forever joined together, or intimately separated, by something whose name is neither hatred nor love, though it contains elements of both. I am trying to say, I guess, that back in Montana I felt *at home:* as uncomfortable as any returned prodigal sitting down at the family table and listening once more to the old jokes tinged with hostility or tenderness, whose original occasion no one quite remembers.

What else to do under such circumstances except to note (with a kind of desperate if undefined hope) the few small things which had actually changed: a new bridge replacing an old one from which a friend once nearly jumped to her death; a new highway scarring the side of a hill where my two oldest boys at five or six or seven used to play among poisonous ticks for which we would search the hairline at the back of their necks just before bedtime; a new First National Bank, astonishingly elegant, and thus, as it were, a kind of inadvertent reproach to the rest of the crummy storefronts along the main drag; and, finally, the stench of pollution from the pump mill—and the cloud from its chimneys, multicolored and ugly-beautiful as a bruise, hanging trapped between the flanks of Mount Sentinel and Mount Jumbo.

But none of this made any real difference, as we discovered (at this point my wife had joined me) lunching in the Florence Hotel, where without looking up, we could identify the voices at the surrounding tables, and guess the precise note of concern and malice with which they would ask about our current difficulties with the Law, after the initial, "Well, I never—" It was not, however, the smallness of Missoula I had come to find, but the hugeness of Montana—especially the flanks of the surrounding valleys, rock and pine and scrub to their rim of endless sky, places where we had walked and built fires and swum and napped in the sun, though never—despite the importunities of sportsman friends—killed anything larger than an ant or a fly. I think what I would have liked best, given as they say there "my druthers," would have been a trip to the Buffalo Preserve at Moiese and a last encounter with the old albino bull, into whose unreadable blear eyes I used to look through the wire fence, feeling myself each time I returned a little more like that totem beast—a little shaggier, a little heavier, a little whiter.

But he had died in our absence, and so we had to content ourselves (the weather was very hot, very still, very dry, and the heat lightning at night threatened forest fires) with wading across or riding the current of those rivers, still icy though at low, low water, whose names I would sometimes say to myself like a litany or a spell, falling asleep in Buffalo on the shores of a dying lake: the Rattlesnake, the Bitterroot, the Blackfoot, the Clark Fork. A river, however, is for people like me only a place to play in; as, indeed, is the whole high, wide, and handsome expanse of Montana, except for little, tight Missoula, where even the trains come less and less frequently to disturb the real estate agents selling each other property and the lawyers waiting in the wings to sue. Like those agents and lawyers (who at least fished and hunted on weekends), I neither planted nor raised stock, neither cut down trees nor dug into the earth for minerals—only, in the West as in the East, read and talked, wrote and listened, taught and learned.

And so, sandy and bruised but exhilarated somehow, I went back to Missoula, to stand on the edge of the University campus, looking up at the "M" made of white-washed stones on the side of Mount Sentinel, and wondering who had won the five dollar prize this year for suggesting "the best new tradition." But I did not walk into the heart of the Oval, its grass already burned brown by summer, turning instead in the direction of the house in which we had lived for two decades. It had become, I knew, having made the sale after some hesitation, the Meeting House of the Unitarian Fellowship, who, I was pleased to discover, kept faithfully painted on its board fence the four-toed foot which is our family emblem, and which used to bug our neighbors nearly out of their minds. But I could not enter here either, or stay long, for I had remembered what else I did in Missoula, which is to say, drink.

And so I went finally where I had to: to the street which represented for me always the true mythic center of Missoula—not the businessmen's center, nor the lawyers', nor the shopping ladies', but the drinkers', which, when I first arrived in 1941, had seemed to my sentimental Easterner's eye the last remnant of the Old West, the West of the movies I had sat through during all those lost Saturday afternoons of my childhood in Newark, New Jersey. I went to Woody Street, where once the bars and whorehouses had provided a meeting place, a common ground for young instructors escaped from their books, students still trying to leave home, and winos just off of the freights.

But Woody Street was gone. The signs on the corners still said its name, and the same old cracked asphalt street still ran up from the N.P. train station in the same old way; but in place of the open doors and brightly lit windows of saloons were boarded-up fronts and gaps full of dusty rubble. Dorazi's was gone, where the Indians had felt free to come even when they were still being hasseled in other bars; and where we would sit, four or five of us, after the last Friday classes to hear Joe Kramer (now eighty-five!) remind us in his comedian's Yiddish accent of the wisdom we had, it would become clear to us as he shouted us down, travestied or denied all week long. And the Sunshine was closed, too, where—with a couple of electrified guitars and a mike—one indistinguishable cowboy group or other had so filled the place with sound that walking in cold sober felt like walking into a well.

But who in the Sunshine had ever been cold sober? I remember staggering out of its doors one night, as blind drunk and happy as I have ever been in my life, my wife sagging on my arm, equally happy I hope (it was, I recall, a wedding anniversary); and there were a pair of cops waiting to greet us—and, in that lovely time before the fall of us all—to drive us home in jovial solicitude. "Now take it easy, Doc, you're gonna be all right in the morning." But everything changed, as God knows it had to; and before disappearing completely, the Sunshine (or maybe it was that bar next door whose name I could never remember, no matter) was taken over for a while by some university kids from the East, interested in listening, over cups of coffee—along with, I suppose, an occasional joint—to what they called "folk music," i.e., the kind of music the drunks in the Sunshine had always danced to or sung, scarcely knowing there was any other.

It was, however, the Maverick I really wanted to walk into just one more time, having long dreamed of coming back to find Spider still behind the bar: his flattened pug's face turning slowly from side to side as he kept an eye out for trouble; and his back to the pasted-up clipping on the mirror behind him, the article in which I had mentioned his saloon. He would recognize me for sure (I told myself), call me by name or just "Hey, Professor"; and buy me a drink—a bourbon and ditch, what else—which I would nurse for a long time in a back booth between the bandstand, on which that same schoolmarmish-looking lady with the specs would be doing a chorus of "Cold Clear Water" to her own piano accompaniment, and the poker table, at which the same five old men, three shills and a couple of suckers, would be playing poker close to their vests. But the Maverick was dark and empty, too, and I could see nothing between the boards nailed over its broken front window—only imagine I heard a rat skittering through the rubbish inside.

Well, it seemed necessary to drink to Spider dead—to buy myself a drink, since he would not be setting them up again; and raising my glass to the image of myself in some bar-mirror make whatever toast came to mind. But where to buy a drink, *where?* I could not go back to the Florence Hotel or the polite "cocktail bars" on Front Street, and all the other places I knew seemed to be gone. So, I walked down Higgins Avenue toward the Station, until finally there were lights, and a sign saying "Bill's" or "Ed's" or "Jim's," some name I knew even then I would not remember. It was a new place, opened up only a year or two before; but the bartender, it turned out, was an old student of mine, the one in fact who had taken the mad picture of me reproduced on the jacket of *Love and*

Death in the American Novel; and the walls of the saloon were decorated with his more recent photographs—huge blowups of assorted old-timers: cowboys, drifters, Indians, and just plain drunks.

Stupidly, I kept walking up and down before them, looking for my own face, and pursued the whole time by a very large Indian lady who kept loudly admiring the curls on the back of my neck—as if I were in fact already developed, fixed, printed, and hung on the wall: one more old-timer from a Montana that no longer existed outside the world of art, if, indeed, it ever had. I was cold sober, had forgotten even to order a drink; but I rushed into the street and shouted up toward the dark mountains, "God damn it, *hier oder nirgends ist Amerika,* here or nowhere is America," to which echo answered (or maybe I just imagine the whole scene, dreaming over a desk in Paris), *"Nirgends ist Amerika."* And only now, writing this, do I know that this means not, as I first thought, "America is nowhere" but rather, "Nowhere is America." "Nowhere" which in Greek is "Utopia."

Nowhere
Friday the Thirteenth
1984   minus 14

FIFTEEN

An Almost Imaginary Interview:
Hemingway in Ketchum

> But what a book they both agreed, would be
> the real story of Hemingway, not those he
> writes but the confessions of the real
> Ernest Hemingway . . .
>
> *The Autobiography of Alice B. Toklas*

I AM WRITING NOW the article which I have known for months I must someday write, not merely because he is dead but because there sits on the desk before me a telegram from a disturbed lady whom I can not quite remember or despise. "Your confiding reminiscences of Papa Hemingway," it reads, "reminiscent of Louella (Hearst)." The clichés of "Papa" and "Hearst" date but do not identify the sender; and the fact that she has wired her malice from Seattle only confuses me. Why Seattle? Surely the few cagey remarks I have made to a reporter about my experiences in Ketchum, Idaho do not constitute "confiding reminiscences"—dictated as they were as much by a desire to conceal as to reveal, and concerned as they were with my own dismay rather than the details of Hemingway's life. How did they get to Seattle? And in what form?

I am aware, of course, of having told over the past six months in at least as many states the story of my inconclusive encounter with Hemingway last November. I have never been able to tell it until after the third drink or the fourth, and then always to those who, I was convinced, would understand that I was talking about a

151

kind of terror which rather joined me to than separated me from a stranger whose voice I have known all my adult life—a stranger obviously flirting with despair, a stranger whose destruction I could not help feeling my own calamity, too. After all, I was only talking the way everyone talks all the time about American letters, the plight of the American writer. What could be more banal or harmless?

But I can tell from the poor conventional ironies of the telegram before me what I have come to suspect already from my need to say over and over precisely how it was in Ketchum: that what is at stake is an image by which we have all lived—surviving haters of Hearst, middlebrow adulators of *For Whom the Bell Tolls,* Jews who have managed somehow to feel closer to Jake Barnes than to Robert Cohn—the lady from Seattle, and I. That image I must do my best to shatter, though on one level I cannot help wishing that it will survive my onslaught.

I do not want ever to see the newspaper article that cued the wire. I am willing to accept responsibility for whatever the press in its inaccuracy and confusion made of my own inaccuracy and confusion; but I want to accept it without having read it. If amends are to be made for pieties offended, they must be made by setting down the best version of what I am able to remember, by my writing this piece which perhaps already is being misunderstood by those who have managed to get so far.

I went to see Hemingway just after Hallowe'en last year along with Seymour Betsky, a colleague from Montana State University, the university attended briefly by one of Hemingway's sons; and, much more importantly, the one from which Robert Jordan took off for the War in Spain in *For Whom the Bell Tolls.* From a place as much myth as fact, from Hemingway's mythical home (I am told that during his last trip to Spain he signed tourist autographs, "E. Hemingway, Red Lodge, Montana"), I set out across the three hundred miles to his last actual home near Sun Valley, a winter resort out of season. We were charged with persuading Hemingway to give a public lecture at our school, to make the kind of appearance he had resolutely refused to make, to permit—like a good American —a larger audience to look at him than would ever read him, even in *Life.* Actually, we felt ourselves, though we did not confess it aloud, neither professors nor promoters, but pilgrims—seeking the shrine of a God in whom we were not quite sure we believed.

I had long since put on record my only slightly begrudged acknowledgment of Hemingway's achievement: his invention of a major prose style viable in the whole Western world, his contrivance of the kind of short story young writers are not yet done imitating, his evocation in *The Sun Also Rises* of a peculiar terror and a special way of coming to terms with it that must seem to the future the very hallmark of our age. But I had also registered my sense of his mindlessness, his sentimentality, his failure to develop or grow. And I could not help recalling as I hurtled half-asleep beside the driver through the lucid air of not-yet winter, up and down the slopes of such mountains as haunted Hemingway, a symposium in Naples just ten years before. I had been arguing in a tongue not my own against what I took to be the uncritical Italian veneration of Hemingway; and I was shouting my protest to one of those young writers from Rome or Palermo or Milan who write in translated Hemingwayese about hunting and *grappa* and getting laid—but who have no sense of the nighttime religious anguish which makes Hemingway a more Catholic writer than most modern Italians. "Yes," I remembered saying, "yes—sometimes he puts down the closest thing to silence attainable in words, but often what he considers reticence is only the garrulousness of the inarticulate." This I hoped at least I was managing to say.

What really stirred in me on that long blue ride into dusk and the snowless valley (there was near dismay in the shops and cafés since the season was at hand and no snow had fallen) was an old resentment at those, chiefly but not exclusively Europeans, unable to understand that Hemingway was to be hated and loved not merely as a special American case, but more particularly as a Western writer, even as an imaginary Montanan. It seemed only fair that revolutions and illness and time bring him to Sun Valley to die, to the western slopes of America, rather than to Spain or Africa or Cuba; and it was scarcely ironical that his funeral be held in a tourists' haven, a place where the West sells itself to all comers.

Hemingway never wrote a book set in the Mountain West, but he wrote none in which innocence and nobility, heroism and cowardice, devotion and passion (not love but *aficion)* are not defined as they are in the T.V. Westerns which beguile a nation. The West he exploited is the West not of geography but of our dearest and most vulnerable dreams, not a locale but a fantasy, whose meanings do not change when it is called Spain or Africa or Cuba. As long as the hunting and fishing is good. And the women can be left behind. In Gary Cooper, all at which Hemingway merely hinted was made explicit; for Cooper was what Hemingway only longed to be, the West made flesh—his face, in its inarticulate blankness, a living equivalent of Hemingway's prose style.

It is not at all odd to find a dramatist and a favorite actor collaborating in the creation of character and image; what Tennessee Williams imagines, for instance, Marlon Brando is—or has obligingly become. But a similar collaboration between novelist and actor seems to me unparalleled in literary history— a little strange, though in this case inevitable. How aptly the paired deaths of Cooper and Hemingway, each greeted as a national calamity, climaxed and illuminated their relationship, their joint role in sustaining on upper cultural levels an image of our character and fate common enough in pulps, comic books and T.V. That they did not manage to see each other before Cooper died seemed to the press (and to me) a more than minor disaster, mitigated perhaps by the fact that the one did not long survive the other. And like everyone else, I was moved by Hemingway's telegram offering Cooper odds of two to one that he would "beat him to the barn."

Death had presided over their association from the start, since their strongest link was Robert Jordan, invented by one, played by the other: the Westerner as fighter for Loyalist Spain, the anti-Fascist cowboy, the Montana innocent in a West turned oddly political and complex, a land ravaged not by the conflict of outlaw and sheriff but by the struggle between Communist and Nazi. In such a West, what can the Western Hero do but—despite the example of his immortal prototypes—die? Unlike the War for the American West, the War in Spain was lost by Our Side; and finally only its dead seemed true heroes. Hemingway's vision in *For Whom the Bell Tolls* is something less than tragic; but his self-pity is perhaps more adequate than tragedy itself to an age unsure of who its heroes are or what it would like to do with them.

Only a comic view could have been truer to our times, and this Hemingway notoriously lacks. He never knew how funny the Westerner had come to seem in cur world, whether played by Roy Rogers or Cooper or Hemingway himself—only how sad. Of all his male leads, Jake Barnes comes closest to being redeemed from self-pity by humor—the humor implicit in his comic wound. And consequently Jake could no more have been played by Cooper than could the Nick Adams of the earliest stories, or the old men of the last books. Never quite young, Cooper was not permitted to grow really old—only to betray his age and suffering through the noncommital Montana mask. He represents ideally the protagonists of Hemingway's middle novels, Lieutenant Henry and, of course, Jordan; but he will not do for anything in *To Have and Have Not,* a Depression book and, therefore, an ill-conceived sport sufficient unto Humphrey Bogart. The roles on either side of middle age, Hemingway was able to play himself, off the screen yet in the public eye: the beautiful young man of up to twenty-three with his two hundred and thirty-seven wounds, the old stud with his splendid beard and his guns chased in silver. We cannot even remember the face of his middle years (except as represented by Cooper), only the old-fashioned photographs of the youth who became the "Papa" of cover-stories in *Look* and *Life:* his own doomed father, his own remotest ancestor as well as ours.

At any rate, it was a pilgrimage we contemplated, my colleague and I, leaving Missoula some twenty-five years after the fictional departure of Robert Jordan. But it was also—hopefully—a raid: an expedition intended to bring Hemingway home to Montana, where he might perhaps succeed in saying what he had never been able to say to outlanders, speak the meanings of the place in which we had been born or had improbably chosen to live. It was, I suppose, *my* Western I hoped Hemingway would play out (becoming for me what Cooper had been for him); and there would have been something appropriately comic, after all, in casting the boy from Oak Park, Illinois in a script composed by the boy from Newark, New Jersey, both of them on location in the Great West. But, of course, the first words we exchanged with Hemingway made it clear that if he had ever been able to speak in public, he was unable to do so now; that if he did, indeed, possess a secret, he was not about to reveal it from the platform. And how insolent, how absurd the quest seems in retrospect—excused only by a retrospective sense that what impelled us was a need to identify with an image we thought we despised. If it was not an act of love we intended, it was a more typical American effort magically to establish something worthy of love. *Here or Nowhere is America.* Surely the phrase rang some-place in the back of my head as we approached Ketchum; but Here turned out to be Nowhere and Hemingway in the middle of it.

At first, however, we were elated, for we were able to reach quickly the young doctor we had been told was Hemingway's friend and hunting companion; and we were as much delighted as embar-rassed (everything seemed to be composing itself more like a poem than a mere event) by the fact that he was called, symbolically, Dr. Saviers. They hunted together during the afternoons, Dr. Saviers told us, though Hemingway could no longer crouch in a blind, only walk in search of birds, his last game. Hemingway worked morn-ings, but perhaps he would adjust his routine, find some time for us the next day before noon . . . after all, we had driven three hundred miles . . . and even though he never made public ap-pearances, still . . . .

We sat that night in a half-deserted bar, where the tourists had not yet come and the help waited on each other, making little in-group jokes. No one noticed us nursing over our drinks the elation about which we scarcely dared speak. God knows what unworthy elements fed our joy: a desire for scraps of gossip or occasions for articles, a secret yearning to be disappointed, to find the world figure fatuous or comic or—No, surely there were motives less ig-noble at its root: a genuine hope that emanating from greatness (the word came unbidden to our minds) there would be a *mana* we could share, a need somehow to verify the myth. We entered Hem-ingway's house through a back porch in character with the legend —limp ducks hanging from the rafters, a gun against the wall—the home of the hunter; but to step into the kitchen was to step out of the mythic world. There were the neatly wrapped trick-or-treat packages left over from the week before, loot unclaimed by kids; *The Readers Digest, The T.V. Guide* open on tables; and beyond, the nondescript furniture of a furnished house, a random selection of meaningless books on the half-empty shelves.

And the Hemingway who greeted us, framed by the huge blank television screen that dominated the living room, was an old man with spectacles slipping down his nose. An old man at sixty-one.

For an instant, I found myself thinking absurdly that this must be not the Hemingway we sought but his father, the ghost of that long-dead father—materialized at the age he would have been had he survived. Hemingway's handclasp I could scarcely feel; and I stood there baffled, a little ashamed of how I had braced myself involuntarily for a bone-crushing grip, how I must have yearned for some wordless preliminary test of strength. I had not known, I realized standing dumb before one even dumber, how completely I had been victimized by the legend Hemingway had worn himself out imagining, writing, living.

Why should he not, after all, inhabit a bourgeois house, sit before T.V. with a drink in his hand, while his wife passed out Hallowe'en packages to children? Why the hell not? But he dwindled so abruptly, so touchingly from the great red and white head to his spindly legs, accentuated by tapered pants, legs that seemed scarcely able to hold him up. Fragile, I found myself thinking, breakable and broken—one time too often broken, broken beyond repair. And I remembered the wicked sentence reported by Gertrude Stein, "Ernest is very fragile, whenever he does anything sporting something breaks, his arm, his leg, or his head." The scar of one more recent break was particularly evident on his forehead as he stood before us, inarticulately courteous: a scar just above the eyes that were the wrong color—not blue or grey as they should have been, not a hunter's eyes at all, but the eyes of a poet who dreamed of hunters, brown, soft, scared. . . .

These, at least, I knew could not have changed. Whatever had recently travestied him, whatever illness had ravaged his flesh, relaxed his handclasp, could not have changed his eyes. These must have been the same always, must always have tried to confess the secret he had perhaps more hoped than feared would be guessed. "But Jake Barnes is in some sense then a self-portrait," I almost said aloud. "And that's why *The Sun Also Rises* seems your truest book, the book of fear and fact, not bravado and bullshit." I did not speak the words, of course, and anyhow he was saying in a hesitant voice, after having listened politely to our names, "Fiedler? Leslie Fiedler. Do you still believe that st— st— stuff about Huck Finn?"

He did not stammer precisely but hesitated over the first sounds of certain words as if unsure he could handle them, or perhaps only a little doubtful that they were the ones he really wanted. And when I had confessed that yes, I did, did still think that most American writers, not only Twain but Hemingway, too (naturally, we did not either of us mention his name in this context), could imagine an ennobling or redemptive love only between males in flight from women and civilization, Hemingway tried to respond with an appropriate quotation. "I don't believe what you say," he tried to repeat, "but I will defend to the death your right to say it." He could not quite negotiate this platitude, however, breaking down somewhere in the neighborhood of "defend." Then—silence.

I knew the motives of my own silence though I could only speculate about his. I had been cast, I could see, in the role of The Critic, hopelessly typed; and I would be obliged to play out for the rest of our conversation not the Western I had imagined, but quite another fantasy: the tragicomic encounter of the writer and the mistrusted professional reader upon whom his reputation and his survival depend. That Hemingway was aware at all of what I had written about him somehow disconcerted me. He was, I wanted to protest, a character in my *Love and Death in the American Novel;* and how could a character have read the book in which he lived? One does not imagine Hamlet reading the play that bears his name. But I was also, I soon gathered, a semifictional character—generically, to be sure, rather than particularly—a Hemingway character, an actor in his imaginary world. So that finding me before him made flesh, he felt obliged to play out with me a private drama, for which he would, alas, never be able to frame quite appropriate sentences, an allegorical quarrel with posterity. At least, for an hour he could get the dialogue out of his haunted head.

He had read or glanced at, I could soon see, not only my essays but practically everything anyone had written on the modern novel in the United States. I fancied him flipping the pages, checking the indexes (or maybe he got it all out of book reviews in *Time),* searching out the most obscure references to himself, trying to find the final word that would allay his fears about how he stood; and discovering instead, imbedded in the praise that could never quite appease his anguish, qualifications, slights, downright condemnations. "T-tell Norman Mailer," he said at one point, "I never got his book. The mails in Cuba are— are— terrible." But who would have guessed that Hemingway had noticed the complaint in *Advertisements for Myself* about his never having acknowledged a presentation copy of *The Naked and the Dead*. And yet the comment was not out of character; for at another point he had said, really troubled, "These d-damn students. Call me up in the middle of the night to get something they can h-hang me with. So they can get a Ph.D." And most plaintively of all, "Sometimes when a man's in—when he can stand it least, they write just the things that—"

Between such observations, we would regard each other in the silence which seemed less painful than talk until Seymour Betsky would rescue us. I did not really want to be rescued, it seems to me now, finding silence the best, the only way of indicating that I knew what was racking the man I faced, knew his doubt and torment, his fear that he had done nothing of lasting worth, his conviction that he must die without adequate reassurance. It was not for Hemingway that I felt pity; I was not capable of such condescension. It was for myself, for all American writers. Who, *who,* I kept thinking, would ever know in these poor United States whether or not he had made it, if Hemingway did not. I may even have grown a little angry at his obtuseness and uncertainty.

"A whole lifetime of achievement," I wanted to shout at him, "a whole lifetime of praise, a whole lifetime of reveling in both. What do you want?" But I said nothing aloud, of course, only went on to myself. "Okay, so you've written those absurd and trivial pieces on Spain and published them in *Life.* Okay, you've turned into the original old dog returning to his vomit. But your weaknesses have never been a secret either from us, or, we've hoped at least, from you. We've had to come to terms with those weaknesses as well as with your even more disconcerting strengths—to know where we are and who, where we go from here and who we'll be when we get there. Don't we have the right to expect the same from you? Don't we have the right to—" But all the while he kept watching me warily, a little accusingly, like some youngster waiting for the reviews of his first book and trying desperately not to talk about it to one he suspects may be a reviewer.

And what could I have told him, I ask myself now, that might have helped, and what right did I really have anyhow, brought there by whim and chance? What could anyone have said to him that had not already been repeated endlessly and without avail by other critics or by sodden adulators at bars. The uncertainty that Hemingway betrayed was a function surely of the depression that was about to destroy him; but, in a deeper sense, that depression must have been the product of the uncertainty—of a lifetime of uncertainty behind the bluster and the posturing, a lifetime of terror indissoluble in alcohol and action, a lifetime of fearing the leap out of the dark, never allayed no matter how many beasts he brought down in bush or boondocks.

It was only 9:30 A.M. but, after a longer than customary lapse in our talk, Hemingway broke out a bottle of wine to help ease us all. "Tavel—a fine little wine from the Pyrenees," he said, without, apparently, any defensive irony or even any sense of the comic overtones of the cliché. Silence and platitude. Platitude and silence. This was the pattern of what never became a conversation. And I felt, not for the first time, how close Hemingway's prose style at its best was to both; how it lived in the meager area of speech between inarticulateness and banality: a triumph wrung from the slenderest literary means ever employed to contrive a great style—that great decadent style in which a debased American speech somehow survives itself.

"It's hard enough for me to wr-write much less—talk," he said twice I think, obviously quoting a favorite platitude of his own invention; and, only once, but with equal satisfaction, "I don't want to talk about literature or politics. Once I talked about literature and I got—sick." One could hear in his tone how often he must, in similar circumstances, have used both; but he meant the first of them at least. The word "articulate" became in his mouth an insult, an epithet. Of Norman Mailer, for instance, he said between pauses, quietly, "He's s-so— articu— late—" and there was only a little envy to mitigate the contempt. But he wanted to talk about literature really, or, more precisely, wanted to talk about authors, his colleagues and rivals. Yet his comments on them boiled down to two only: the first for writers over fifty, "Great guy, you should've known him!"; the second for those under that critical age, "That boy has talent!" Vance Bourjaily, I recall, seemed to him the "boy" with the most "talent." The one author he did not mention ever was himself, and I abided by the taboo he tacitly imposed, though, like him I fear, more out of cowardice than delicacy.

When I noticed in a particularly hard moment the *T.V. Guide* beside me open to the Saturday Night Fights, I welcomed the cue, tried to abandon Bourjaily in favor of Tiger Jones, though I really admire the style of the one not much more than that of the other. "Terrible what they make those boys do on television," Hemingway responded, like the joker next to you at the bar who baffles your last attempt at communication. And it didn't help a bit when Mrs. Hemingway entered to apologize in an attractive cracked voice for the state of the house. "If I had only known that someone was coming. . . ." But why was everyone apologizing and to whom?

It was the *politeness* of the whole affair which seemed some-how the final affront to the legend. Hemingway was like a well-be-haved small boy, a little unsure about the rules, but resolved to be courteous all the same. His very act of asking us to come and talk during his usual working hours and at a moment of evident distress was a gesture of genuine courtesy. And he fussed over the wine as if set on redeeming our difficult encounter with a show of formality. At one point, he started to pour some Tavel into my glass before his own, then stopped himself, put a little into his glass, apologized for having troubled to remember protocol, apologized for apologiz-ing—finally insisted on drinking to my next book, when I lifted my glass to his.

But what were we doing talking of next books when I could not stop the screaming inside of my head, "How will anyone ever know? How will I ever know unless the critics, foolish, biased, bored, tell me, tell us?" I could foresee the pain of reading the re-views of my first novel, just as I could feel Hemingway's pain read-ing the reviews of his later work. And I wanted to protest in the name of the pain itself that not separated but joined us: The critic is obliged only to the truth though he knows that truth is never completely in his grasp. Certainly he cannot afford to reckon with private anguish and despair in which he is forbidden to believe, like the novelist, inventing out of his friends and his own shame Lady Brett or Robert Cohn.

And I looked up into Hemingway's smile—the teeth yellowish and widely spaced, but bared in all the ceremonious innocence of a boy's grin. He was suddenly, beautifully, twelve years old. A tough, cocky, gentle boy still, but also a fragile, too-often-repaired old man, about (how could I help knowing it?) to die. It puzzled me a little to discover him, who had never been able to invent a tragic protagonist, so much a tragic figure himself—with meanings for all of us, meanings utterly different from those of his myth, meanings I would have to figure out later. . . . Yet he seemed, too, as we had always suspected, one who had been *only* a boy and an old man, never what the rest of us for too wearily long must endure being— all that lies between. I could not help recalling the passage where Gertrude Stein tells of Hemingway at twenty-three crying out that he was too young to be a father. And I could hear him now in my inner ear crying out that he was too young to be an old man. Too young to be an ancestor.

But he was not too young to be my ancestor, not too young for me to resent as one resents what is terribly there when he is born. I would not be able to say the expected kind things about him ever, I knew, not even after he was dead. And who would understand or believe me when I was ready to say what I could: that I loved him for his weakness without ceasing to despise him for his strength.

We had left Seymour Betsky's car in town, and as the four of us looked at each other now, more than ready to be done with our meeting, Hemingway and his wife offered to drive us back in to pick it up. He had to do some small chores, chiefly go to the bank. But it was a Saturday, as we had all forgotten; and Betsky and I stood for a moment after we had been dropped off watching Hemingway bang at the closed glass doors, rather feebly perhaps but with a rage he was obviously tickled to be able to feel. "Shit," he said finally to the dark interior and the empty street; and we headed for our car fast, fast, hoping to close the scene on the first authentic Hemingway line of the morning. But we did not move quite fast enough, had to hear over the slamming of our car door the voice of Mrs. Hemingway calling to her husband (he had started off in one direction, she in another), "Don't forget your vitamin tablets, Daddy."

—1962

SIXTEEN

On Remembering Freshman Comp

I TOOK, as they say, Freshman Composition at New York University Heights in 1938 and 1939, sitting with some twenty-five or thirty others before a teacher whom I can only imagine now as scared and baffled, though glad surely to have a job—however ill-paid—in those Depression days. The indignities he endured in graduate school (I am not certain he ever made it to a Ph.D.) he visited upon us in kind: a minor Terror never quite equivalent to the major Terror he lived with beyond our ken and on his own time. We scarcely suspected this, having no way of knowing that the dictator who threatened us with failure for a single comma fault or run-on sentence might cringe before his thesis director or wake at nights to worry about his prelims. Not realizing the nature of his suffering, I could not know a chief reason for the existence of a freshman course in composition—as therapy for graduate students and recent Ph.D.'s. Just as the aggrieved workingman was once permitted to beat his wife and children on Saturday nights, so the doctoral candidate was once allowed to bully a classful of freshmen. But social progress has changed all of that. The workingman is no longer aggrieved—and the graduate student, then customarily celibate, is now almost required to have a wife and children, on whom surely he vents a good deal of his legitimate spite. And what use to him, therefore, is a class of freshmen? No wonder there is talk of eliminating the comp course altogether.

What assaults of wit we quivered under! What ironical sallies bowed our heads! Sometimes—not sure we understood the nuances of his rancor—our instructor would explain to us how we had just been insulted, translating down for our benefit and his own. It was

163

only then that he confessed we did not speak a common language —though he never gave up the pretense that we *should* speak one, persisted in maintaining the hoax that there was one to speak. He seemed to believe that such a language was actually to be found in the back pages of *Harper's Magazine,* to which he aspired—or in which he had been published once, or was about to be published— we were never sure. At that moment, I was myself seeking a language of my own in magazines like *transition,* which is to say, I was working hard to learn a not-quite-up-to-date international art jargon—which appealed to my seventeen-year-old desire to use writing more for the purposes of concealment than revelation. As if one could ever be understood too easily or too soon! As for the rest of the class, they strove dumbly to protect the living language which was their heritage: a language which moved at the pace of city life, which was grayed to the tones of city light, which erupted into the dull horror of city violence—but which kept also the rhythms of an almost forgotten Yiddish.

But we were forbidden Yiddishisms as we were forbidden slang; and though we had our censors outnumbered, our ignorance and shame kept us powerless. We were, some eighty-five or ninety or ninety-five per cent of us, urban Jews; our instructor and his colleagues were one hundred per cent Western or Midwestern or back-country *goyim,* who had (not so long before) abandoned their Midwestern or Western or back-country dialects for a nonfunctional, unreal Academese, acceptable on its more formal levels in the pages of *PMLA*—and on its more relaxed levels in *Harpers* or *Atlantic Monthly* or *The Saturday Review of Literature.* It all seemed to us a familiar way of choosing up sides for an old unfair game. We had played by similar not quite kosher rules in grade school and in high school, becoming in self-defense bilingual— though already our first language, our native schoolyard tongue had begun to slip away from us. But we were not yet fully at home with the lifeless classroom language whose shape was determined by antiquated rules of etiquette (usually called "grammar") rather than by aesthetic principles or organic needs.

Nobody had ever told us that the American language was still to be invented—was always to be invented—as it has been invented and reinvented by urban Jews of approximately my own generation, Saul Bellow, for instance, and Bernard Malamud, Delmore Schwartz and Grace Paley; and as it had been invented earlier out of their own dialects by Hemingway and Faulkner, Melville and Whitman and Henry James. Our world extended from Beowulf to Thomas Hardy, and the language we studied was called misleadingly "English." How could we discover what was living in our own tongue reading *The Mayor of Casterbridge* (which we did not really like) or *Martin Chuzzlewit* (which we renamed *Martin Chuzzleberg* and managed to love), or learning the scholarly way to crib from Sir Sidney Lee in "research papers" on Shakespeare's *Sonnets*. It was once, I suppose now, the function of freshman comp classes precisely to convince all Americans, farm boys and city dwellers, Slavs and Swedes, Italians and Jews, that they had a common literary language which was quite (or almost) the same as that used by "our British Ancestors." It was simply a matter of straightening out that difficulty about "different than." But the British were not by a long shot *our* ancestors, and we resented the melting pot brainwashing that culminated for us in the first year of college. Here or nowhere our (approximately) Anglo-Saxon mentors had decided, we would be convinced we spoke a common tongue with them: a language capable of uttering only the most correctly tepid Protestant banalities no matter what stirred in our alien innards.

All this I was scarcely aware of then—thinking rather of my private war against gentility and "good taste." In that war, the Enemy included my fellow students, too: those would-be doctors and lawyers eager to be accepted by a world of other doctors and lawyers, a world more polite and less passionate than that of their parents and grandparents. But it was the teachers who represented especially the standards of an established alien taste, represented it as my fellow students could not, partly by virtue of their degree—but chiefly by virtue of certain inflections and idioms as foreign to us as their neckties. Writing my weekly themes on the subway, jostled by elbows and haunted by haggard faces I would stop sometimes to sketch in the little pad I carried with me like a charm—I would know what I wrote against as well as for: against their taste as well as for our own. I can remember now only two of the themes I wrote on "forbidden subjects," risking an F if I did not make an

A. In our classroom, women and love were taboo like the teacher and the course—too sacred to touch without the threat of flunking; but I was seventeen and even on the Lexington Avenue Express it was somehow spring in April and May. Both my remembered efforts were stories, for exposition irked me and I longed to be delivered from the Description of a Process ("How I Tie My Shoes").

The first of my stories described the strange life and death of a woman who had an orgasm every time she passed through a subway turnstile—and who in her last moments attained the ultimate ecstasy, imagining the crucifix above her hospital bed whirling madly against her as she passed into Heaven. The other concerned a man who married a seal but was unable to find a way to consummate their union and perished (along with his bride) of sheer frustration. But the latter was a translation only and lacked the real point of an original version which I had composed in uncertain French—after I had discovered that the French word for seal was *phoque*. On each paper in indignant red pencil my instructor wrote "Good taste!" It seems a naïve enough time from the vantage point of an age in which similar stories would evoke psychoanaltyic interpretations by instructors with subscriptions to the *Partisan Review*. "Good taste!" It was from fellow students I learned about Freud, as it was a fellow student (shortly thereafter dropped from the School of Engineering) who told me on the library steps about a writer called Kafka—and set me to limping through *The Castle* in German. And this is the way it should be, I cannot help believing still: the world of Them, of the Others, of the Past defined in the classroom; the world of Us, of the Young, sought and fought for outside. But having gained certain things we desired (there are now Jewish Chairmen of English Departments, and conservative girls from old-fashioned schools are bullied into saying "It's me" instead of "It is I."), we have lost others we cannot so easily spare. Now in what is called Freshman Composition, students may be asked to read casebooks on Ezra Pound or even the Beats—and are certainly urged in one way or another to pursue the up-to-date, hand in hand with teachers eager to prove that their youth, though longer used, is quite as vigorous as that of the dewiest of their students.

So another traditional function of the classical freshman composition course is abandoned: the attempt to impose yesterday's taste and yesterday's usage on tomorrow's writers, thus defining a world against which the future can define itself. But we have lived long enough to create a world in which everyone inhabits the future and the past belongs to the past—a world in which there is scarcely a freshman teacher who would have nerve or sense enough to flunk the Scott Fitzgerald of this generation. And what is the function of the comp course whose ends are *not* Initiation through Terror, Melting Pot, Brainwashing, and the Induction into Gentility? How we flounder these days in search of a *raison d'être:* functional linguistics, semantics, "close reading," the battle against Mass Culture; how appallingly often new texts with guaranteed new approaches appear. I was in on the birth of one of the first at the University of Wisconsin. Only six years after I was myself a freshman, I found myself teaching a comp course, but one utterly different from what I had endured. Our text (still mimeographed then) was S. I. Hayakawa's adaptation of Korzybski to classroom uses, and we called the course not Composition at all but "Language in Action." "Cow$_1$ is not Cow$_2$ . . ." we taught our students to repeat and somewhere in the background floated a dream of world understanding and no war.

If I permit myself a certain nostalgia for 1938, it is not because I forget the grimmer aspect of the comp course in a school whose unconfessed aim was the final liquidation of the ghetto in favor of the suburb, the conversion of the children of greenhorns into subscribers to *Time* and *Newsweek*. It is only because I appreciate—belatedly—the lovely innocence of those terrible times. We were in some ways, I will not deny, like a class in an occupied country, a group of Alsatians or Czechs, say, under a German master. And we felt ourselves captives, prisoners in the classroom, in a way which it is hard to remember; because outside there was simply nothing—no jobs, no openings, a world without possibility and therefore a world of violence. In the classroom, too, violence seemed always barely tamped down, just ready to explode; but when it came, it came from an unexpected quarter. I think all of us believed that a certain large Italian boy, who slept quietly in the first row (he drove a truck all night) except when browbeaten awake by the lash of our instructor's wit, would someday spectacularly erupt. But oddly enough it was in the biology class that he took his stand, declaring one day in the midst of a lecture that he could not abide being taught natural science by a virgin (we saw his point) and walking out. No, in comp class it was a fifteen-year-old stammerer who blew up for us all, hurling himself at some kid behind him who snickered when he stuck in the middle of explaining, perhaps, the difference between "it's" and "its."

Outside of class, he could usually make it through a sentence at the cost of a little wheezing here and there; but on his feet before a teacher, he would be overwhelmed by all the pressures that had driven him to skip three years of the long way toward a B.A. and certified membership in genteel America. His mouth opened grotesquely and his breath terrifyingly audible, he would seem someone who tried to scream rather than speak, someone who tried to wake from a nightmare—and the clowns around him who did not know that there was a nightmare from which to wake would mock him. When he jumped that day halfway across the room and his mocker went down under him, we all leaped, too, our *Martin Chuzzlebergs* flying; and whether we wanted to make peace or compound the violence we could not have said. Only the teacher stood outside the melee, frozen into silence, alone. . . . It is this scene which possesses me whenever I try to call up the faces and voices of those days, and I like to think that it is somehow a parable. But I should hate to be called on to explain its meanings.

Athens, Greece
—1962

SEVENTEEN

Academic Irresponsibility

To ARGUE in favor of freedom for the teacher seems at first the most pointless sort of preaching to the converted, since everybody —as everybody hastens to assure you—is already convinced. Difficult enough under the best of conditions, everybody explains, teaching would be virtually impossible without a large degree of liberty. But everybody then adds, at the point where piety ends and candor begins, that the teacher obviously must be "responsible" as well as free; the clear implication is that freedom is *limited* by responsibility—to which everybody else assents, with the sole exception, it sometimes seems, of me.

In my objections to responsibility, I find myself not only lonelier and lonelier but more and more distant from those I had long thought my natural allies. From my earliest reading years, I had understood that Babbitt was the enemy of freedom, and responsibility his hypocritical watchword. Of this I had been assured not only by Sinclair Lewis, who baptized him, but by John Dos Passos in *U.S.A.,* by James Thurber in *The Male Animal,* by the whole consort of writers who had sentimentalized and mythicized the early academic victims of Rotarians, chambers of commerce and boards of trustees—from Thorstein Veblen to Scott Nearing and innumerable other half-forgotten half heroes fired from university posts for defending Tom Mooney and Sacco and Vanzetti or for criticizing monopoly capitalism and the war.

The campaign of vilification and harassment directed against certain leftish academics in the time of Joe McCarthy seemed the climax and confirmation of the whole thing. After the total discrediting of McCarthy, when political liberty for professors was pretty generally won and Babbitts everywhere had gone into retreat, an occasional rear-guard action on their part seemed more comic and pathetic than sinister or threatening. Picking up, for instance, a Kiwanis Club pamphlet labeled "Freedom," I am tickled rather than dismayed to discover no reference to anything that I mean by freedom, only an appeal to teachers to transmit to the young "an understanding of responsible citizenship, principles of free enterprise and values of our spiritual heritage. . . ." "Free" as in enterprise, but "responsible" in everything; it is quite what the literature I grew up on taught me to expect—something comfortably unchanged in our disconcertingly changeable world.

There is, however, one area at least where the Babbitts, even in retreat, continue to pose a real threat to freedom—a threat because the academic community is on their side. When social behavior rather than politics is involved—especially in matters of sex or the use of banned drugs (associated inevitably with sex in the fantasies of the repressors) and especially when faculty members seem to advocate, or condone, or encourage or simply permit unconventional student practices in these matters—then the faculties of universities tend to speak the same language as the Kiwanis Club. And here I am eternally shocked and disheartened.

For almost a decade now, there has been instance after instance, from the notorious firing of Timothy Leary at Harvard, through the dismissal of certain young "homosexual" instructors at Smith, to the recent failure to rehire the poet Robert Mezey at Fresno State College. Often the real issues are camouflaged, as in Leary's case; the charge pressed was not that Leary had become a published advocate of LSD but that he failed to meet his classes regularly. Or they tend to be blurred, as in Mezey's case; the fact that he opposed the war in Vietnam and defended black power might suggest the recurrence of simple old-fashioned McCarthyism, were it not that thousands of academic opponents of the most unjust of American wars continue to be reappointed or promoted so long as they do not also happen to advocate changes in the existing marijuana laws.

Sometimes the underlying issues are totally hushed up, out of ostensible regard for the reputation of the victims, who, accepting dismissal in order to avoid scandal, provide their colleagues with the possibility of copping out; so that no advocate of academic freedom is called upon to take a principled stand on freedom for potheads or queers; no libertarian is forced to confront the limits of his own tolerance. I am aware of only a single case of this kind fought hard enough and far enough to compel the American Association of University Professors to rethink its own position, defining—from a teacher's presumable point of view—the competing claims of freedom and responsibility: the now nearly forgotten Koch case.

On March 18, 1960, Leo Koch, an assistant professor of biology at the University of Illinois, wrote a letter to the campus paper in which, after some reflections—more banal and less witty than he obviously thought them—on "a Christian code of ethics already decrepit in the days of Queen Victoria," he concluded:

> With modern contraceptives and medical advice readily available at the nearest drugstore, or at least a family physician, there is no valid reason why sexual intercourse should not be condoned among those sufficiently mature to engage in it without social consequences and without violating their own codes of morality and ethics.
>
> A mutually satisfactory sexual experience would eliminate the need for many hours of frustrating petting and lead to much happier and longer-lasting marriages among our younger men and women.

Whether the course of action that Professor Koch advocated would, indeed, have led to the happiness and marital stability he promised remains yet to be proved, since he inspired no general movement to lead openly the sort of sexual life that many students, whether "sufficiently mature" or not, have been leading covertly, anyhow. If Koch was espousing anything new in his manifesto, it was presumably the abandonment of concealment and that unconfessed pact by which students make it possible for their teachers to pretend they do not know what their students pretend they do not know those teachers know.

Yet his letter had results, all the same, for it brought about a chain of events that ended in his being fired. And his firing, in turn, produced a series of statements and counterstatements about morality and freedom from the president of the university, its board of trustees, the faculty senate and many individual members of the teaching staff. This intramural debate was followed by a prolonged investigation under the auspices of the American Association of University Professors of what had become by that time "the Koch case," an investigation not finally reported on in full until three years later. The report, which appeared in the *A.A.U.P. Bulletin* of March 1963, reveals a division of opinion among college professors themselves, symptomatic of a confusion on the issues involved, that not only divides one academic colleague from another but splits the individual minds of many Americans inside the universities and out.

More interesting to me, however, and more dismaying than any of the disagreements, was a substantial area of agreement between the president and the board of trustees of the University of Illinois (who thought Koch should be fired), the faculty senate of that institution (who thought he should only be reprimanded) and Committee A of the A.A.U.P., the professed guardians of academic freedom (who thought the whole case should have been thrown out of court because of lack of due process). All four agreed that Koch was guilty of a "breach of academic responsibility" and that, regardless of his guilt or innocence, his academic freedom, like everyone else's, was and should have been limited by the academic responsibility that he was accused of having flouted. What academic responsibility means was nowhere very clearly defined in the dispute but was apparently understood by everyone involved to signify an obligation on the part of any professor to keep his mouth shut or only moderately open in cases where there is a clear danger of offending accepted morality, i.e., public opinion.

But how odd it was to find in the conservative and anti-intellectual camp a committee specifically charged with the protection of professors' rights—rights which the committee has often unyieldingly defended. What, then, moved it this time to grant that ". . . we can hardly expect academic freedom to endure unless it is matched by academic responsibility"? Surely, the topic of Koch's letter had something to do with it, and not merely the fact that his thoughts were neither well reasoned nor cogently expressed. If all cases of academic freedom involved the justification of documents as dignified and compelling as, say, Milton's *Areopagitica,* to defend liberty would be as easy as to attack it; but this, as the A.A.U.P. must have learned in its long career, is far from the truth. No, it was the subject of Koch's expostulation that made the difference; for when sex and students are simultaneously evoked, even the hardiest campus civil libertarian seems willing to cry "responsibility" with all the rest.

And the larger community has sensed this, moving in to attack —even when political motives play a considerable role—only when sex and drugs are involved. The young instructors at Michigan State University who helped edit a radical magazine called *Zeitgeist* may have offended their colleagues and administrators in many ways; but when their contracts were not renewed, a year or so ago, it was only the dirty words they had printed that were marshaled as evidence against them. And when, some years before that, Mulford Sibley, a well-known pacifist and political dissident, was brought under attack at the University of Minnesota, what was quoted against him was a speech in which he suggested that the university might be healthier if it could boast "a student Communist club, a chapter of the American Association for the Advancement of Atheism, a Society for the Promotion of Free Love . . . and perhaps a nudist club."

Predictably enough, communism and atheism tended to be soft-pedaled in the accusations brought against him, which lingered most lovingly over the fact that he was "agitating for nudist clubs" and added, apparently as the final proof of his perfidy, that "Dr. Sibley assigned books to his students resembling 'Lady Chatterley and Her Love Affairs.' " I know how disabling such a charge can be in academic circles, since, in an early encounter of my own with a really concerted effort to silence me in the classroom (the only time I ever really ran into trouble before the recent attempt to manufacture a case against me on the grounds of "maintaining a premise where marijuana is used"), I was accused not only of contempt for my then-fellow Montanans but also of having written a "dirty" poem called *Dumb Dick* and a "dirty" story called *Nude Croquet,* which was "subsequently banned in Knoxville, Tennessee." Alas, some of my former colleagues, willing enough to stand with me on political grounds, were shaken by being informed that I was a "dirty writer."

Pornography and nudity, along with trafficking in drugs and indulging in homosexuality, as well as refusing to condemn any or all
of these to students, are the stock charges in latterday assaults
against the freedom of the teacher by elements in the business community sophisticated enough to know that in our time, old-fashioned accusations of being Red or "soft on Reds" are likely to be
laughed out of the court of public opinion and have no status at all
in courts of law. But there are statutes that can be invoked against
offenses of the former sort, as in the recent police harassment of
Leonard Wolf, a member of the English department of San Francisco State College, charged with "contributing to the delinquency
of minors."

Wolf is the founder of Happening House, an institution set up
to maintain a dialogue between the kind of kids who inhabit the
Haight-Ashbury district of San Francisco and the local academic
community. During a conference on the problem of runaways,
some of those kids, members of a performing dance group, took off
all their clothes onstage. Wolf, who was the most convenient adult
on the premises, was arrested. He was subsequently tried and acquitted because the prosecution could not prove him responsible for the
students' disrobing, but from the start, the intent of the police seems
to have been quite clearly to impugn Wolf both as the founder of
Happening House and as a teacher. Why else charge him with acting
in a way that "causes, tends to cause or encourages unknown juve-
niles to lead immoral or idle lives"? Whatever college officials
thought of his classroom performance or his outside activities, a court
conviction would make him a criminal in their eyes—and, as such,
his position in the college, as well as his status in the community,
would be endangered. And just as clearly, it wasn't only Wolf who
was being put on trial, but all teachers who, insofar as they are true to
their profession, seek to release their students from parochialism and
fear, thus laying themselves open to charges of "corrupting the
young" or "contributing to the delinquency of minors." A printed
statement from the Leonard Wolf defense recognizes this fact—
though it states the dilemma ineptly and misleadingly by insisting
that in his case, "The limits of any teacher's responsibility are at
stake" and that "If the attack on Professor Wolf proves successful
. . . the limits of responsibility will have been unfairly extended in
the service of repressive interests."

One cannot effectively fight an opponent whose language, along with its assumptions, has been uncritically accepted. And to grant —even implicitly—that there are just and proper limits somewhere, sometimes, to the teacher's freedom is to give the game away to those ready and eager to seize any show of weakness on the teacher's part. This is especially dangerous these days, when we are threatened on two sides, not just on one, as we have long been accustomed. On the one hand, there are the traditional "repressive interests," plus the courts and cops whom they largely control, to whom a free faculty seems always on the verge of going over to the enemy, i.e., the young, whom they think of as swinging back and forth between an unwholesome flight from reality and untidy demonstrations in the streets. And, on the other hand, there are the young themselves, or at least the revolutionaries among them, to whom the much-vaunted "academic freedom" of their teachers seems only a subterfuge, a cover-up for their subservience to the *real* enemy, i.e., the old, who, if they do not actually wage imperialist war and exploit labor, apologize for both.

I sit at the moment looking mournfully at an "Open Letter" directed to the faculty at the University of Sussex, an English university in which I spent last year as a visiting professor. The document is signed by "The February 21 Committee," a group whose chief political activity was throwing a can of red paint over a speaker from the American Embassy who had attempted to defend United States intervention in Vietnam. An early paragraph reads, in part: "Students say 'free inquiry' or 'free speech' mean that academics must permit their institution to be used for any purpose, this freedom ends logically in irresponsibility. . . ." Syntax and punctuation have broken down a little, but the meaning is clear—and disheartening. Whether Kiwanis Clubber, A.A.U.P. member or Maoist student, one touch of responsibility makes them all kin to one another, and alien to me.

Yet there is a difference, of course, between the Babbitts and the *enragés,* those who boast themselves sane and those who like to think of themselves as mad. Both demand restrictions on political freedom, one from the right and one from the left; but the students, at least, are on the side of erotic and imaginative freedom, in favor of love and dreams—and when such issues are involved or can be evoked, the free professor will find them on his side. In that area, indeed, they are more dependable allies than his own colleagues, since even the most liberal professors have tended to be equivocal on the subject of social, as opposed to intellectual, freedom, for both students and themselves. To the young, more important than the freedom to read what books or take what courses they please is the freedom to make love as they please; and it was therefore quite proper that the recent student revolt in France was touched off at the University of Nanterre by protest over restricted visiting privileges between boys' and girls' dormitories.

This fundamental inconsistency of viewpoint toward social rather than academic freedom has tended to sap the integrity of certain faculty, and sowed a deepening distrust in the minds of students, who, in response, have been on occasion as cavalier about the political rights of their teachers as their teachers have been about their personal liberties. But there is an even more fundamental source of confusion in the definition of responsibility that the academic community—professors first of all, and now the students—has accepted, without sufficient wariness, from the larger community that surrounds and often resents it.

Once the teacher has granted the theory that responsibility equals restriction, restraint, censorship, taboo, he has lost in advance all those "cases" to which he must in due course come. At best, he commits himself to endless wrangles about exactly where freedom (understood as the right to express what he believes without hindrance) yields to responsibility (understood as the obligation to curtail his expression), lest he offend the taste, the conventions or the religious, political, and moral codes of the community that sustains him.

There is no way out of such wrangles and not much point in going on to further debates about who (the teacher, the community, or some impartial referee) is to draw the line between freedom and responsibility, once these have been postulated as opposites. And surely there is even less point in debating after the fact how harshly the "irresponsibles" are to be treated, whether by a lopping of heads or a mere slapping of wrists; i.e., whether they are to be dismissed or reprimanded. I propose, therefore, to define responsibility in quite a different way—as a matter of fact, in two quite different ways—in order to put the problem in a new light and deliver everyone from the frustration and ennui of having endlessly to re-hash the old arguments.

Let me begin with a positive definition of "academic responsi-bility" as the teacher's obligation to *do* something, rather than not to. The teacher—not exclusively, perhaps, but, without doubt, es-pecially—has a single overwhelming responsibility: the responsibil-ity to be *free,* which is to say, to be what most men would call *irre-sponsible.* For him, freedom and responsibility are not obligations that cancel each other out but one and the same thing; and this unity of academic freedom and academic responsibility arises from the teacher's double function in our society: first of all, to extend the boundaries of knowledge by questioning *everything,* including the truths that most men at any given point consider sacred and timeless; and, finally, to free the minds of the young, so that they can continue the same task beyond what he himself can imagine.

I shall not linger over the traditional "research" function of the teacher, since its necessity is granted, with whatever secret reserva-tions, by almost everyone except certain backward students, much given to complaining that their teachers spend more time on re-search than on them—not understanding that there would be noth-ing for those teachers to give them if independent investigation and lonely meditation were ever suspended or drastically curtailed. Thorstein Veblen, prototype of the free teacher, thought it was a mistake to attempt to combine in a single person the schoolmaster and the scholar; but American universities have long since made the decision to try, and it is incumbent on the scholar-schoolmaster to be clear in his own mind, and to make clear to everyone else concerned, the priorities of his commitments. Few of them have been as candid about it as was Robert Frost, himself a schoolmaster for some 50 years, who always insisted from the platform that the teacher's first duty was to himself, his second to his subject matter and only his third to the student. And no one who begins with an understanding of the free teacher's peculiar obligation to the free student could possibly challenge this order.

The problem to begin with is: What can, and what should be, taught? From that start, it was clear to me that teaching was a pas-sion, not a science, and that methods, therefore, are meaningless in the classroom, that lesson plans and pedagogical strategy are vanity and illusion. But it has taken me nearly three decades of teaching to realize that even the subject matter one teaches is quickly—and, in most cases, quite correctly—forgotten, gone, certainly, with the last exam. It should no longer be considered a scandalous secret that the students believe they are hiding from teachers—or vice versa —that course subject matter is at best optional, at worst totally irrelevant.

What is required of the teacher is not that he impart knowledge but that he open up minds, revealing to his students possibilities in themselves that they had perhaps not even suspected, and confirming in them a faith in their own sensibilities and intelligence; not suffering their foolishness or indulging their errors, but all the time revealing to them the double truth that, though the student can often be wrong, he has, like his teacher, the *right* to be wrong; and that, if he is willing to live a life of intellectual risk, he may someday know more, see further and feel more acutely than any of the elders of the community, including his teachers. It is the credo of the free and truly "irresponsible" teacher that no truth except this (not even the ones he most dearly believes in) is final, since the advance of human thought is potentially unlimited.

Such a teacher addresses his students, confronts them, engages with them, in the hope that they will someday go beyond the limitations of vision built into him by the limitations of his training and his time; and that they will even escape the trap of believing that their new vision is a final one, to be imposed forever after on the generations who succeed them. My ideal teacher must teach his students, in short, to be free—which is something quite different from persuading them to write in their notebooks, "Be free!," since freedom cannot be acquired by rote any more than it can be established by law. Freedom cannot be taught by preaching it—as, by writing this, I have betrayed myself into doing—but by acting it out, living it in full view. Once we have realized that the teacher is not just a guide, much less a substitute parent or a charming entertainer (though he can be all of these things, too, if he is so moved), but a model; and that what is learned in the classroom is *him,* the teacher, we will understand that the teacher must become a model of the free man.

And yet how many of our own teachers do we remember as having been even in aspiration, much less in fact, anything like free? How many do we recall with love for having freed us from those fears and doubts about ourselves and our world that we brought with us into school, inextricably intertwined with our ignorance and bravado? There have been only a handful among the scores I encountered in my own school career: one or two in high school, none at all in college, and one in graduate school, whom I cannot forbear naming. Author of once-admired but now-forgotten poems and a splendid book about the shape of his own life, *The Locomotive God,* William Ellery Leonard once gave me, by his splendid example, certain illusions about what teaching and teachers were like that brought me into the university in the first place; and then left me, with even more splendid tact, to find out the truth for myself.

But why have so many, so large a majority not merely of my teachers but of everybody's teachers, failed in their obligation to choose to be free? It is tempting, but finally unsatisfactory to say, in easy cynicism: Well, everyone fails at everything, so why not they? Certainly there are pressures on them from all sides to be of "service" to the community as a whole, or to the past, to the present, to God, to the Revolution, etc. Wherever the free teacher turns, he confronts men, sometimes his own colleagues, convinced that the function of the university is not to free the mind but to inculcate a set of values, to indoctrinate or—as we say when somebody else's values are concerned—to brainwash the student.

But the wielders of such pressures are, in a sense, not hard to resist, especially when they speak from the conservative tradition; since there are habits of response built into most professors from earliest youth that stir a reflex of resistance against movements to ban books by, say, Allen Ginsberg and William Burroughs on the one hand, or by Ché Guevara and Mao Tse-tung on the other, or to fire those who ask students to read them. Whatever our disagreements with the lovers of such literature, we tend to feel them on our side. No, the most conspicuous failure of professors in this regard has been their refusal to protect the dissident right-wingers among them under attack from antilibertarians on our side. Surely one of the most scandalous events of recent academic history has been the quiet dismissal of a distinguished rightist teacher of political science from an equally distinguished Ivy League college, whose own silence was bought by buying up his contract and whose colleagues' silence apparently did not have to be bought at all.

Obviously, those who advocate reticence or "responsibility" from our side are more insidious—and sometimes, it would appear, impossible to resist. For it is our loyalty, rather than our timidity, on which such academic enemies of "irresponsibility" insist: asking us to limit ourselves (lest we give aid and comfort to a common opponent) in the free investigation, say, of the interconnections between the homosexual revolution and the first stages of the civil rights movement, or the importance of anti-Semitism and racism in the later black-power movement. Similarly, they urge us not to take away from the progressive forces certain symbolic heroes of the historical left—not, for instance, to follow up the evidence that at least Sacco, and possibly Vanzetti as well, was guilty as charged in the famous case that mobilized most decent men on their side; and that many of the organizers of the protests against their condemnation already knew the fact and strategically concealed it.

And when the voices that plead with us to lie a little about the importance of Negroes in our history, or to mitigate a little the harsh truth about the last country to betray some revolution in which we once thought we believed, are the voices of our own students, the voices of the young—how even harder it is to resist. We know that their cause, too, will be betrayed, as all causes are ultimately betrayed, but it seems churlish and unstrategic to tell them so; their strength and weakness is precisely not to know this, as our strength and weakness is to know it. And these strengths and weaknesses are complementary, make social life and intercourse between the generations not merely possible but necessary. Why, then, should we not lie to them a little when they come to us, as they do between periods of absolute rejection?

In a way, we are better off, safer, from our own point of view and theirs, when they turn their backs on us, muttering, "Old men, all we want you to do for us is *die!*" But a moment later, they return (being in need of uncles and grandfathers if not fathers: Marcuses and McLuhans and Norman O. Browns), crying, "Underwrite, sanction our revolt, tell us we are righter than you!" Indeed, how could they fail to be righter than we are still, wrong as we were at their age? But it is not our function as free teachers to tell them only how they are right; it is also imperative that we say (at the risk of being loved less, even of finally losing their ear altogether) how they are wrong—what in their movement, for instance, threatens the very freedom that makes it possible, and what threatens to freeze into self-righteousness.

Spokesmen for the "future" forget, even as they fight for it, that the "future" quickly becomes the present, then the past; and that soon they are only fighting for yesterday against the proponents of the day before yesterday. This is why the teacher dedicated to freedom must tell them *right now* the same thing he tells the Kiwanians when they howl down or propose to ban some speaker, some uncongenial idea: If any kind of truth or pursuit of truth— however misguided, however wrong—seems threatening to a cause we espouse, it is time to re-examine that cause, no matter how impressive its credentials. It is also to ourselves, of course, that we're speaking, since without constantly reminding ourselves of this simple principle we will yield to some pressure group, right, left or center. But even taken together, such groups are not our deepest and most dangerous enemy.

What gets us, as teachers, into final trouble is the enemy of our freedom that ordinarily we do not perceive at all: inhibiting forces that are as impersonal and omnipresent and invisible as our total environment or our very selves. Indeed, they are a large and growing part of that total environment, especially in the United States, where more and more education for more and more people remains an avowed goal of society. There are, however, inhibitory and restrictive tendencies built into the very school system to which almost everyone born in America is condemned by the fact of his birth—condemned beyond the possibility of appeal, since what he may feel as a prison was dreamed for him by his forebears as utopia.

For better or worse, in any event, young Americans these days find themselves sentenced by law to a term lasting from their fourth or fifth birthday to their sixteenth—and, by custom and social pressure, to a good deal more: time added, as it were, for good behavior. But though students in large numbers are dimly aware of all this, they have tended to resist it as outlaws rather than as revolutionaries, i.e., to drop out rather than to raise as a slogan, an immediate demand, the right not to go to school. Students have been primarily—and quite properly, as far as it goes—concerned with failures of the school system to provide them with the kinds of freedom to which that system itself is theoretically pledged: the right to demonstrate or petition, to participate and advise, to control in part, at least, their own destinies *in* the schools; but the existence of those schools, and even their traditional function, they have largely taken for granted.

To me, however, the root problem, the essential restriction of freedom, seems compulsory education itself—on both the primary and the secondary levels, where it is enforced by statute and truant officers; and on the higher levels, where it is, more and more broadly, customary and enforced by the peer group plus parents and teachers. Everything begins with the assumption by the community (or some auxiliary private enterprise) of the role traditionally played in the lives of the young by their families, aided and abetted by medicine men, prophets or kindly passing strangers; and is confirmed beyond hope of reform when that community sets up ever more rigid and bureaucratized institutions to do that job for it.

From this initial requirement follows most of what is dangerously restrictive throughout the school system: the regulation of every moment of a student's day (especially in high schools) and a good part of a student's nights (especially for female students, all the way to the university level). This involves, first of all, required attendance, tardiness reports, classes artificially divided into periods and rung off and on by a centrally controlled bell system, proctored examinations and blackmail by grades. And it implies, in the second place, a host of "disciplinary regulations" beginning with the banning of cigarettes on school grounds, or alcohol at school dances, or pot and the pill in dormitories, and ending with petty decrees—totally unconnected to the laws of the larger community— about the length of skirts and pants and hair. Hair, especially, seems the concern of school authorities, whether on the head or on the face—as if somewhere in the collective mind of those authorities, the image persisted of youth as a sort of Samson who to be en-slaved must be shorn.

Students have, of course, protested against this; and a good deal of what moves them, plus more that might or should move them, has been beautifully formulated by Edgar Z. Friedenberg, begin-ning with a book titled *The Vanishing Adolescent*. But their cry of "No more *loco parentis*" is undercut by their clearly contradictory wishes on this score. In general, they seem to want the schools to maintain a certain parental role in warding off police prosecution, yet to surrender that role in maintaining internal discipline. In any case, the protesters do not begin far enough back; for the American school system is essentially—by definition and tradition—*in loco parentis*. And nothing fundamental is solved by persuading it to be-come a permissive rather than an authoritarian parent—that is, to make itself more like students' actual parents and less like their ac-tual grandparents.

It is, alas, precisely those "permissive" parents who have made the whole school system, from kindergarten to university, what it is, insisting that it act out for them the dark side of their own ambiva-lence toward their children—be the bad parent they feel guilty for not being—and for wanting to be. If our schools are, in fact, totali-tarian under their liberal disguises, more like what the sociologists call "total institutions" (jails, mental hospitals, detention camps) than small democratic communities or enlarged families, this is be-cause the parents of the students in them *want* them to be what they are. Certainly any parent, any full adult in our society, is at least dimly aware of the tendency in himself and his neighbors to project upon children and adolescents sexual and anarchic impulses denied in himself. These impulses he asks his children both to act out and to be blamed for, relieving him of his own double guilt—and providing in its place the double pleasure of vicarious self-in-dulgence and the condemnation of sin.

In addition, there is the sexual jealousy that inevitably troubles those home-tied by jobs or children, or oppressed by the meno-pause and the imminence of death when they confront others just emerging into puberty, as well as the desperation of those unable to persuade their children of the value of moral codes in which they only theoretically believe—a desperation that ends in calling out the law to enforce what love could not achieve. And, finally, there is the strange uncertainty of our society about just when a child becomes an adult (whatever that elusive term may mean)—at puberty, at 16, 18, 21; when he votes, drinks legally, goes into the Army or simply becomes capable of reproducing himself. Out of this uncertainty emerge those absurd social regulations that turn the girls' dormitory into a police state, the rules whose goal is to keep those we claim we have to regulate (because they are still "children") from getting pregnant, i.e., from proving to us that biologically, at least, they are fully mature.

Small wonder, then, that our schools and universities have become, like our jails and hospitals and asylums, institutions whose structure works against their own avowed ends—leading not to the free development of free men but to the depersonalization of the student, to his conversion into a code number and an IBM card punched full of data, a fact that he may forget in the midst of the small pleasures that punctuate his boredom but of which he is reminded once, twice, even three times a year by the degrading rituals of examination and registration. The damage done the student by this system we have all begun to notice, as the resentment of his indignity has driven him to construct barricades and hurl fire bombs; but the similar damage done to his teachers we tend to ignore, since they typically respond with silence or statements read only to one another at annual meetings.

It is not merely that the teacher, too, is regulated, right down to such trivial matters as wearing a tie or smoking in class, but that also—and, finally, more critically—he, like the prison guard or the asylum attendant, becomes the prisoner of the closed world he presumably guards, a world in which he begins talking at the ping of one bell and stops at the clang of another, meanwhile checking attendance, making sure no one cheats or lights a cigarette under a NO SMOKING sign or consumes hard liquor or drugs, or, God forbid, takes off his clothes in public. All of this, however, makes him a jailer or a cop, who notoriously resemble their charges; and insofar as he resists, turns him into a hypocrite, acknowledging only the infractions that someone else—the press, a planted police spy, an indignant parent—has noticed first.

How can the teacher who accepts such a system talk freedom to the students before him? Or how can he demand it for himself—academically, politically, personally—at the very moment he is denying it—socially, erotically—to those he asks to emulate his model? The historical struggle of teachers for what has been called "academic freedom"—that is, their own freedom—has been impugned throughout by their hypocrisy. No community, not even a school, can exist one-tenth absolutely free and nine-tenths half slave. It is an unendurable fraud, of which most of us manage to remain absurdly unaware, until some notorious "case"—the Leary case, the Koch case, the Mezey case—forces us to confront it, to confront the contradiction in ourselves. By then, however, it is too late.

Inevitably, at that point we tend to compromise or totally betray for one of us the principles we have already learned to compromise and betray for the students to whom we are, after ourselves, chiefly responsible. And here we have come, at long last, to responsibility. To avoid the word at this juncture would be as abject as having taken refuge in it earlier, since to be responsible means, in the new context, not to be restricted, which is to say, less free— but to be *answerable,* which is to say, more free.

Until a man has learned to be truly free, he cannot begin to be responsible in this deep etymological sense of the word, since the only thing for which a teacher is properly answerable is his own freedom, his necessary prior *ir*responsibility. A slave or a man under restraint, an indoctrinated indoctrinator, a civil servant brainwashed to brainwash others, is answerable for nothing. No matter what charges are brought against him, he can plead innocent; for he is the agent of another, a despicable tool, just another Eichmann, dignified beyond his worth by being brought to the dock.

The free teacher, on the other hand, must not merely suffer but welcome, even invite, criticism of what he espouses and teaches, for his job is to change the minds of the young—which those in established positions seem to view as a kind of "corruption." For him, freedom does not mean freedom from consequences; he takes, as the old Spanish proverb has it, what he wants but he pays his dues. Wanting nothing free of charge, he denies to no one the right to disagree with what he says, to criticize, to try to rebut, even to threaten sanctions. He must always be willing to argue against all comers the basic case for his freedom, which is never, and can never be, won finally and forever. But he must also be prepared to defend—one by one and each on its own merits—all of the tenets, views, opinions and analyses he finds himself free to offer.

Above all, when his ideas are proved wrong, to his own satisfaction, in the debate with those who challenge him, he must feel free to confess his error without in any way diminishing his right to have held those ideas; for he has never had any real freedom at all unless he has been free from the start to be wrong and unless he remains free to the end to change his mind. If, in the debate he has occasioned, however, he continues to believe in his position, he must—with all the assurance that comes of knowing his fallibility as well as that of his opponents—continue to maintain that position. It does not matter at all if a majority is against him, or even everybody; for even everybody has, on occasion, turned out to be wrong, and he is, in any case, not answerable to a popular vote.

He dares not betray the facts as he has learned from his teachers and his colleagues to determine them, but he must always be aware that those "facts" exist finally in his own head. And he is equally answerable to posterity—which means, for a teacher, his students—not those before him at any moment but those yet to come; best of all, those not yet born; and these, too, he must remember live only inside his skull. It is to the unborn, then, that the free man, the true teacher, is finally answerable; but it is the living students, their parents and the community that he inhabits rather than the one he dreams, that judge him and can make him suffer. If that community—parents or students or both—desires to visit sanctions on him, he must not pretend surprise or feel dismay.

Yet they are not hard to please, really, the spokesmen of the past or those of the present; all they ask is a show of subservience either to long-established conventions or to the very latest life style. Only an allegiance to the ever-receding future dismays both; for, driven to imagine a time to come, the responsibles, both old and young, feel their authority slipping from them as they realize that someday they will be dead. But it is precisely this realization that exhilarates some men, making them feel free enough to be irresponsible, irresponsible enough to be free.

—1968

EIGHTEEN

The New Mutants

A REALIZATION that the legitimate functions of literature are bewilderingly, almost inexhaustibly various has always exhilarated poets and dismayed critics. And critics, therefore, have sought age after age to legislate limits to literature—legitimizing certain of its functions and disavowing others—in hope of insuring to themselves the exhilaration of which they have felt unjustly deprived, and providing for poets the dismay which the critics at least have thought good for them.

Such shifting and exclusive emphasis is not, however, purely the product of critical malice, or even of critical principle. Somehow every period is, to begin with, especially aware of certain functions of literature and especially oblivious to others: endowed with a special sensitivity and a complementary obtuseness, which, indeed, give to that period its characteristic flavor and feel. So, for instance, the Augustan Era is marked by sensitivity in regard to the uses of diction, obtuseness in regard to those of imagery.

What the peculiar obtuseness of the present age may be I find it difficult to say (being its victim as well as its recorder), perhaps toward the didactic or certain modes of the sentimental. I am reasonably sure, however, that our period is acutely aware of the sense in which literature if not invents, at least collaborates in the invention of time. The beginnings of that awareness go back certainly to the beginnings of the Renaissance, to Humanism as a self-conscious movement; though a critical development occurred toward the end of the eighteenth century with the dawning of the Age of Revolution. And we may have reached a second critical point right now.

At any rate, we have long been aware (in the last decades uncomfortably aware) that a chief function of literature is to express and in part to create not only theories of time but also attitudes toward time. Such attitudes constitute, however, a politics as well as an esthetics; or, more properly perhaps, a necessary mythological substratum of politics—as, in fact, the conventional terms reactionary, conservative, revolutionary indicate: all involving stances toward the past.

It is with the past, then, that we must start, since the invention of the past seems to have preceded that of the present and the future; and since we are gathered in a university at whose heart stands a library[1]—the latter, like the former, a visible monument to the theory that a chief responsibility of literature is to preserve and perpetuate the past. Few universities are explicitly (and none with any real degree of confidence) dedicated to this venerable goal any longer. The Great Books idea (which once transformed the University of Chicago and lives on now in provincial study groups) was perhaps its last desperate expression. Yet the shaky continuing existence of the universities and the building of new college libraries (with matching Federal funds) remind us not only of that tradition but of the literature created in its name: the neo-epic, for instance, all the way from Dante to Milton; and even the frantically nostalgic Historical Romance, out of the counting house by Sir Walter Scott.

Obviously, however, literature has a contemporary as well as a traditional function. That is to say, it may be dedicated to illuminating the present and the meaning of the present, which is, after all, no more given than the past. Certainly the modern or bourgeois novel was thus contemporary in the hands of its great inventors, Richardson, Fielding, Smollett and Sterne; and it became contemporary again—with, as it were, a sigh of relief—when Flaubert, having plunged deep into the Historical Romance, emerged once more into the present of Emma Bovary. But the second function of the novel tends to transform itself into a third: a revolutionary or

[1] "The New Mutants" is a written version of a talk given at the Conference on the Idea of The Future held at Rutgers, in June, 1965. The conference was sponsored by *Partisan Review* and the Congress for Cultural Freedom, with the cooperation of Rutgers, The State University.

prophetic or futurist function; and it is with the latter that I am here concerned.

Especially important for our own time is the sense in which literature first conceived the possibility of the future (rather than an End of Time or an Eternal Return, an Apocalypse or Second Coming); and then furnished that future in joyous or terrified anticipation, thus preparing all of us to inhabit it. Men have dreamed and even written down utopias from ancient times; but such utopias were at first typically allegories rather than projections: nonexistent models against which to measure the real world, exploitations of the impossible (as the traditional name declares) rather than explorations or anticipations or programs of the possible. And, in any event, only recently have such works occupied a position anywhere near the center of literature.

Indeed, the movement of futurist literature from the periphery to the center of culture provides a clue to certain essential meanings of our times and of the art which best reflects it. If we make a brief excursion from the lofty reaches of High Art to the humbler levels of Pop Culture—where radical transformations in literature are reflected in simplified form—the extent and nature of the futurist revolution will become immediately evident. Certainly, we have seen in recent years the purveyors of Pop Culture transfer their energies from the Western and the Dracula-type thriller (last heirs of the Romantic and Gothic concern with the past) to the Detective Story especially in its hard-boiled form (final vulgarization of the realists' dedication to the present) to Science Fiction (a new genre based on hints in Poe and committed to "extrapolating" the future). This development is based in part on the tendency to rapid exhaustion inherent in popular forms; but in part reflects a growing sense of the irrelevance of the past and even of the present to 1965. Surely, there has never been a moment in which the most naïve as well as the most sophisticated have been so acutely aware of how the past threatens momentarily to disappear from the present, which itself seems on the verge of disappearing into the future.

And this awareness functions, therefore, on the level of art as well as entertainment, persuading quite serious writers to emulate the modes of Science Fiction. The novel is most amenable to this sort of adaptation, whose traces we can find in writers as various as

William Golding and Anthony Burgess, William Burroughs and Kurt Vonnegut, Jr., Harry Matthews and John Barth—to all of whom young readers tend to respond with a sympathy they do not feel even toward such forerunners of the mode (still more allegorical than prophetic) as Aldous Huxley, H. G. Wells and George Orwell. But the influence of Science Fiction can be discerned in poetry as well, and even in the polemical essays of such polymath prophets as Wilhelm Reich, Buckminster Fuller, Marshall McLuhan, perhaps also Norman O. Brown. Indeed, in Fuller the prophetic-Science-Fiction view of man is always at the point of fragmenting into verse:

> men are known as being six feet tall
> because that is their tactile limit;
> they are not known by how far we can hear them,
> e.g., as a one-half mile man
> and only to dogs are men known
> by their gigantic olfactoral dimensions. . . .

I am not now interested in analyzing, however, the diction and imagery which have passed from Science Fiction into post-Modernist literature, but rather in coming to terms with the prophetic content common to both: with the myth rather than the modes of Science Fiction. But that myth is quite simply the myth of the end of man, of the transcendence or transformation of the human—a vision quite different from that of the extinction of our species by the Bomb, which seems stereotype rather than archetype and consequently the source of editorials rather than poems. More fruitful artistically is the prospect of the radical transformation (under the impact of advanced technology and the transfer of traditional human functions to machines) of *homo sapiens* into something else: the emergence—to use the language of Science Fiction itself —of "mutants" among us.

A simpleminded prevision of this event is to be found in Arthur C. Clarke's *Childhood's End,* at the conclusion of which the mutated offspring of parents much like us are about to take off under their own power into outer space. Mr. Clarke believes that he is talking about a time still to come because he takes metaphor for fact;

though simply translating "outer space" into "inner space" reveals to us that what he is up to is less prediction than description; since the post-human future is now, and if not we, at least our children, are what it would be comfortable to pretend we still only foresee. But what, in fact, are they: these mutants who are likely to sit before us in class, or across from us at the dinner table, or who stare at us with hostility from street corners as we pass?

Beatniks or hipsters, layabouts and drop-outs we are likely to call them with corresponding hostility—or more elegantly, but still without sympathy, passive onlookers, abstentionists, spiritual cata- tonics. There resides in all of these terms an element of truth, at least about the relationship of the young to what we have defined as the tradition, the world we have made for them; and if we turn to the books in which they see their own destiny best represented *(The Clockwork Orange,* say, or *On the Road* or *Temple of Gold),* we will find nothing to contradict that truth. Nor will we find any- thing to expand it, since the young and their laureates avoid on principle the kind of definition (even of themselves) for which we necessarily seek.

Let us begin then with the negative definition our own hostility suggests, since this is all that is available to us, and say that the "mutants" in our midst are nonparticipants in the past (though our wisdom assures us this is impossible), dropouts from history. The withdrawal from school, so typical of their generation and so in- scrutable to ours, is best understood as a lived symbol of their rejection of the notion of cultural continuity and progress, which our graded educational system represents in institutional form. It is not merely a matter of their rejecting what happens to have hap- pened just before them, as the young do, after all, in every age; but of their attempting to disavow the very idea of the past, of their seeking to avoid recapitulating it step by step—up to the point of graduation into the present.

Specifically, the tradition from which they strive to disengage is · the tradition of the human, as the West (understanding the West to extend from the United States to Russia) has defined it, Humanism itself, both in its bourgeois and Marxist forms; and more especially, the cult of reason—that dream of Socrates, redreamed by the Ren- aissance and surviving all travesties down to only yesterday. To be sure, there have long been antirational forces at work in the West, including primitive Christianity itself; but the very notion of literary culture is a product of Humanism, as the early Christians knew (setting fire to libraries), so that the Church in order to sponsor poets had first to come to terms with reason itself by way of Aquinas and Aristotle.

Only with Dada was the notion of an antirational antiliterature born; and Dada became Surrealism, i.e., submitted to the influence of those last neo-Humanists, those desperate Socratic Cabalists, Freud and Marx—dedicated respectively to contriving a rationale of violence and a rationale of impulse. The new irrationalists, however, deny all the apostles of reason, Freud as well as Socrates; and if they seem to exempt Marx, this is because they know less about him, have heard him evoked less often by the teachers they are driven to deny. Not only do they reject the Socratic adage that the unexamined life is not worth living, since for them precisely the unexamined life is the only one worth enduring at all. But they also abjure the Freudian one: "Where id was, ego shall be," since for them the true rallying cry is, "Let id prevail over ego, impulse over order," or—in negative terms—"Freud is a fink!"

The first time I heard this irreverent charge from the mouth of a student some five or six years ago (I who had grown up thinking of Freud as a revolutionary, a pioneer), I knew that I was already in the future; though I did not yet suspect that there would be no room in that future for the university system to which I had devoted my life. Kerouac might have told me so, or Ginsberg, or even so polite and genteel a spokesman for youth as J. D. Salinger, but I was too aware of what was wrong with such writers (their faults more readily apparent to my taste than their virtues) to be sensitive to the truths they told. It took, therefore, certain public events to illuminate (for me) the literature which might have illuminated them.

I am thinking, of course, of the recent demonstrations at Berkeley and elsewhere, whose ostensible causes were civil rights or freedom of speech or Vietnam, but whose not so secret slogan was all the time: *The Professor is a Fink!* And what an array of bad antiacademic novels, I cannot help reminding myself, written by disgruntled professors, created the mythology out of which that slogan grew. Each generation of students is invented by the generation of teachers just before them; but how different they are in dream and fact—as different as self-hatred and its reflection in another. How different the professors in Jeremy Larner's *Drive, He Said* from those even in Randall Jarrell's *Pictures from an Institution* or Mary McCarthy's *Groves of Academe.*

To be sure, many motives operated to set the students in action, some of them imagined in no book, however good or bad. Many of the thousands who resisted or shouted on campuses did so in the name of naïve or disingenuous or even nostalgic politics (be careful what you wish for in your middle age, or your children will parody it forthwith!); and sheer ennui doubtless played a role along with a justified rage against the hypocrisies of academic life. Universities have long rivaled the churches in their devotion to institutionalizing hypocrisy; and more recently they have outstripped television itself (which most professors affect to despise even more than they despise organized religion) in the institutionalization of boredom.

But what the students were protesting in large part, I have come to believe, was the very notion of man which the universities sought to impose upon them: that bourgeois-Protestant version of Humanism, with its view of man as justified by rationality, work, duty, vocation, maturity, success; and its concomitant understanding of childhood and adolescence as a temporarily privileged time of preparation for assuming those burdens. The new irrationalists, however, are prepared to advocate prolonging adolescence to the grave, and are ready to dispense with school as an outlived excuse for leisure. To them work is as obsolete as reason, a vestige (already dispensable for large numbers) of an economically marginal, pre-automated world; and the obsolescence of the two adds up to the obsolescence of everything our society understands by maturity.

Nor is it in the name of an older more valid Humanistic view of man that the new irrationalists would reject the WASP version; Rabelais is as alien to them as Benjamin Franklin. Disinterested scholarship, reflection, the life of reason, a respect for tradition stir (however dimly and confusedly) chiefly their contempt; and the Abbey of Theleme would seem as sterile to them as Robinson Crusoe's Island. To the classroom, the library, the laboratory, the office conference and the meeting of scholars, they prefer the demonstration, the sit-in, the riot: the mindless unity of an impassioned crowd (with guitars beating out the rhythm in the background), whose immediate cause is felt rather than thought out, whose ultimate cause is itself. In light of this, the Teach-in, often ill understood because of an emphasis on its declared political ends, can be seen as implicitly a parody and mockery of the real classroom: related to the actual business of the university, to real teaching, only as the Demonstration Trial (of Dimitrov, of the Soviet Doctors, of Eichmann) to real justice or Demonstration Voting (for one party or a token two) to real suffrage.

At least, since Berkeley (or perhaps since Martin Luther King provided students with new paradigms for action) the choice has been extended beyond what the earlier laureates of the new youth could imagine in the novel: the nervous breakdown at home rather than the return to "sanity" and school, which was the best Salinger could invent for Franny and Holden; or Kerouac's way out for his "saintly" vagrants, that "road" from nowhere to noplace with homemade gurus at the way stations. The structures of those fictional vaudevilles between hard covers that currently please the young *(Catch 22, V., A Mother's Kisses),* suggest in their brutality and discontinuity, their politics of mockery, something of the spirit of the student demonstrations; but only Jeremy Larner, as far as I know, has dealt explicitly with the abandonment of the classroom in favor of the Dionysiac pack, the turning from *polis* to *thiasos,* from forms of social organization traditionally thought of as male to the sort of passionate community attributed by the ancients to females out of control.

Conventional slogans in favor of "Good Works" (pious emendations of existing social structures, or extensions of accepted "rights" to excluded groups) though they provide the motive power of such protests are irrelevant to their form and their final significance. They become their essential selves, i.e., genuine new forms of rebellion, when the demonstrators hoist (as they did in the final stages of the Berkeley protests) the sort of slogan which embarrasses not only fellow travelers but even the bureaucrats who direct the initial stages of the revolt: at the University of California, the single four-letter word no family newspaper would reprint, though no member of a family who could read was likely not to know it.

It is possible to argue on the basis of the political facts themselves that the word "fuck" entered the whole scene accidentally (there were only four students behind the "Dirty Speech Movement," only fifteen hundred kids could be persuaded to demonstrate for it, etc., etc.). But the prophetic literature which anticipates the movement indicates otherwise, suggesting that the logic of their illogical course eventually sets the young against language itself, against the very counters of logical discourse. They seek an antilanguage of protest as inevitably as they seek antipoems and antinovels, end with the ultimate antiword, which the demonstrators at Berkeley disingenuously claimed stood for FREEDOM UNDER CLARK KERR.

Esthetics, however, had already anticipated politics in this regard; porno-poetry preceding and preparing the way for what Lewis Feuer has aptly called porno-politics. Already in 1963, in an essay entitled *"Phi Upsilon Kappa,"* the young poet Michael McClure was writing: "Gregory Corso has asked me to join with him in a project to free the word FUCK from its chains and strictures. I leap to make some new freedom. . . ." And McClure's own "Fuck Ode" is a product of this collaboration, as the very name of Ed Sanders' journal, *Fuck You,* is the creation of an analogous impulse. The aging critics of the young who have dealt with the Berkeley demonstrations in such journals as *Commentary* and the *New Leader* do not, however, read either Saunders' porno-pacifist magazine or *Kulchur,* in which McClure's manifesto was first printed —the age barrier separating readership in the United States more effectively than class, political affiliation, or anything else.

Their sense of porno-esthetics is likely to come from deserters from their own camp, chiefly Norman Mailer, and especially his recent *An American Dream,* which represents the entry of antilanguage (extending the tentative explorations of "The Time of Her Time") into the world of the middle-aged, both on the level of mass culture and that of yesterday's ex-Marxist, post-Freudian *avant-garde.* Characteristically enough, Mailer's book has occasioned in the latter quarters reviews as irrelevant, incoherent, misleading and fundamentally scared as the most philistine responses to the Berkeley demonstrations, Philip Rahv and Stanley Edgar Hyman providing two egregious examples. Yet elsewhere (in sectors held by those more at ease with their own conservatism, i.e., without defunct radicalisms to uphold) the most obscene forays of the young are being met with a disheartening kind of tolerance and even an attempt to adapt them to the conditions of commodity art.

But precisely here, of course, a disconcerting irony is involved; for after a while, there will be no Rahvs and Hymans left to shock —antilanguage becoming mere language with repeated use and in the face of acceptance; so that all sense of exhilaration will be lost along with the possibility of offense. What to do then except to choose silence, since raising the ante of violence is ultimately self-defeating; and the way of obscenity in any case leads as naturally to silence as to further excess? Moreover, to the talkative heirs of Socrates, silence is the one offense that never wears out, the radicalism that can never become fashionable; which is why, after the obscene slogan has been hauled down, a blank placard is raised in its place.

There are difficulties, to be sure, when one attempts to move from the politics of silence to an analogous sort of poetry. The opposite number to the silent picketer would be the silent poet, which is a contradiction in terms; yet there are these days nonsingers of (perhaps) great talent who shrug off the temptation to song with the muttered comment, "Creativity is out." Some, however, make literature of a kind precisely at the point of maximum tension between the tug toward silence and the pull toward publication. Music is a better language really for saying what one would prefer not to say at all—and all the way from certain sorts of sufficiently cool jazz to Rock and Roll (with its minimal lyrics that defy understanding on a first hearing), music is the preferred art of the irrationalists.

But some varieties of skinny poetry seem apt, too (as practised, say, by Robert Creeley after the example of W. C. Williams), since their lines are three parts silence to one part speech:

> *My lady*
> *fair with*
> *soft*
> *arms, what*
> *can I say to*
> *you—words, words . . .*

And, of course, fiction aspiring to become Pop Art, say, *An American Dream* (with the experiments of Hemingway and Nathanael West behind it), works approximately as well, since clichés are almost as inaudible as silence itself. The point is not to shout, not to insist, but to hang cool, to baffle all mothers, cultural and spiritual as well as actual.

When the Town Council in Venice, California was about to close down a particularly notorious beatnik cafe, a lady asked to testify before them, presumably to clinch the case against the offenders. What she reported, however, was that each day as she walked by the cafe and looked in its windows, she saw the unsavory types who inhabited it "just standing there, looking—nonchalant." And, in a way, her improbable adjective does describe a crime against her world; for nonchaleur ("cool," the futurists themselves would prefer to call it) is the essence of their life style as well as of the literary styles to which they respond: the offensive style of those who are not so much *for* anything in particular, as "with it" in general.

But such an attitude is as remote from traditional "alienation," with its profound longing to end disconnection, as it is from ordinary forms of allegiance, with their desperate resolve not to admit disconnection. The new young celebrate disconnection—accept it as one of the necessary consequences of the industrial system which has delivered them from work and duty, of that welfare state which makes disengagement the last possible virtue, whether it call itself Capitalist, Socialist or Communist. "Detachment" is the traditional name for the stance the futurists assume; but "detachment" carries with it irrelevant religious, even specifically Christian overtones. The post-modernists are surely in some sense "mystics," religious at least in a way they do not ordinarily know how to confess, but they are not Christians.

Indeed, they regard Christianity, quite as the Black Muslims (with whom they have certain affinities) do, as a white ideology: merely one more method—along with Humanism, technology, Marxism—of imposing "White" or Western values on the colored rest of the world. To the new barbarian, however, that would-be post-Humanist (who is in most cases the white offspring of Christian forebears), his whiteness is likely to seem if not a stigma and symbol of shame, at least the outward sign of his exclusion from all that his Christian Humanist ancestors rejected in themselves and projected mythologically upon the colored man. For such reasons, his religion, when it becomes explicit, claims to be derived from Tibet or Japan or the ceremonies of the Plains Indians, or is composed out of the non-Christian submythology that has grown up among Negro jazz musicians and in the civil rights movement. When the new barbarian speaks of "soul," for instance, he means not "soul" as in Heaven, but as in "soul music" or even "soul food."

It is all part of the attempt of the generation under twenty-five, not exclusively in its most sensitive members but especially in them, to become Negro, even as they attempt to become poor or prerational. About this particular form of psychic assimilation I have written sufficiently in the past (summing up what I had been long saying in chapters seven and eight of *Waiting for the End)*, neglecting only the sense in which what starts as a specifically American movement becomes an international one, spreading to the *yé-yé* girls of France or the working-class entertainers of Liverpool with astonishing swiftness and ease.

What interests me more particularly right now is a parallel assimilationist attempt, which may, indeed, be more parochial and is certainly most marked at the moment in the Anglo-Saxon world, i.e., in those cultural communities most totally committed to bourgeois-Protestant values and surest that they are unequivocally "white." I am thinking of the effort of young men in England and the United States to assimilate into themselves (or even to assimilate themselves into) that otherness, that sum total of rejected psychic elements which the middle-class heirs of the Renaissance have identified with "woman." To become new men, these children of the future seem to feel, they must not only become more Black than White but more female than male. And it is natural that the need to make such an adjustment be felt with especial acuteness in post-Protestant highly industrialized societies, where the functions regarded as specifically male for some three hundred years tend most rapidly to become obsolete.

Surely, in America, machines already perform better than humans a large number of those aggressive-productive activities which our ancestors considered man's special province, even his *raison d'être*. Not only has the male's prerogative of making things and money (which is to say, of working) been preempted, but also his time-honored privilege of dealing out death by hand, which until quite recently was regarded as a supreme mark of masculine valor. While it seems theoretically possible, even in the heart of Anglo-Saxondom, to imagine a leisurely, pacific male, in fact the losses in secondary functions sustained by men appear to have shaken their faith in their primary masculine function as well, in their ability to achieve the conquest (as the traditional metaphor has it) of women. Earlier, advances in technology had detached the wooing and winning of women from the begetting of children; and though the invention of the condom had at least left the decision to inhibit fatherhood in the power of males, its replacement by the "loop" and the "pill" has placed paternity at the mercy of the whims of women.

Writers of fiction and verse registered the technological obsolescence of masculinity long before it was felt even by the representative minority who give to the present younger generation its character and significance. And literary critics have talked a good deal during the past couple of decades about the conversion of the literary hero into the nonhero or the antihero; but they have in general failed to notice his simultaneous conversion into the non- or antimale. Yet ever since Hemingway at least, certain male protagonists of American literature have not only fled rather than sought out combat but have also fled rather than sought out women. From Jake Barnes to Holden Caulfield they have continued to run from the threat of female sexuality; and, indeed, there are models for such evasion in our classic books, where heroes still eager for the fight (Natty Bumppo comes to mind) are already shy of wives and sweethearts and mothers.

It is not absolutely required that the antimale antihero be impotent or homosexual or both (though this helps, as we remember remembering Walt Whitman), merely that he be more seduced than seducing, more passive than active. Consider, for instance, the oddly "womanish" Herzog of Bellow's current best seller, that Jewish Emma Bovary with a Ph.D., whose chief flaw is physical vanity and a taste for fancy clothes. Bellow, however, is more interested in summing up the past than in evoking the future; and *Herzog* therefore seems an end rather than a beginning, the product of nostalgia (remember when there were real Jews once, and the "Jewish Novel" had not yet been discovered!) rather than prophecy. No, the post-humanist, post-male, post-white, post-heroic world is a post-Jewish world by the same token, anti-Semitism as inextricably woven into it as into the movement for Negro rights; and its scriptural books are necessarily *goyish,* not least of all William Burroughs' *The Naked Lunch.*

Burroughs is the chief prophet of the post-male post-heroic world; and it is his emulators who move into the center of the relevant literary scene, for *The Naked Lunch* (the later novels are less successful, less exciting but relevant still) is more than it seems: no mere essay in heroin-hallucinated homosexual pornography—but a nightmare anticipation (in Science Fiction form) of post-Humanist sexuality. Here, as in Alexander Trocchi, John Rechy, Harry Matthews (even an occasional Jew like Allen Ginsberg, who has begun by inscribing properly anti-Jewish obscenities on the walls of the world), are clues to the new attitudes toward sex that will continue to inform our improbable novels of passion and our even more improbable love songs.

The young to whom I have been referring, the mythologically representative minority (who, by a process that infuriates the mythologically inert majority out of which they come, "stand for" their times), live in a community in which what used to be called the "Sexual Revolution," the Freudian-Laurentian revolt of their grandparents and parents, has triumphed as imperfectly and unsatisfactorily as all revolutions always triumph. They confront, therefore, the necessity of determining not only what meanings "love" can have in their new world, but—even more disturbingly—what significance, if any, "male" and "female" now possess. For a while, they (or at least their literary spokesmen recruited from the generation just before them) seemed content to celebrate a kind of *reductio* or *exaltatio ad absurdum* of their parents' once revolutionary sexual goals: The Reichian-inspired Cult of the Orgasm.

Young men and women eager to be delivered of traditional ideologies of love find especially congenial the belief that not union or relationship (much less offspring) but physical release is the end of the sexual act; and that, therefore, it is a matter of indifference with whom or by what method ones pursues the therapeutic climax, so long as that climax is total and repeated frequently. And Wilhelm Reich happily detaches this belief from the vestiges of Freudian rationalism, setting it instead in a context of Science Fiction and witchcraft; but his emphasis upon "full genitality," upon growing up and away from infantile pleasures, strikes the young as a disguised plea for the "maturity" they have learned to despise. In a time when the duties associated with adulthood promise to become irrelevant, there seems little reason for denying oneself the joys of babyhood—even if these are associated with such regressive fantasies as escaping it all in the arms of little sister (in the Gospel according to J. D. Salinger) or flirting with the possibility of getting into bed with papa (in the Gospel according to Norman Mailer).

Only Norman O. Brown in *Life Against Death* has come to terms on the level of theory with the aspiration to take the final evolutionary leap and cast off adulthood completely, at least in the area of sex. His post-Freudian program for pansexual, nonorgasmic love rejects "full genitality" in favor of a species of indiscriminate bundling, a dream of unlimited subcoital intimacy which Brown calls (in his vocabulary the term is an honorific) "polymorphous perverse." And here finally is an essential clue to the nature of the second sexual revolution, the post-sexual revolution, first evoked in literature by Brother Antoninus more than a decade ago, in a verse prayer addressed somewhat improbably to the Christian God:

> *Annul in me my manhood, Lord, and make*
> *Me woman sexed and weak . . .*
> > *Make me then*
> *Girl-hearted, virgin-souled, woman-docile, maiden-meek . . .*

Despite the accents of this invocation, however, what is at work is not essentially a homosexual revolt or even a rebellion against women, though its advocates seek to wrest from women their ancient privileges of receiving the Holy Ghost and pleasuring men; and though the attitudes of the movement can be adapted to the antifemale bias of, say, Edward Albee. If in *Who's Afraid of Virginia Woolf* Albee can portray the relationship of two homosexuals (one

in drag) as the model of contemporary marriage, this must be because contemporary marriage has in fact turned into something
much like that parody. And it is true that what survives of bourgeois marriage and the bourgeois family is a target which the new
barbarians join the old homosexuals in reviling, seeking to replace
Mom, Pop and the kids with a neo-Whitmanian gaggle of giggling
camerados. Such groups are, in fact, whether gathered in coffee
houses, university cafeterias or around the literature tables on campuses, the peacetime equivalents, as it were, to the demonstrating
crowd. But even their program of displacing Dick-Jane-Spot-Baby,
etc., the WASP family of grade school primers, is not the fundamental motive of the post-sexual revolution.

What is at stake from Burroughs to Bellow, Ginsberg to Albee,
Salinger to Gregory Corso is a more personal transformation: a
radical metamorphosis of the Western male—utterly unforeseen in
the decades before us, but visible now in every high school and college classroom, as well as on the paperback racks in airports and
supermarkets. All around us, young males are beginning to retrieve
for themselves the cavalier role once piously and class-consciously
surrendered to women: *that of being beautiful and being loved.*
Here once more the example of the Negro—the feckless and
adorned Negro male with the blood of Cavaliers in his veins—has
served as a model. And what else is left to young men, in any case,
after the devaluation of the grim duties they had arrogated to themselves in place of the pursuit of loveliness?

All of us who are middle-aged and were Marxists, which is to
say, who once numbered ourselves among the last assured Puritans,
have surely noticed in ourselves a vestigial roundhead rage at the
new hair styles of the advanced or—if you please—delinquent
young. Watching young men titivate their locks (the comb, the
pocket mirror and the bobby pin having replaced the jackknife,
catcher's mitt and brass knuckles), we feel the same baffled resentment that stirs in us when we realize that they have rejected work.
A job and unequivocal maleness—these are two sides of the same
Calvinist coin, which in the future buys nothing.

Few of us, however, have really understood how the Beatle
hair-do is part of a syndrome, of which high heels, jeans tight over

the buttocks, etc., are other aspects, symptomatic of a larger retreat from masculine aggressiveness to female allure—in literature and the arts to the style called "camp." And fewer still have realized how that style, though the invention of homosexuals, is now the possession of basically heterosexual males as well, a strategy in their campaign to establish a new relationship not only with women but with their own masculinity. In the course of that campaign, they have embraced certain kinds of gesture and garb, certain accents and tones traditionally associated with females or female impersonators; which is why we have been observing recently (in life as well as fiction and verse) young boys, quite unequivocally male, playing all the traditional roles of women: the vamp, the coquette, the whore, the icy tease, the pure young virgin.

Not only oldsters, who had envisioned and despaired of quite another future, are bewildered by this turn of events, but young girls, too, seem scarcely to know what is happening—looking on with that new, schizoid stare which itself has become a hallmark of our times. And the crop-headed jocks, those crew-cut athletes who represent an obsolescent masculine style based on quite other values, have tended to strike back blindly; beating the hell out of some poor kid whose hair is too long or whose pants are too tight—quite as they once beat up young communists for revealing that their politics had become obsolete. Even heterosexual writers, however, have been slow to catch up, the revolution in sensibility running ahead of that in expression; and they have perforce permitted homosexuals to speak for them (Burroughs and Genet and Baldwin and Ginsberg and Albee and a score of others), even to invent the forms in which the future will have to speak.

The revolt against masculinity is not limited, however, to simple matters of coiffure and costume, visible even to athletes; or to the adaptation of certain campy styles and modes to new uses. There is also a sense in which two large social movements that have set the young in motion and furnished images of action for their books—movements as important in their own right as porno-politics and the pursuit of the polymorphous perverse—are connected analogically to the abdication from traditional maleness. The first of these is nonviolent or passive resistance, so oddly come back to the land of its inventor, that icy Thoreau who dreamed a love which ". . . has not much human blood in it, but consists with a certain disregard for men and their erections. . . ."

The civil rights movement, however, in which nonviolence has found a home, has been hospitable not only to the sort of post-humanist I have been describing; so that at a demonstration (Selma, Alabama will do as an example) the true hippie will be found side by side with backwoods Baptists, nuns on a spiritual spree, boy bureaucrats practicing to take power, resurrected socialists, Unitarians in search of a God, and just plain tourists, gathered, as once at the Battle of Bull Run, to see the fun. For each of these, nonviolence will have a different sort of fundamental meaning—as a tactic, a camouflage, a passing fad, a pious gesture—but for each in part, and for the post-humanist especially, it will signify the possibility of heroism without aggression, effective action without guilt.

There have always been two contradictory American ideals: to be the occasion of maximum violence, and to remain absolutely innocent. Once, however, these were thought hopelessly incompatible for males (except, perhaps, as embodied in works of art), reserved strictly for women: the spouse of the wife beater, for instance, or the victim of rape. But males have now assumed these classic roles; and just as a particularly beleaguered wife occasionally slipped over the dividing line into violence, so do the new passive protesters— leaving us to confront (or resign to the courts) such homey female questions as: *Did Mario Savio really bite that cop in the leg as he sagged limply toward the ground?*

The second social movement is the drug cult, more widespread among youth, from its squarest limits to its most beat, than anyone seems prepared to admit in public; and at its beat limit at least inextricably involved with the civil rights movement, as the recent arrests of Peter DeLissovoy and Susan Ryerson revealed even to the ordinary newspaper reader. "Police said that most of the recipients [of marijuana] were college students," the U.P. story runs. "They quoted Miss Ryerson and DeLissovoy as saying that many of the letter packets were sent to civil rights workers." Only fiction and verse, however, has dealt with the conjunction of homosexuality, drugs and civil rights, eschewing the general piety of the press which has been unwilling to compromise "good works" on behalf of the Negro by associating them with the deep radicalism of a way of life based on the ritual consumption of "pot."

The widespread use of such hallucinogens as peyote, marijuana, the "Mexican mushroom," LSD, etc., as well as pep pills, goof balls, airplane glue, certain kinds of cough syrups and even, though in many fewer cases, heroin, is not merely a matter of a changing taste in stimulants but of the programmatic espousal of an antipuritanical mode of existence—hedonistic and detached—one more strategy in the war on time and work. But it is also (to pursue my analogy once more) an attempt to arrogate to the male certain traditional privileges of the female. What could be more womanly, as Elémire Zolla was already pointing out some years ago, than permitting the penetration of the body by a foreign object which not only stirs delight but even (possibly) creates new life?

In any case, with drugs we have come to the crux of the futurist revolt, the hinge of everything else, as the young tell us over and over in their writing. When the movement was first finding a voice, Allen Ginsberg set this aspect of it in proper context in an immensely comic, utterly serious poem called "America," in which "pot" is associated with earlier forms of rebellion, a commitment to catatonia, and a rejection of conventional male potency:

> *America I used to be a communist when I was a kid I'm not sorry.*
> *I smoke marijuana every chance I get.*
> *I sit in my house for days on end and stare at the roses in the closet.*
> *When I go to Chinatown I . . . never get laid . . .*

Similarly, Michael McClure reveals in his essay, *"Phi Upsilon Kappa,"* that before penetrating the "cavern of Anglo-Saxon," whence he emerged with the slogan of the ultimate Berkeley demonstrators, he had been on mescalin. "I have emerged from a dark night of the soul; I entered it by Peyote." And by now, drug-taking has become as standard a feature of the literature of the young as oral-genital love-making. I flip open the first issue of yet another ephemeral San Francisco little magazine quite at random and read: "I tie up and the main pipe [the ante-cobital vein, for the clinically inclined] swells like a prideful beggar beneath the skin. Just before

I get on it is always the worst." Worse than the experience, however, is its literary rendering; and the badness of such confessional fiction, flawed by the sentimentality of those who desire to live "like a cunning vegetable," is a badness we older readers find it only too easy to perceive, as our sons and daughters find it only too easy to overlook. Yet precisely here the age and the mode define themselves; for not in the master but in the hacks new forms are established, new lines drawn.

Here, at any rate, is where the young lose us in literature as well as life, since here they pass over into real revolt, i.e., what we really cannot abide, hard as we try. The mother who has sent her son to private schools and on to Harvard to keep him out of classrooms overcrowded with poor Negroes, rejoices when he sets out for Mississippi with his comrades in SNCC, but shudders when he turns on with LSD; just as the ex-Marxist father, who has earlier proved radicalism impossible, rejoices to see his son stand up, piously and pompously, for CORE or SDS, but trembles to hear him quote Alpert and Leary or praise Burroughs. Just as certainly as liberalism is the LSD of the aging, LSD is the radicalism of the young.

If whiskey long served as an appropriate symbolic excess for those who chafed against Puritan restraint without finally challenging it—temporarily releasing them to socially harmful aggression and (hopefully) sexual self-indulgence, the new popular drugs provide an excess quite as satisfactorily symbolic to the post-Puritans —releasing them from sanity to madness by destroying in them the inner restrictive order which has somehow survived the dissolution of the outer. It is finally insanity, then, that the futurists learn to admire and emulate, quite as they learn to pursue vision instead of learning, hallucination rather than logic. The schizophrenic replaces the sage as their ideal, their new culture hero, figured forth as a giant schizoid Indian (his madness modeled in part on the author's own experiences with LSD) in Ken Kesey's *One Flew Over the Cuckoo's Nest.*

The hippier young are not alone, however, in their taste for the insane; we live in a time when readers in general respond sympathetically to madness in literature wherever it is found, in established writers as well as in those trying to establish new modes. Surely it is not the lucidity and logic of Robert Lowell or Theodore Roethke or John Berryman which we admire, but their flirtation with incoherence and disorder. And certainly it is Mailer at his most nearly psychotic, Mailer the creature rather than the master of his fantasies who moves us to admiration; while in the case of Saul Bellow, we endure the theoretical optimism and acceptance for the sake of the delightful melancholia, the fertile paranoia which he cannot disavow any more than the talent at whose root they lie. Even essayists and analysts recommend themselves to us these days by a certain redemptive nuttiness; at any rate, we do not love, say, Marshall McLuhan less because he continually risks sounding like the body-fluids man in *Dr. Strangelove*.

We have, moreover, recently been witnessing the development of a new form of social psychiatry[2] (a psychiatry of the future already anticipated by the literature of the future) which considers some varieties of "schizophrenia" not diseases to be cured but forays into an unknown psychic world: random penetrations by bewildered internal cosmonauts of a realm that it will be the task of the next generations to explore. And if the accounts which the returning schizophrenics give (the argument of the apologists runs) of the "places" they have been are fantastic and garbled, surely they are no more so than, for example, Columbus' reports of the world he had claimed for Spain, a world bounded—according to his newly drawn maps—by Cathay on the north and Paradise on the south.

In any case, poets and junkies have been suggesting to us that the new world appropriate to the new men of the latter twentieth century is to be discovered only by the conquest of inner space: by an adventure of the spirit, an extension of psychic possibility, of which the flights into outer space—moonshots and expeditions to Mars—are precisely such unwitting metaphors and analogues as the voyages of exploration were of the earlier breakthrough into the Renaissance, from whose consequences the young seek now so des-

---

[2] Described in an article in the *New Left Review* of November-December, 1964, by R. D. Laing who advocates "ex-patients helping future patients go mad."

perately to escape. The laureate of that new conquest is William
Burroughs; and it is fitting that the final word be his:

> "This war will be won in the air. In the Silent Air with Image
> Rays. You were a pilot remember? Tracer bullets cutting the
> right wing you were free in space a few seconds before in blue
> space between eyes. Go back to Silence. Keep Silence. Keep
> Silence. K.S. K.S. . . . From Silence re-write the message that
> is you. You are the message I send to The Enemy. My Silent
> Message."
> The Naked Astronauts were free in space. . . .

—1965

Index

Aaron, Daniel, 44
Academic freedom, 169-86
Act of Darkness, 45, 67, 70-78, 280
Adams, Henry, 107, 108
*Adventures of Huckleberry Finn,
    The,* 105, 122
Aeneid, 124
After the Fall, 98
Agee, James, 45
Albee, Edward, 201-2, 203
Algren, Nelson, 59
Alienated artist concept, 90-92
All the King's Men, 51
All the Sad Young Men, 71
Alpert, Richard, 206
"America," 205
American, The, 116-17
American Association of Univer-
    sity Professors (A.A.U.P.),
    171-73
American Dream, An, 98, 195, 197
American Jitters, 53, 65
American Writers' Congress, 52
Americana, 50
Amter, Israel, 61, 62
Anderson, Sherwood, 52, 54
Another Country, 102
Antin, Mary, 82
Antirationalism, 191-208
Anti-Semitism, 38, 41, 107, 180,
    200
Antiwar literature, 32-42, 79
Antoninus, Brother, 201

Aquinas, St. Thomas, 192
Aristotle, 26, 192
Assistant, The, 59
Auden, W. H., 20-21
Augustine, St., 49

Babbitt, 169-70, 175
Baldwin, James, 48, 102, 107-8,
    204
Balso Snell, 45
Barbary Shore, 61
Barbusse, Henri, 33
Barnes, Djuna, 129
Barth, John, 133-38, 190
Beatles, the, 102, 202
Beats, 44, 96, 166, 191, 197, 204
    See also Hippies
Beecher, Henry Ward, 105
Bellow, Saul, 48, 51, 59, 64, 99,
    165, 199-200, 203
Belmondo, Jean-Paul, 46
Berkeley protests and demonstra-
    tions, 187, 194-95
Berryman, John, 51, 207
Betsky, Seymour, 152, 162
Beyond Desire, 54
Billy Budd, 123
Bishop, John Peale, 45, 64-78, 80
Blacks, *see* Negroes
Bloor, (Mother) Ella Reeve, 61,
    62
Blues for Mr. Charlie, 102

Bogart, Humphrey, 46, 155
Bourjaily, Vance, 160, 161
Brando, Marlon, 154
Brighton Rock, 129
Brown, Charles Brockden, 136
Brown, Norman O., 180, 190, 201
Browne, Sir Thomas, 136
Buchanan, Thomas G., 93-94
Buckminster Fuller, Richard, *see* Fuller, Richard Buckminster
Burgess, Anthony, 190, 191
Burke, Kenneth, 52
Burns, James MacGregor, 55
Burroughs, William, 61, 179, 190, 202, 203, 206, 208
By-Ways of Europe, 108

Cabell, James Branch, 65-66
Cahan, Abraham, 82, 88
Caldwell, Erskine, 52
Call It Sleep, 44, 71, 79-87
Camp, 43-44, 203
Can You Hear Their Voices?, 50
Cannibal, The, 128
Capote, Truman, 64, 66
Cassady, Neal, 61
Castaway, 57-58, 71
Castle, The, 166
Catch-22, 194
Celebrated Jumping Frog and Other Sketches, The, 104
Céline, L.-F., 45
Ceremony in Lone Tree, 133
Chambers, Whittaker, 50
Chaucer, Geoffrey, 34
Chekhov, Anton, 21
Childhood's End, 190-91
Civil rights movement, 47, 192, 194, 198, 204, 206
Clarel, 124
Clarke, Arthur C., 190-91
Clarke, Donald Henderson, 82
Clemens, Samuel, *see* Twain, Mark
Clockwork Orange, 191
Collected Poems, 68

Communism (Communist Party), 10, 50ff., 61-67, 173, 174
    Rosenberg case, 7-17
    See also Marx, Karl; Marxism (Marxists)
Confidence Man, The, 115
Connecticut Yankee in King Arthur's Court, A, 104
Conroy, Jack, 48
Cool Million, A, 45, 57, 80-81
Cooper, Gary, 46, 89, 154, 155
Cooper, James Fenimore, 108, 122
Coplon, Judith, 10
Corso, Gregory, 194, 202
Cowley, Malcolm, 53, 54, 65
Cozzens, James Gould, 57-58, 71
Crane, Stephen, 33, 90
Creeley, Robert, 48, 196
Cult of the Orgasm, 200-1
Cultural relations, European-American, 88-92, 93-103, 104-19
Culture in Crisis, 51-54
Custis, George Washington, 72

Dahlberg, Edward, 52, 128
Dante Alighieri, 34, 98, 107, 108, 121, 122, 141, 188
David Levinsky, 81
Davidson, Donald, 65-66
Davis, Sammy, Jr., 45
Day of the Locust, The, 45, 48, 56
Death of a Salesman, The, 59
Death on the Installment Plan, 45
Delissovoy, Peter, 204
Dismantling of Lemuel Pitkin, The. See Cool Million, A
Don Giovanni, 37, 38
Don Quixote, 37
Dos Passos, John, 44, 52, 59, 80, 169
Dostoevski, Feodor M., 21
Dr. Strangelove, 207
Dream Life of Balso Snell, The, 45
Dreiser, Theodore, 52, 81
Drive, He Said, 48, 193, 194

Drugs (drug culture), 47, 61, 170, 174, 204-8
Durrell, Lawrence, 137

Einstein, Albert, 131
Eliot, T. S., 91, 106
  anti-Semitism, 107
  influence, 72, 94-95
End of the Road, 134
Enormous Room, The, 36
Erotic literature and films, 124-25, 137
  See also Pornography
Esquire, 59
Exile's Return, 53, 54, 64

Fable, A, 33
Fairbanks, Mary Mason, 111
Falstaff, 37, 38, 40
Farewell to Arms, A, 33, 36
Farrell, James T., 44, 52, 59, 80, 84-85
Faulkner, William, 55, 67, 98, 134, 165
  influence, 65-66, 71, 72, 73, 98
"February 21 Committee" 175
Feu, Le, 33, 36
Feuer, Lewis, 195
Fielding, Henry, 188
Fitzgerald, F. Scott, 43, 44, 90-91, 107, 167
  Bishop and, 67, 68-69, 71
Flanagan, Hallie, 50
Flaubert, Gustave, 188
Floating Opera, The, 134
Following the Equator, 104
Fontamara, 45
For Whom the Bell Tolls, 152, 154-55
Franklin, Benjamin, 106, 193
Freud, Sigmund (Freudianism), 131, 166, 192, 200, 201
Friedenberg, Edgar Z., 183
Frost, Robert, 177

Fuchs, Daniel, 44, 64, 80
"Fuck Ode," 195
Fuck You, 195
Fuller, Richard Buckminster, 190

García Lorca, Federico, 95
Garfield, John, 46
Genet, Jean, 203
Ginsberg, Allen, 95, 179, 192
  homosexuality and new literature, 200, 202, 203
  link to the thirties, 61-63
  psychedelics and dreams, 205
Giovanni's Room, 102, 107
Glasgow, Ellen, 65-66
Go Tell It On the Mountain, 102
Goethe, Johann Wolfgang von, 98
Gold, Michael (Mike), 45, 64
Golden Boy, 45
Golding, William, 190
Good Soldier Schweik, The, 32-42
Goodbye, Mr. Chips, 82
Goose on the Grave, The, 128
Grapes of Wrath, The, 46, 80
Great Gatsby, The, 68
Greene, Graham, 105, 129
Gregory, Horace, 70, 81
Groves of Academe, 193
Guevara, Ché, 179
Guttman, Allen, 44, 55

Hamlet, 94-103, 125-26
Hamlet of A. MacLeish, The, 98
Hammett, Dashiel, 46, 52, 102
Happening House, 174
Hardy, Thomas, 165
Harper's Magazine, 164
Harte, Bret, 105, 109
Hasek, Jaroslav, 34-42
Hawkes, John, 127-32
Hawthorne, Nathaniel, 99, 106, 107, 109, 122, 123
Hayakawa, S. I., 167
Heart Is A Lonely Hunter, The, 67

Hemingway, Ernest, 4, 46, 52, 71, 80, 106, 134, 165, 197, 199
   interview, 151-62
   war novels, 33, 34, 36, 37, 55
Heraclitus, 134-35
Herzog, 99, 199-201
Hilton, James, 82
Hippies (hip; hipsters), 44, 96, 191, 206
   See also Beats
Hiss, Alger, 10, 11, 12, 14, 50
Hitler, Adolf (Nazism; Nazis), 32, 55
Homage to Blenhot, 44, 80
Homer, 120-21, 124, 125
Homosexuality, 74, 75, 170, 174, 180, 199, 201-2, 203-4
Honey in the Horn, 79
"Hot Afternoons Have Been in Montana," 45
Howells, William Dean, 108, 111, 112
Howl, 60-62
Huckleberry Finn, 105, 122
Hughes, Langston, 52
Humanism, 187, 191, 192, 193, 197-98
Huntsmen Are Up in America, The, 72-73, 75-76
Huxley, Aldous, 190
Hyman, Stanley Edgar, 195-96

I Was a Fugitive from a Chain Gang, 46
"If Only," 73-74
Iliad, 124
I'll Take My Stand, 51, 64-65
In Dubious Battle, 80
Innocents Abroad, 104-19
Irrationalism, 191-208
Irving, Washington, 106, 107

James, Henry, 106, 107, 116-17, 122, 165
Jarrell, Randall, 193

Jesus Christ, 98, 99
Jewish-American writers, 79-85
   See also specific writers by name
Jewish character stereotypes, *see* Anti-semitism
Jews Without Money, 45, 64
John Reed clubs, 51
Johnson, Lyndon B., 60
Joyce, James, 141
   influence, 70
   and myths, 70

Kaddish, 62
Kafka, Franz, 41, 166
Kaplan, H. J., 107
Kazin, Alfred, 44
Kempton, Murray, 94
Kennedy, Jacqueline, 60
Kennedy, John F., 49, 60, 93-94
Kenyon Review, 51, 65
Kerouac, Jack, 61, 191, 192, 194
Kesey, Ken, 206
Krushchev, N. S., 47
King, Martin Luther, 194
Kinsey report, 21, 25
Koch, Leo, 171-72, 185
Korzybski, Alfred, 167
Kramer, Joe, 148
Kulchur, 195

Lady Chatterley's Lover, 50
Laing, R. D., 207
Lampedusa, Giuseppe di, 135
Larner, Jeremy, 48, 193, 194
Lawrence, D. H., 50, 105, 137, 200
   Indians and Negroes, 101
Leary, Timothy, 170, 185, 206
Leaves of Grass, 95, 124
Leonard, William Ellery, 179
Leopard, The, 135
Leopold, Nathan (Leopold and Loeb), 43
Let Us Now Praise Famous Men, 45
Lewis, Sinclair, 169

Liberalism, 51
Life (magazine), 155, 159
Life Against Death, 201
Lime Twig, The, 129-32
Lion and the Fox, The, 55
Locomotive God, The, 179
Loeb, Richard (Leopold and Loeb), 43
Logan, 136
Long, Huey, 51, 64, 79
Longfellow, Henry W., 107
Look Homeward, Angel, 80
Lorca, *see* García Lorca, Federico
Lost Horizon, 82
Louis Beretti, 82
Love Among the Cannibals, 133
Love and Death in the American Novel, 150, 158
Low Company, 44
Lowell, Robert, 206
LSD, 47, 205, 206
    See also Drugs (drug culture)

McCarthy, Joseph R. (McCarthyism; McCarthy era), 169-70
McCarthy, Mary, 44, 193
McClure, Michael, 195, 205
McCullers, Carson, 66, 67
Macdonald, Dwight, 44
McLuhan, Marshall, 51, 64, 180, 190, 207
Mailer, Norman, 48, 137
    dreams and myths, 98
    and Hemingway, 159, 160
    Negroes, 102
    porno-esthetics, 195, 197, 201
    radicalism, 61
    war novels, 33-34
Malamud, Bernard, 59, 107, 165
Male Animal, The, 169
Maltese Falcon, The, 46
Many Thousands Gone, 73
Mao Tse-tung, 179
Marble Faun, The, 109
Marching! Marching!, 49, 54, 79
Martin Chuzzlewit, 165

Marx, Karl, 61, 134, 192
Marxism (Marxists), 18, 61, 64, 65, 67, 191, 197, 202
Masaryk, Jan, 38
Matthews, Harry, 190, 200
Mayor of Casterbridge, The, 165
Melville, Herman, 98-99, 106, 107, 115, 165
    Moby Dick, 120-26
Mezey, Robert, 170, 185
Michelangelo, 107, 108
Miller, Arthur, 59, 98
Miller, Henry, 95, 128, 137
Millie, 82
Milton, John, 188
Miss Lonelyhearts, 45, 48, 56, 71
Moby Dick, 88, 120-26
Monroe, Harriet, 67
Montana, 139-44, 145-50
Morris, Wright, 133-34
Mother's Kisses, A, 194
Muni, Paul, 46

Naked and the Dead, The, 33-34, 159
Naked Lunch, The, 200
Narrative of A. Gordon Pym, The, 121
Nazism, *see* Hitler, Adolf (Nazism; Nazis)
Neal, John, 136
Nearing, Scott, 61
Negroes, 90, 125, 197, 198, 202
    Black Muslims, 197
    Black Power movement, 180
    Civil Rights movement, 180, 204
    Southern literature, 65, 66, 73-78
    stereotypes, 65, 66, 198, 202
    writers, 95, 102-3
New Masses, 64, 79, 80, 82
New Yorker, 59
Notes of a Native Son, 102

O'Connor, Flannery, 66
Odets, Clifford, 45

O'Donnell, George Marion, 65
Odyssey, 120-21
Of Time and the River, 80
On the Road, 191, 194
Onassis, Jacqueline Kennedy, 60
One Flew Over the Cuckoo's Nest, 206
Orwell, George, 190
Oswald, Lee Harvey, 100

Paley, Grace, 165
Panza, Sancho, 37
Part of Our Time, 44
Partisan Review, 51, 59, 128, 139
Patchen, Kenneth, 128
Personal Recollections of Joan of Arc, 104
"Phi Upsilon Kappa," 195, 205
Pictures from an Institution, 193
Pierre, 98, 99, 100
Plato, 26
Playboy, 59
Plenipotentiaries, The, 107
Plutzik, Hyam, 98
Poe, Edgar Allan, 90-91, 99, 106, 121, 136, 189
Poet in New York, The, 95
Poetry, 67
Pop (mass) art and culture, 43, 189, 197
Popular Front novels, 80
Pornography, 195-208
    See also Erotic literature and films
Porter, Katherine Anne, 52
Portrait of the Artist as a Young Man, 70
Pound, Ezra, 95, 98, 106, 107, 116, 166
Power of Sympathy, The, 98
Prince and the Pauper, The, 104
Proletarian literature, 54-63, 79-80
Promised Land, The, 82
Psychedelics, *see* Drugs (drug culture); LSD

Rabelais, François, 136, 193
Radical Novel in America, The, 44, 54
Rahv, Philip, 195-96
Ransom, John Crowe, 51
Rechy, John, 200
Red Badge of Courage, The, 33
Reed, John, clubs, 51
Reich, Wilhelm, 190, 200, 201
Rexroth, Kenneth, 128
Richardson, Samuel, 124
Rideout, Walter, 44, 54
Rise of David Levinsky, The, 81
Robinson, Edward G., 48-49
Rock (Rock and Roll) music, 196
Roethke, Theodore, 207
Roosevelt, Franklin D. (New Deal era), 48, 49-50, 51, 52, 53, 55-60
Rosenberg, Ethel, 4-5, 7-17
Rosenberg, Harold, 56
Rosenberg, Julius, 4-5, 7-17
Roth, Henry, 52, 59, 64, 65
    Call It Sleep, 44, 71, 79-87
Roth, Philip, 84
Roughing It, 113
Rukeyser, Muriel, 56
Ryerson, Susan, 204

Sacco and Vanzetti case, 54-55, 62, 169, 180
Sade, Marquis de, 56, 136
Salinger, J. D., 192, 194, 199, 201, 202
Sanctuary, 66, 71, 72
Sanders, Ed, 195
Saviers, Dr., 156
Scarlet Letter, The, 222
Schlesinger, Arthur, Jr., 49
Schwartz, Delmore, 165
Science fiction, 189-91, 200
Scott, Sir Walter, 34, 188
Scottsboro Boys case, 54, 62
Sexual Revolution, 200-4, 205, 206

Shakespeare, William, 3, 34, 75, 77, 94, 98, 100-2, 107, 108, 123, 125-26
Shapiro, Karl, 51, 102
Sherman, Philip Henry, 105
Sherman, Stuart P., 111-12, 117, 118
Sibley, Mulford, 173
Siegel, Eli, 45
Silone, Ignazio, 45
1601, 137
Slesinger, Tess, 45
Smollett, Tobias George, 188
Socrates, 191, 192, 196
Soldier's Pay, 33
Some Like It Hot, 43
Sot-Weed Factor, The, 134-38
Sound and the Fury, The, 65, 68
Southern Review, The, 52, 64, 79
"Speaking of Poetry," 75-76
Stalin, Joseph (Stalinism; Stalinists); 32, 47, 51, 64, 88, 89, 91
Steffens, Lincoln, 52
Stein, Gertrude, 157, 162
Steinbeck, John, 44, 80, 102
Sterne, Laurence, 126, 188
Stevenson, Adlai, 60
Stowe, Harriet Beecher, 110-11
Straight Fight, 18-31
"Stranger in the Village, A," 107
Studies in Classic American Literature, 101
Studs Lonigan, 80
Summer in Williamsburg, 44
Sun Also Rises, The, 153, 157
Superman, 49

Tate, Allen, 51, 67, 68, 72
Taylor, Bayard, 108
Tempest, The, 100
Temple of Gold, 191
Tender Is the Night, 107
"That Evening Sun," 66
This Side of Paradise, 67

Thomas Aquinas, St., 192
Thoreau, Henry David, 106, 204
Thurber, James, 169
"Time of Her Time, The," 195
To Have and Have Not, 46, 71, 80, 155
"Toadstools Are Poison," 66
Tom Sawyer Abroad, 104
Tramp Abroad, A, 104
Treasure of the Sierra Madre, The, 46
Trocchi, Alexander, 200
Twain, Mark, 97, 158
  erotic theme, 109-11, 137
  Innocents Abroad, 104-19

Undertaker's Garland, The, 68
Unpossessed, The, 45
U.S.A., 80, 169

V., 194
Vanishing Adolescent, The, 183
Veblen, Thorstein, 169
Vietnam War, 60, 100, 170, 175
Vonnegut, Kurt, Jr., 190
Voter Decides, The, 18-31
Voting, 18-31

Walk on the Wild Side, A, 59
Walton, Eda Lou, 80, 85
War novels, 33
Warren, Robert Penn, 51, 65, 66, 67, 79
Warren Commission report, 94
Waste Land, The, 72
Weatherwax, Clara, 49, 54, 79, 80
Wells, H. G., 190
Welty, Eudora, 66
Werther, 98, 136
West, Nathanael, 45, 48, 50, 56-57, 65, 71, 197
  rediscovery of, 44, 45, 64
  Roth and, 80-81, 83-84

What Price Glory, 38
While Rome Burns, 82
Whitman, Walt, 21, 94-97, 102, 106, 124, 134, 165, 199, 202
Whittier, John G., 111, 112
Who Killed Kennedy?, 93-94
Who's Afraid of Virginia Woolf, 201-2
Williams, Tennessee, 154
Williams, William Carlos, 95, 196
Wilson, Edmund, 52, 53-54, 65 and Bishop, 67, 78, 72
Winterset, 45
Wolf, Leonard, 174

Wolfe, Thomas, 80
Woollcott, Alexander, 82
Wound in the Heart, The, 44
Wright, Richard, 52
Writers on the Left, 44

Young Logan, 84-85

Zeitgeist, 173
Zolla, Elémire, 205
Zukofsky, Louis, 95